Praise for

NOTHING SHORT (

'Very, very good. It's all here. Reacher is keeping an eye on this guy. In the rear-view mirror for now, but that's closer than most'
Lee Child, number one *New York Times* bestselling author of *Make Me* and other books in the Jack Reacher series

'A singular new talent! Storey's *Nothing Short of Dying* is nothing short of brilliant. It grabs you from page one and simply doesn't let go. This man is a born storyteller!'
Jeffery Deaver, number one international bestselling author of *The Bone Collector* and *The Coffin Dancer*

'Clyde Barr – remember the name, because he could become just as famous as Lee Child's anti-hero Jack Reacher. Utterly compelling ... for my money, it will become a world-wide sensation'
Daily Mail

'Erik Storey's writing is exceptional. This is a splendid debut – harsh and gripping throughout'
The Times

'*Nothing Short of Dying* takes you into the underbelly of the American West where some things haven't changed since the gunfight at the O.K. Corral. The novel features great action scenes, fast pacing, and well-drawn characters, with sharp and blunt dialogue that always rings true'
Nelson DeMille, number one *New York Times* bestselling author of *The Lion's Game* and *Nightfall*

'*Nothing Short of Dying* may be the year's best debut thriller. It leaps at you like a wolf, sinks its teeth in, and won't let go. Fans of Jack Reacher will love Clyde Barr, a dark, classic hero who can hold his own against any evil'

Times
author
s Keep

'*Nothing Short of Dying* contains furious, non-stop action that paints the mountains and gorges of Western Colorado red with blood'

C.J. Box, *New York Times* bestselling author of *Badlands* and *Off the Grid*

'Immensely enjoyable ... [Clyde is] a Grail Knight in disguise, rescuing the good and punishing the bad ... Encounters with bad guys are appropriately, cinematically violent, and the rich, sensory descriptions enhance a well-told story'

Booklist

'Grandly cinematic ... What makes Clyde Barr great isn't just that he's haunted, driven, and lethal, but that he's paired with a strong, independent, and capable woman who refuses to be a victim – Allie Martin is exactly my kind of gal. Together, they make a modern-day "Bonnie and Clyde" out for their own kind of justice'

Taylor Stevens, *New York Times* bestselling author of *The Informationist*

'A thrill ride – Erik Storey's *Nothing Short of Dying* hits the ground running. Clyde Barr isn't the usual protagonist, he's a man who has been knocked down but keeps getting back up with a vengeance, so buckle up and hang on because you're in for one hell of a read'

Craig Johnson, *New York Times* bestselling author of the Longmire Mysteries

'Nothing short of thrilling ... Erik Storey is a gene splice of Lee Child and Joe Lansdale. In this modern-day gunslinger classic everyone is a bad guy and Clyde Barr is the baddest of them all'
Scott Sigler, *New York Times* bestselling author of *Contagious* and *Alive*

ERIK STOREY

NOTHING SHORT OF DYING

**SIMON &
SCHUSTER**

London · New York · Sydney · Toronto · New Delhi

A CBS COMPANY

First published in Great Britain by Simon & Schuster UK Ltd, 2016
This paperback published 2017
A CBS COMPANY

1 3 5 7 9 10 8 6 4 2

Simon & Schuster UK Ltd
1st Floor
222 Gray's Inn Road
London WC1X 8HB

www.simonandschuster.co.uk

Simon & Schuster Australia, Sydney
Simon & Schuster India, New Delhi

A CIP catalogue record for this book is available from the British Library.

Paperback ISBN: 978-1-4711-4686-2
eBook ISBN: 978-1-4711-4685-5

Printed and bound by CPI Group (UK) Ltd, Croydon, CR0 4YY

MIX
Paper from
responsible sources
FSC® C020471

Simon & Schuster UK Ltd are committed to sourcing paper that is made
from wood grown in sustainable forests and support the Forest Stewardship
Council, the leading international forest certification organisation. Our
books displaying the FSC logo are printed on FSC certified paper.

For Stephanie, for taking my hand and walking with me down the root-strewn path of life. Without you this book would not exist.

Love beyond words,

E

CHAPTER ONE

It started with a phone call in the Utah wilderness, about a week after I'd been released from prison.

I'd been enjoying one of those perfect spring mornings in the mountains. Baby-blue skies, soft breeze out of the northwest, sweet sage dripping with dew, and wildlife that practically ran from the trail into the frying pan. A great morning, I thought, on the way to many more like it in the Yukon, where I planned to live in the peace and cold.

I'd spent the morning tracking and then shooting a young mule deer buck. He led me through creeks swollen with muddy runoff, across hillsides so slick with fallen aspen leaves that I took a few ungraceful dives, and into a meadow of young lupine, where I pulled the trigger on my big African rifle as he turned broadside with his nostrils flaring.

The rest of the day was spent cutting the buck into steaks for dinner and strips to be smoked and air dried for later use. That night I built a small campfire out of wrist-size branches of juniper and sat staring at the flames as I fidgeted with the little hunk of plastic and wires I'd bought to contact my sisters as I passed through.

I'd hoped for a storybook homecoming—me calling them

and telling them I was home and them suggesting I come over straightaway so they could cook for me. In my daydreams we'd have a merry old time catching up and talking like the family we used to be. In reality Deb didn't answer and Angie told me I could go to hell. Jen wasn't in any phone book, so I didn't call her. Odds were good that if I did, she'd tell me something similar, so I put the phone away and set about cooking the steak.

I was sitting in a camp chair, listening to the crickets and the night wind, and had just finished rubbing salt and pepper into the meat, when the damned plastic contraption started chirping in my pocket. The sound was like an Atari video game, and I couldn't push buttons fast enough to make it stop.

"This is Barr," I said.

"Clyde." It was Jen, her voice barely a whisper. "I need you to come get me."

I looked up at the night sky, pulling on my beard. As happy as I was to hear her voice, the tone scared the hell out of me and lured me back to a time of fear. It was the same tone and pleading I'd heard as a child on the bad nights. The nights that Mom and Dad—or Mom and some new guy—were fighting, or when one of those guys, drunk and out of control, chose to hurt us.

Back then Jen would often crawl into my room and wake me with a trembling whisper. Together, we'd push the dresser against the door, huddle in a corner, and ride out the storm.

"Where are you?"

"Clyde, you need to *hurry*. He's going to kill me. After I help him, I'm dead."

"Who's going to kill you? Help who with what?" I had absolutely no idea what she was talking about or where she was.

"Jesus, Clyde." Even though she whispered, I could hear her panic. "After I help him get inside a week from now, I'm no use to him. Please, *please* get me the hell out of here. You owe me."

She was right about the obligation. "Okay. Tell me where you are."

"Promise me. *Promise* you'll come get me."

This part was important, and she knew it. If I gave my word, nothing short of dying would stop me. It hadn't *yet*. I stood and watched the constellations disappear, blanketed by invisible clouds. "I promise," I said. "Now, where the hell are you?"

Suddenly there was a muffled shout and what sounded like a crash. I heard a male voice, then silence.

"Jen?"

There was no reply. I looked at the phone's screen. The call-time numbers were still running. "Jen?" I said, louder.

Nothing.

There was a faint click and the line went dead. I flipped the phone shut and shoved it in my pocket.

As the night wind stirred the trees, I pulled a soft pack of straights from my flannel shirt pocket and shook out one of the last cigarettes. After touching it to a glowing ember from the fire, I stood in the darkness next to a sweet-smelling serviceberry bush.

One of my resolutions had been to quit smoking when I went into the backcountry. It was reassuring knowing there's no better counter to the bad habit than fresh air and open spaces. But this new development put my vow on hold.

As reluctant as I was to delay my journey north, I'd made a promise. And this time it was to my sister—not some villager or desperate campesino in one of the many jungles I'd

3

hacked my way through. My own flesh and blood—whatever the hell that meant.

I limped back to the fire and tossed the butt into the flames. From the valley came the lonely cry of coyotes. The wind rustled up the smells of melting snow and slowly caressed the pines as I looked back up at the stars and wondered what Jen had done this time.

Like me, and unlike our straitlaced sisters, she'd always been a troublemaker. She had a knack for finding the wrong people, the wrong times, and the wrong places. When we were young it had been us against the world. But then I left—left her to fend for herself, because I'd been selfish.

Now I had a chance to make up for it. First though, I needed a direction. A track I could follow. I called Angie again.

No answer, so I called Deb.

I got another one of those mechanical voices telling me to leave a message, so I did. I wasn't sure Deb would call back, so I went ahead and started breaking camp. The tent came down in the same amount of time it takes most people to strip their beds. It and my sleeping bag went in my big bag, a beat-up ruck I'd hauled halfway around the world.

I limped over and shoveled dirt on the fire. As the last few embers suffocated under the soil, I silently said good-bye to the oak brush, aspen, and pines that had been my home this last week. I tipped my hat to Mount Lena, who'd let me sleep on her for the last couple of days. It was the closest I'd been to a woman in three years.

The phone rang as I began climbing into the truck. I stepped back out into the cold mountain air and pushed buttons until the ringing stopped.

"Barr," I said.

"This is Nick."

I didn't know any Nicks.

"Deb's husband."

"Oh," I said.

"Stop calling. She doesn't want to talk to you. Ever. Got it?"

I nodded, watched the moon start to peek over the ragged horizon. Nick went on to tell me that I was a worthless bastard who'd abandoned his family. When his rant was over, I informed him what Jen had said. He told me that she was just as bad as I was and that he couldn't care less what happened to her. I eventually prodded him into telling me that he'd seen her in Clifton with "her lowlife friends" and that she was using drugs again.

"Okay, well, thanks for—" He broke off the call before I could finish.

I got back in the truck, threw the phone on the cracked dash, then turned the key in the ignition. Nothing. I got back out, kicked the door, kicked the side panels, then slammed a fist on the hood. Satisfied with my mechanic skills, I got back behind the wheel and tried the ignition again. The dilapidated engine turned over, started, and made unhealthy grinding noises as I headed south.

I drove off the mountain, under a brilliant moon, back toward the country I thought I'd left for good. I smacked my hands against the steering wheel and felt both it and the truck wobble. The grimy wheel was connected by an iffy steering rod to a junk pickup that I'd bought for two hundred bucks from the coyote who'd driven me across the border. Listening to the creaks and moans of the aging steel, I wondered if either of us would survive the trip.

My eyes burned and the road blurred in front of me. I wanted to stop and crawl into my sleeping bag but decided on a drink instead. I grabbed the paper bag that sat on the passenger seat, pulled the bottle out, put it between my legs, and then took a big, long pull.

After the liquor hit, driving away from my Yukon dreams and back toward the place I'd grown up didn't feel so bad. But deep down I knew I was kidding myself. The truth was, Jen's call had surfaced memories that I'd buried under many years and thousands of miles. With one phone call, she'd made me remember what I wanted to forget.

When our dad left, and our mom died, I did something stupid that almost got me killed. Jen did something worse that saved my life. If anyone ever found out what we'd done, we'd both be serving life sentences. Jen's keeping quiet kept me free. Because of that, and of what we'd endured together, I'd do whatever she asked.

CHAPTER TWO

I awoke in a tangle of sweaty sheets. The screams of women and children and the popping of Kalashnikovs faded slowly back into the realm of dreams as the morning light filtered in through the slightly drawn curtains. Though I'd come to consciousness coiled for action, I relaxed when I spotted a cheap television perched on a nearby entertainment stand.

It was the TV that told me what country I'd woken up in.

The soft bed beneath me was another tip-off. I wasn't surrounded by snoring people wrapped in dirty blankets and crowding all of the available floor space. And there were no chickens or goats. I scratched my flat naked belly, felt the reassuring cold steel of the rifle by my side, and shook my head, amazed by what the developed world takes for granted.

Water heaters, for instance. I loved water heaters. Their existence meant I could take a gloriously long shower without any work. I was absolutely filthy. A week on the mountain swirled around my feet and down the drain in a black slurry. After toweling off, I wiped condensation from the bathroom mirror and used my scissors to trim back my unruly hair and beard. The sight of gray tufts mixed with black should have been depressing, but I had a slightly different thought—how much I'd changed in the years I'd been away. I was staring at a naked ape with wide straight shoulders, hard sinewy limbs, and hairy tanned skin. I actually looked *too* lean. If I didn't get some calories in soon, I'd drop to under two hundred pounds for the first time since high school.

After pulling on a pair of jeans and a denim shirt, I sat down and drew a little notebook out of my pack. I bit the inside of my cheek and flipped through the pages, staring at the phone numbers written inside. *Who do I call first?*

I decided to call Juan. He was my only real friend from Riverside High. While other kids focused on geometry and biology, Juan taught me how to steal cars and pick locks. In return I taught him how to shoot and brawl. I hoped he still had his family connections.

"This is Barr," I said when Juan picked up on the third ring.

"Barr?" There was a brief silence, then hushed Spanish. *"Seriously?"*

"Yeah. I need some help."

"Well, I'm good, thanks for asking."

"Sorry," I said. "How you been?"

"Good, man. It's been a *lot* of years. Where have you—"

"I'll fill you in later. Right now I need info."

"What kind?" Juan asked warily.

"Jen's in trouble—*again*. Maybe mixed up with somebody very dangerous."

"I'm not sure how much help I can be, now that we're outside of it."

"We?"

"Me and Maria."

I didn't say anything for several moments, tried to ignore the punch to the gut.

"Oh, man . . . you didn't know?" Juan said.

"You still live in the same place?" I asked.

"Yeah, but, Clyde . . ."

"I'll be there in thirty," I said, and hung up.

TWENTY MINUTES AND A STOP for smokes later, I pulled into Riverside, Colorado, and stopped in the public park. The cottonwoods were finally beginning to leaf out and the grass was short and green. On the far side of the park, protecting the town from the river, was the levee where kids played and rode their bikes on the crest. From behind it wafted the sweet, earthy scent of the mighty Colorado.

The park nearly overflowed with very large families in the middle of various get-togethers, birthday parties, and picnics. I got out, leaned on the hood of my truck, and lit a fresh cigarette. Most of the folks were Hispanic, happy, and boisterous. I could have been standing in a village in any of the Latin countries I'd wandered through, but I wasn't. I was home, staring at the central gazebo that had changed my life. Memories of this place came flooding back, as if the levee had suddenly given way.

Down the street, Juan's house sat next door to the one Maria had grown up in—Maria, the girl I'd dated all through high school, the one who'd taken my virginity with relish and let loose feelings I'd never had before.

Sixteen years ago, I'd sat with Maria under that gazebo, my arms wrapped tight around her thin waist, and told her I was leaving. She didn't cry, just looked into my eyes and nodded. It was inevitable, she'd told me. She said I needed to escape, run away.

Is that what I'd been doing all this time? *Running away?*

9

I crushed out my cigarette, got in the truck, and drove to Juan's.

I WAS SITTING IN HIS backyard, in a flimsy white plastic chair, my chukkas propped up on a cooler, drinking a Bud Light, and trying to pretend I wasn't uncomfortable as hell.

"So, I can try to help, but like I said, we're out of the life now," Juan said.

I took a sip of beer. "About this *we*—"

"Sorry you didn't know. We would have invited you, but no one knew where you were."

I looked at the ground.

"Really," he said. "You can't be *that* mad, right? I mean, you've been gone for almost . . . When *did* you leave?"

"A year after high school," I said.

Juan shook his head. "Sixteen years, then. So, you gonna hit me or just drink all my beer?"

"You happy? Is *she* happy?" I asked.

"Of course, man. Especially now. Two little ones running around, her finally finishing nursing school. I just got a raise at the shop."

"Then that's all that matters." I reached into the cooler for another beer, popped the tab on another can of Bud. "I thought you guys only drank Coronas?"

"That horse piss? You probably assume we eat burritos three times a day, too."

"You mean you *don't*?" I said.

Juan laughed. "Well, that's what we're having tonight."

Maria came out then carrying paper plates loaded with food that smelled of cumin and pepper. Flies flitted around the burritos. I couldn't meet her gaze, stared at the top of my beer can instead. She and Juan exchanged love sonnets in a fast Spanglish that I had a hard time following. I told her thanks, but she ignored me and walked back inside. My eyes followed her soft retreat, imagining a past that could have been. I took one bite, then finished the burrito in three more.

"I'll call my cousins," Juan said. "My brothers, too. They still got a hand in all that. See what they can find out."

I nodded, not really paying attention. The house, the kids, the jobs. They were living the American dream, one I could have had if I'd stayed.

"So I'll call you," Juan said.

"Sure," I said, draining the dregs of my beer.

When I finished, I crushed the can, tossed it into a steel drum set out for that purpose, and stood. "Thanks, man. And, uh . . . tell Maria she's beautiful, okay?"

CHAPTER THREE

The sun finally gave up for the day as I cruised down the interstate toward Clifton. In the rearview mirror I could see the tired old ball of atoms settle down in its bed of rocks and sand, pulling its pink-and-red blankets over its head, then finally turning off the light. It would be a while until the moon arrived to take its place. Both windows were down and I could feel the temperature drop immediately, as it always does in the desert. In the cool air I smelled the faint river scents start to push away the god-awful gasoline smog that had been plaguing my nose all day.

The lights of the city were glowing now, overpowering the stars and making the world look upside down. The truck rattled and squeaked off I-70, and together we stopped at the first motel we came to. It was one of those leftovers from an era when car travel was exciting. It even had one of those names: Travel Lodge. All dark brown wood with a small faded sign that showed they had all the modern conveniences, like air-conditioning and color TVs. My kind of place.

Juan called after I'd checked in and unloaded my bags.

"I asked around," he said. "Found out some things. They reminded me why I decided to get out of this shit. My oldest brother, Alejandro, remember him? He's still running a crew in Clifton. Mostly sells pot and a little crank. He used to sell it out of a place on F and Susan called the Cellar. Know it? Anyway, about a year ago a new guy came to town, some white dude with a lot of muscle, and he ran Alejandro out."

"What's this got to do with Jen?" I asked with a sinking feeling. Getting involved in stuff like this was the reason I'd wound up in prison.

"This big honcho, he disappeared a week ago. And the last time he was spotted he was with Jen."

"Oh," I said.

"Yeah. And everyone is looking for him. He stopped the flow of good meth. Word is, he's making something even better, but he's cut off any trade in it until it's done so that the tweakers will be jonesing real good when the new batch comes out."

"What's this honcho's name?"

"Didn't ask. I don't want to know specifics, 'cause I'm out of the life, remember?"

"Yeah. So I should start looking at the Cellar?"

"That's what Alejandro said. The big honcho is missing, but his little brother runs the place, slings crank out of there when he has supply. Alejandro suggests you try talking to the main bartender there, a pretty brunette named Allie Martin. Just be careful."

"You know me," I said. "Safety first."

"I *do* know you. That's why I said to be careful. Don't go stepping on rattlers, Barr. You might get bit."

"Uh-huh."

"One more thing," Juan said. "Chopo got out a while back and he's heading this way to help my brother. I know you guys did some business years ago. He might be willing to lend a hand."

"I got it for now, Juan, thanks. And tell—"

"Yeah, yeah, I'll tell her. Stay alive, man." He hung up.

A HALF HOUR LATER I paused at the front entrance to the Cellar and felt under my Carhartt jacket, first to my right and then to my left, for my six-inch Green River butcher knife and my compact .40 caliber. I walked in slowly, letting my eyes adjust to the gloom. The place smelled of piss and mildew and stale beer. There was something else, too: the acrid sweat of the strung out—a smell that reminded me of the little cantinas in Bolivia where people in the coca trade use booze to come down from the powder cloud that gets them through the long shifts. If broken souls had an odor, they'd smell like the Cellar.

A single bar on the right ran the entire length of the building: twelve bar stools, five occupied by men. And to the left of the bar was a group of tables, one of which propped up three people—two women and a guy—who looked like they were passed out. The bartender, a good-looking young woman with a ponytail, was yelling at a man whose elbows were propped on the bar. He stomped outside after the reaming, and I headed toward his abandoned seat.

The four men who remained on the stools glowered as I walked past and sat down. The bartender pretended to ignore me. After she waited the predetermined time it took to show the four men whose side she was on, she walked over and took my order. A Canadian whiskey with a cheap beer back. My version of a boilermaker.

The four men fidgeted, animated about something or other, eyes constantly searching, seeing and cringing at the spiders on the walls and the mothmen in the corners. All four tweakers were white, thin, and tall. And close to the same age. All wore baggy shirts and baggy pants, and their flat-brimmed ball caps were crooked. When they spoke it was clipped and fast and they used hand gestures that looked like bad karate. Occasionally they'd look my way, make a gesture, laugh, and sneer. One spit at my feet. I smiled, nodded, and held up my whiskey.

The three at the table must have been coming down from "a long time on the moon," as the meth heads called the time they spent tweaked. Their heads were cradled on skinny folded arms and one, the guy, snored.

"You Allie?" I asked the bartender as she pulled a bottle down from the top shelf and wiped an inch of dust off it.

"Maybe."

"You know a girl named Jen Barr?"

She smiled, a strange smirk that told me she knew a lot of things. After putting the bottle back on the shelf, she said, "I might. You a cop?"

I pulled up my coat sleeves, showing her scars and green ink. "Do I look like a cop?"

She laughed. "Everyone has ink. Cops too."

Which I couldn't argue. When I left, only sailors, bikers, and cons had tattoos. From what I'd seen since I'd returned to this country, everyone and their grandmothers had something scrawled on their skin.

"I don't care much for the law," I said. "I'm just a brother looking for his sister Jen."

"You should ask the owner," she said with that same strange smirk. "He's outside smoking, but he'll be back soon. He might know her."

"Care if I sit here and wait?"

"Be my guest."

So I sat and sipped and waited. "Who owns this dive?" I asked after I finished the whiskey.

"Brent. Everyone here calls him Spike."

"Spike?" The name made me think of a cartoon bulldog.

"Yeah. He got the name when he stopped smoking and started using the needle." She pantomimed someone sticking a syringe into a vein. "It's a stupid name. Fits him well."

"Got it." She either believed that I wasn't a cop or she hated her boss. Or both.

She walked over by the till, shook the empty tip jar, and glared at the four restless men next to me. Grabbing a rag, she started wiping down the bar and made her way back to me.

"Brent's not going to like someone coming into his place and asking questions," she said. "It's not the kind of place where you get answers."

I nodded, not showing any worry, but I was getting restless. This was taking too long. I thought I'd just ask a few questions, then hit the road with a direction. Hunting people was much more frustrating than hunting animals, because it involved talking, which I wasn't very good at. I sipped my beer, resigned myself to a long night, and thought about all the dirty little dive bars I'd been in over the years.

Allie kept wiping, trying to push a puddle of liquor off the bar. I said, "You do know her, though?"

She folded her arms and stared at me with a look of defiance that told me she was done with annoying men for the day. On *her* the expression looked cute.

"Maybe you should ask *him*," she said, looking over my shoulder.

I turned and watched a short guy with fussed-over dusty-brown hair who I assumed was the owner come back into the bar like he'd forgotten something. He strode quickly across the room, quickening his pace further when he saw me. He wore green slacks and a brown T-shirt that was too tight. There were track marks on both of his Popeye arms. The gold Rolex on his wrist wobbled as he cracked his knuckles.

"And who the holy hell are you?" he asked, his voice high-pitched and angry.

"You must be Spike," I said.

"You didn't answer my question, asshole. This is pretty much a private club. No outsiders. You're going to tell me who you are, and why you're here, then you're gonna get your ass off that stool and out of my bar or I swear to God—"

"The name's Clyde Barr," I said, pushing back on the stool a few inches. "I'm looking for someone and thought you could help. Want a beer?"

"No, I don't want no stupid beer. And I don't talk to no cops, either."

This cop thing was getting old.

"He's not a cop, Brent," Allie said. "And don't take out your being pissed at me on him. He's looking for his sister."

"Shut up, bitch, no one asked you. We'll deal with our thing when this is done," Spike, or Brent, said.

Allie threw the wet rag at Brent and walked to the other end of the bar.

"You should watch the language," I said. "But she's right. I'm not a cop and I'm looking for my sister Jen. Know her?"

"I might. She may have been that slut my brother was—"

I'd had enough. I leaped off the stool, grabbed the mouthy prick by the neck, and shoved him up against a carpeted pillar. My eyes caught movement as the four bar-stool guys rushed toward me. I'd forgotten how fast tweakers can move.

So I popped Spike on the ear—hard with a cupped hand—then swung him down and at the feet of the four guys. He dropped, tumbled, then rolled on the floor and caught the feet of three of them. They went down. The fourth moved like a Benzedrine cat and hopped over Spike, came down, and tried to get me with a big right. I stepped inside it and chopped my forearm onto the side of his exposed neck. As he started falling I hit him in the face with my palm and stuck my knee into his ear. He crumpled as the other three got up.

They were fast but not fast enough. I reached back, grabbed a shot glass, and crashed it into the nearest one's temple. Then I smashed my palm under the next guy's jaw, lifting him off his feet and onto his back away from the others. The last man stood and warily came at me in a cage fighter's stance, faking jabs and ready to take me down wrestling-style if I gave him a chance.

I didn't. I faked a big right, stopped it as he started to duck under, then hit him with my left elbow. It rocked him a little and I moved in, hammer-fisting the back and side of his head until he went down. Spike was starting to get up, not very well, clutching his ear, so I stomped on his ankle as if crushing a beer can. Something cracked and Spike passed out. No one was getting up.

I went back over to the bar, sat down, and sipped on my beer. Allie stood wide-eyed by the beer taps, staring at the fallen men.

"You going to call the cops?" I asked, pointing my chin in the direction of the phone on the back wall.

Instead of answering, she started laughing. Sort of. Not girlish giggles, but mirthful mumbles. Then she shook her head and said, "Hell no. We get fights in here all the time. Not like that, but if anyone deserved a beating, it was those assholes."

Other than the sound of her voice, the place was relatively

quiet: snoring from the three people passed out at the table, and an occasional groan from one of the men on the floor.

I finished my beer, thought about getting another, then decided against it. I asked Allie, "Should I leave, or can I ask you a few questions?"

She stood still and calm and collected, then leaned over the bar and studied me. She waited a few beats, then said, "Shoot." She didn't look anything like the tweaker patrons. Instead of being a ghostly white stick figure, she was tan and healthy. There were no signs of the usual mannerisms that went with meth: no shaking, no grinding teeth, no picking at the skin.

"You don't use the stuff they sell in here, do you?"

"Nope," she said proudly. "I'm only here because Brent pays real well, and I have a lot of bills."

For some reason this made me feel as if we were on the same side. I continued admiring her. She had long black hair pulled back and wore a gray sweatshirt and jeans. No makeup, no jewelry, but she didn't need them. Juan had understated how pretty she was.

"So you know Jen. You've seen her?" I said.

She nodded and said, "She's a regular, day crowd. Works nights. I always wondered how she didn't get fired. Guess if you're a janitor, they don't care if you're drunk, or maybe she used enough of the shit Brent sells to stay awake."

I nodded, even though it hurt to think of Jen back on that path. At least she was trying to work.

"I heard that she was last seen in here, hanging out with some big-time guy."

Allie turned and walked to the back bar, and I thought our conversation was over, until she returned with a new beer. When I reached for my money roll, she waved it off and said,

"This one's on me. For taking out the trash. Even if it means I might have to find a new job."

"You know the guy she was last seen with?" I asked, sipping on a beer I didn't need.

More silence while she decided whether she could share with me. I hoped she felt she could—that the two of us were different from the others on the floor.

Finally, after another couple of seconds, she said, "Brent's brother, Lance. The infamous Mr. Alvis. Your sister was here the last time Lance graced us with his presence. He bought her drinks, and they left together, but I didn't pay too much attention because it was a busy night. We pulled in two thousand in a couple hours, and I made three hundred in tips. I haven't seen Lance or Jen since."

"Do you know where they went? Where they'd be now?"

Allie shook her head. "Nope. But either your sister has horrible taste in men or she's in trouble."

"Why do you say that?"

"You haven't heard of Mr. Lance Alvis?"

I said, "If I had, I wouldn't be asking dumb questions. Who is he?"

"You must *not* be a cop," she said, nodding in approval. "Lance is the man when it comes to getting something to snort, shoot up, or smoke. In three states and growing, from what I hear. Story goes that the asshole used to run private security in Iraq, and when he came back he checked out what Brent was doing and decided to change professions. Lance has more talent for the business than his little brother. Some people say there's no bigger supplier."

"You believe them?"

"From what I've seen, yeah. He has three or four of his friends with him everywhere he goes, and they're all mean, hard-looking. Plenty of scars, and scary eyes like yours. They throw money around like it's candy at a parade. I'm pretty sure they roughed up someone in the office a month ago. The jukebox was loud, but I could make out the screams."

I nodded. Brent started to move, then moan, then cry.

"I need a glass of water," I said.

"What for?"

"To pour on Spike, get him to wake up. I need to ask him about his brother."

Allie shook her head, swishing the ponytail across her shoulders. "Won't do any good. Lance keeps Brent in the dark on most things. He gives Brent just enough dope to keep the place running and put some extra cash in his pocket. And even then, the stuff is passed through a middle man. Lance is too smart to actually touch the drugs or the money. No one knows exactly what Lance does or where he goes, except maybe whatever woman he's screwing."

I took out a hundred-dollar bill, pushed it across the bar. "Tip, then," I said. "I'll be poking around town for a while, trying to get a lead on Jen. If you hear anything, or if Spike gets cranky when he wakes up and tries anything, give me a call." I wrote my number on a coaster and stood up. "Want help closing?"

She looked at the men on the floor, some of them now slowly moving. Sighing, she pocketed the hundred and the coaster and shook her head. "Those guys are pretty bad. I'm going to have to call an ambulance." She went back behind the bar, popped the till, took a couple twenties out, and shoved them in her jeans. "I'll wait five minutes after you leave before I do."

I offered my hand, and she took it, surprising me with her workingwoman grip. "Clyde Barr," I said.

"I heard. Five minutes."

I pushed away from the bar, and she shoved the till closed, walked ahead, and opened the door for me, and then I was out in the dark and on the street. Driving back to the motel, I wondered about this girl's cool demeanor. I figured she'd seen her share of ugly people and events. When you've been to hell and back, watching a few tweakers get laid out by a big guy asking questions probably qualifies as just another day at the office.

CHAPTER FOUR

The morning was rung in with church bells. Not the kind that clang out from deep inside mossy stone towers. Rather, loud speakers in fake steeples blasting tinny facsimiles. I tried pulling a pillow over my head, but it made me claustrophobic. Then I was conscious of my full bladder. *Damn.* I shuffled into the bathroom and took a long, glorious piss.

My hands were almost too swollen to button my pants. I'd learned years ago that you shouldn't hit with your fists if you make a living with your hands, so they were less sore than if I'd cracked a knuckle on a skull, but they still ached. My whole body did. Probably not as bad as Spike and his friends, but *everyone* gets hurt when they fight. The winner is the one who hurts less.

I carried my big bag out and threw it in the back of the truck, returned to the room, tossed the room key on the bed, and checked my little bag—a beat-up and scarred Duluth, all leather, with little straps that bit into my shoulders if it was packed too heavy. An old African hand had given it to me when I was young and working on a game reserve in Kenya. Along with the pack, this friend of mine, Cecil, had also given me crucial knowledge of who and what to avoid.

Inside the Duluth I carried my little notebook, my pistol and knife, ammo for my .375 Holland & Holland rifle, a plump first-aid kit, and a couple Nietzsche and Haggard paperbacks. The reassuring bulge of the bag's hidden pocket told me that all my cash was there. Thinking about the money made me suddenly cautious, so I took out the pistol, press checked it to make sure there was a round in the chamber, and placed it in my jacket pocket. I was about to throw my flip phone in the bag but decided to check my messages first. There was just one call—from Allie.

"Hey, Barr, remember me from last night? Brent's awake in St. Mary's and he's called me twice saying he's going to kill me. He thinks I helped you, that we had a master plan or something. What an idiot. He's calling his big brother for reinforcements. Let's talk."

I rubbed my chin and stuffed the phone back in my pocket. Then I sat down on the bed, let out a sigh, and started cleaning my rifle. I didn't need to—I'd cleaned the gun after dressing out the buck on the mountain—but it gave me time to think.

I replayed the phone message in my head. This was another wrinkle in my plans—another person to worry about. But there was no denying that I was the guy who'd put Allie in jeopardy. This was a problem I had to fix.

I finished cleaning and put the supplies away, relishing the sharp smell of gun oil, then stared out the window. Those who needed help always managed to find me, no matter where I hid. They tracked me down and pleaded. And I never refused. Somehow, that always caused bigger problems.

THE DOOR TO MY ROOM clicked shut, and a minute later I was in the lobby. The bored teenage boy at the desk looked at me, carrying the rifle, and at my face, and quickly shifted from bored to nervous. His pimply face trembled and his shaking hand reached for the phone on the desk.

"Don't, kid," I said. "I'm only here to check out. Room 104."

"Oh." Instant relief. He looked at the computer, told me I was good to go, and then asked, "So, you going on safari or something?" His gaze shifted from the rifle to my head. I wore a battered and brown felt hat, with a big crown and old bloodstains speckled on the large dusty brim. A raven feather stuck out of the leather band.

"Or something," I said, then walked out of the motel and got into my truck.

As I drove east, I brooded more on Allie. I had to call her back soon, but I needed to get away from the motel and out of Clifton. It sounded like she did, too. But if we were to meet again it had to be somewhere I chose, somewhere out in the open where I could watch for the people who'd be pursuing us.

The drive was pretty, in the way irrigated land can be. Closed fruit stands, old Victorian houses, peach orchards, and massive leafy vineyards. The road widened, signaling the town proper, and I turned right and drove back down toward the river to a big sprawling park with wide sidewalks, lush green grass, and tall, tough tamarisk that blocked my view of the river.

Next to the main parking lot was a cleared dirt area surrounded by trees with a better view of the river, used occasionally as overflow parking. I drove in and backed the truck into a shady space between two cottonwoods, well away from the main lot. I sat in the cab and returned Allie's call.

She answered on the first ring. "Barr? Where *are* you?"

"In my truck. Have you seen any of them yet?"

"No. I've been in my car, driving all around town, waiting for you to call."

"Okay," I said. There was a firmness in her voice, a sense of resoluteness in the face of fear. All in all, she seemed to be handling it pretty well. It was the second time she'd impressed me.

"I want you to head to Palisade, Riverbend Park, and pull into the main lot on the west side. I'll come get you. What type of car you driving?"

"A white Ford Escort. I should be there in . . . let's see, twenty minutes."

"Good."

"Hey, Barr . . ."

"Yeah."

"When Brent was threatening me he said something weird about your sister. Something about her being 'disposable.' I think maybe you'd better find her fast."

Allie's words scared me, but as soon as an image of what Jen might be facing appeared in front of my eyes, I willed it away. I'd been in enough scrapes over the years to know that you have to solve one problem at a time.

I walked to the paved parking lot to make sure my truck wasn't visible. It wasn't. Then I checked the park. Just one little red sedan parked close to the gazebo. An elderly overweight man with red suspenders, shorts, and long white socks sat on the bench in the gazebo reading a paperback.

No threats yet. Allie wouldn't be arriving for another fifteen minutes, so I walked over to the river's edge.

The Colorado wasn't at its peak, not yet, but it was well on its way. Most of the bank was submerged, and the level of the milk-chocolate-colored water would rise every day. The standing waves built and crashed but appeared to move

neither up- nor downstream. The actual water never stopped
though, just pushed and slammed its way toward the Pacific
without thinking. That's what I loved most about the river—
its constant motion.

It would be nice, after this was over, to take a long raft
trip. Maybe Jen and I could paddle through Westwater and
its ass-clenching rapids, then lounge on the banks in Moab
for a week or two. That would be heaven: a raft trip with a
beer in my hand instead of a rifle.

I heard flapping and looked up. A heron drifted down
from one of the tallest trees and settled onto a muddy flat by
the shore, shook, then extended its little head up on its long
neck. It stuck its thin beak into the air, looked left and right,
then suddenly flapped immense wings, sucking both feet out
of the mud, and headed west.

Someone was coming.

I drifted back to the truck and leaned on the hood, watching the parking lot and the single road leading to it. A white
Escort zipped down the road and made the hard right turn,
sending up a spray of gravel as it came to an abrupt stop at
the edge of the parking lot. Allie got out, cell phone in hand,
and I felt my phone buzz. I didn't answer it.

She walked around the car, looking anxiously at the phone
and around the park. My phone buzzed again. I watched the
road. No one right behind her, no one parking equidistant
to me and the town, playing the same game as me. I continued watching Allie to see how she functioned under fire.
She paced furiously around the car, walked toward the park,
turned around and headed toward the trees, then returned to
the car and sank down, her butt in the dirt and her back to
the door. She held her phone now in both hands and stared
at the screen.

Today she wore shorts and a tank top. It was obvious that she'd never been on the junk. Her body was toned, athletic. I watched her for a little while longer, then surveyed the park. The old man was getting into his car and leaving, so, seeing no new threats, I decided to let Allie off the hook. I pulled out my phone.

"Allie."

"Jesus, Barr, where the hell are you? This doesn't feel—"

"Relax. I'm here. You got a bag in the car?"

She hesitated. "Yeah, but—"

"Get it. Walk west, away from the park and into the trees. I'll be there. And hurry. I'd bet good money you were tailed."

She wasted little time popping the hatch and grabbing her little day backpack. No big suitcase, no duffel bag. Instead, something she could run with. She even put both straps on before marching in my direction. She'd barely made it into the trees—had just spotted me and my truck—when they finally showed up.

CHAPTER FIVE

A sleek blue sports sedan with tinted windows appeared, moving too fast toward the park. I stepped out of the shadows and motioned to Allie, who started running toward me. "Get in the truck and stay there," I said quietly. "I'll be back in a minute."

She hesitated for a moment before opening the passenger door. Her look asked for an explanation.

"We have visitors," I said.

"Barr, we should just *go*."

"If we leave now," I said, "they'll be on our ass the whole time. I'm going to make sure we get a little head start."

"They probably have guns."

"So do I," I said.

AS I SLALOMED MY WAY through the brush toward the parking lot, I checked the pistol in my pocket and considered how I might use it. I decided to try stealth instead. At a point about ten feet from Allie's car, I went to one knee and crouched behind a leafy cottonweed tree. At my feet lay a long branch. I snatched it up and waited for the right moment.

The blue sedan slowly pulled alongside Allie's car and crunched to a stop. Three men got out—two from the back and then the driver. All three were late twenties. The driver, a short man with slicked-back hair and a very full mustache, barked orders. The other two strutted over to Allie's car, one on either side, and peered through the windows. They both had their hands free but kept checking the back of their belts. The driver turned around slowly, carefully looking at the whole park. He kept touching his belt buckle. So he was armed, too. But he carried it in a spot I never really understood. *Better hope that pistol doesn't accidentally fire.*

Eventually he turned back toward the car and started yelling in Spanish at his buddies, telling them to look around, to go search the park. They jogged away, the driver's gaze following them. His back was toward me, and both his buddies were soon out of sight.

I leaped up and ran at the driver, already swinging the branch. He was quick and wary and had turned and pulled his gun halfway out of his pants when the wood connected solidly with his neck. He crumpled to his knees and tried to get his gun up, but I swung the stick down on his arm. The gun fell from his limp fingers and he turned, looking for his friends. I hit him in the ear with the branch, swinging with both hands and putting my hips into it, driving with my legs. There was a crunch and he fell over on his face.

The two buddies had heard our little scuffle and were racing back toward me, as I'd hoped. I ran toward the river and dove into the brush, crawling on my belly to a spot next to a deer trail that led to water. I heard their footsteps, then their accented yelling.

"Where'd he go, man?"

"To the river, I think."

"He got Fernando good, man. That fool is mine."

A starling exploded out of the brush beside the trail.

"That him?"

"I don't know, didn't see nothing."

They entered the path in front of me with their guns out, black poly pistols in the low-ready position. They walked to the river's edge, scanning the shoreline, the surrounding willows, and the weedy brush, then came to a stop on a small cutbank about four feet above the water. They were shoulder to shoulder, guns held in both hands, when I rushed them.

Holding the stick two-handed at chest level, flat in front of me, I crashed into them, sending both of them sprawling into the foamy brown water. Their heads came up within seconds of each other, arms flailing, already fifty feet downstream. I heard them sputter, then swear, and watched as the roaring river carried the two bobbing heads around a bend and out of sight.

I quickly hurried back to Allie's car. The driver was still motionless, lying facedown in the dirt. I picked him up in a fireman's carry and, staggering forward under the man's weight, made it back to the river, where I set him down by the water's edge. I cupped both hands into the water and threw it on his face. Nothing. I did it again, then *again*, and he finally came to.

"You!" he said, his eyes focusing. "I'm gonna kill you. Where is she?"

"Allie? She's long gone now. How about you tell me where Lance is?"

"I ain't gonna tell you nothing, man." He tried to spit at me but only managed to eject a small bit of spittle over his lip that slowly ran down his chin. He put one hand on his head and moaned. "Where is Diego and Jorge? How come you ain't already—"

I cut him off. "They're on their way to Mexico. Want to go, too?"

He squinted at me, thinking about what I'd said. "You bastard."

"That's not very nice, Fernando. Let's try again. Where's Lance? He has a girl named Jen with him, right?" I stepped left, keeping my eyes on him, and grabbed a large, round cobblestone. He watched me closely and his eyes widened.

"What are you gonna do with the rock, man? Come on . . ." I took a step closer and raised the rock. It was light and smooth, a nice chunk of water-worn sandstone. He rocked left and right trying to get up, hands still holding his head. I jumped at him, rock raised, and watched a dark stain spread across the front of his jeans. Then I threw the rock in the river. He wasn't going to tell me anything, so I grabbed him by his slick hair, ignored his screams, and dragged him to the bank. I asked him one last time, "Do you know where Lance is?"

He didn't answer, just broke down in gasping, cracking sobs and shook his head.

Oh well, I *tried*.

I grabbed him under both shoulders and slid him into the moving water. He attempted to swim to shore, despite the head injury, but I didn't see whether or not he made it before the current took him thrashing around the bend. I walked back to my truck.

CHAPTER SIX

We were back on the interstate, headed east, before Allie said anything.

"You going to tell me what happened to those guys?"

"I gave them free swimming lessons."

Her eyes widened. She stared at me a moment, probably wondering what condition they were in when they went into the river. "You think Brent will send anyone else?"

"Not for a while. If he does, we'll make ourselves hard to find. What more do you know about Lance?"

She stared out the window, sighing. "I told you what I know. He's ambitious, and from the little of I've seen of him, he doesn't have much of a conscience. He even treats Brent like shit."

"That doesn't give me a place to start. There must be something else."

Allie shook her head. "He's private about what he's into. He's not the type who's going to shoot his mouth off in a bar. Brent is the bigmouth in the family." She paused, seeming to remember something.

"What?"

"One night, Brent was pretty lit up by whatever junk he

was on and talking big to a couple guys in his crew—something about how Lance has a factory-size lab somewhere. 'Control that lab and you control the meth trade for a thousand miles,' he said."

For the first time, I wondered if this big honcho I was going up against might be too much to handle. The three years I'd spent in Somalia had taught me how to take on a warlord with his own private army, but Lance sounded smarter than the average tribal bully. *Security expertise. Doesn't shoot off his mouth. An empire builder.* What had Jen said when she'd called me two nights ago? *After I help him get inside a week from now, I'm no use to him.* Inside what?

As the highway mile markers continued to tick by, I kept brooding on the possibilities.

Finally, Allie broke the silence. "Jen mentioned you a couple times."

"Yeah, what'd she say?"

"That you ran away to Africa—to play guns with the natives. She said you were a mercenary."

I hated that word. It implied that I fought for money, which I never did—well, not solely. Yeah, I'd put my hunting skills to use over there, but it was usually for a cause.

"Jen doesn't know the real story. None of that matters now anyway. What matters is that I'm sitting in a truck with a girl going . . . come to think of it, I have no idea *where* we're going. And I have no clue where my sister is."

"I'm not a *girl*," Allie said. Her eyes had narrowed to thin slits, and she stared at me as if begging for debate.

"Sure, you're not a girl. Got it." I'd obviously hit a nerve and I wasn't going to argue.

"Let's get something straight, Barr. I've been through more in twenty-six years than most women have in a lifetime."

She looked back out the window, watching the orchards fly by.

I kept driving, waiting for her to say something else.

"My dad died when I was ten," she said in a quiet voice. "Had a heart attack while he was burning ditches. Left me and my mom on our farm. My mom loved me, but she was sick. Smoked two packs a day and didn't have the energy it took to run a place like that. So I did *every* chore, ran *every* tractor, fixed *every* fence. No one gets to call me a girl."

I nodded, gripping the steering wheel tightly as I fought the truck around the corners. Minutes passed. I sensed there was more.

"You want to tell me the rest of it?"

Allie ran a hand through her hair and closed her eyes. "I met an older guy, started dating, and well . . . it turned out *really* bad. Then my mom had a stroke. I'm her only kid, and who else was going to take care of her, right? Only thing is, it's really expensive and it takes all of your time. So I let some Mennonites farm our place, and I spent every second either caring for my mom or working at crap bars until it almost killed me.

"Then I started working at the Cellar. Brent said I brought in customers. He told me I doubled his business. He paid me enough to put Mom up in an assisted-living place. Looks like that's going to unravel pretty quickly."

So there it was again. The pattern of my life was continuing. I'd begun by trying to help Jen, but had already caused a big problem for Allie. *Damn.*

WE WERE OUT OF THE Grand Valley then, rolling through a narrow canyon that the river had carved through brown-and-red sandstone. We drove into a tunnel and I honked the horn, just to hear the echo. The sound startled Allie and she started talking again. "What are we going to do?" Her eyes were red, but her jaw was set.

"I'm going to drop you off, next town," I said, trying to keep the truck between the lines. The wheels weren't cooperating.

Allie kept staring out the window. "I'm staying."

"I'll give you money. You can get a bus, start over somewhere else."

"That's not good enough."

"What do you mean?"

"If I help you, maybe you help *me*?"

"How?" I wasn't sure where she was going with this.

"I've got a feeling you're a guy who gets what he wants. And not just a piece, either—you take the whole thing."

"And why do I need *you*?"

She smiled. "To pull back on the leash? The best solution isn't always going to be to put five people in the hospital or toss three guys in a river."

I pretended I wasn't amused, but I was. "I could just stop the truck right now, throw you out, drive off."

"Doubt it," she said confidently, tossing her ponytail as she turned to look out the window. "You aren't that kind of guy. Not to women. But if you tried . . ."

"What?" I asked.

"I'd punch you in the dick."

The truck wandered from the white line, across the yellow, and almost onto the opposite shoulder before I got it back under control. Allie looked across, repeated her question. "So what are we going to do?"

Score one for her.

I shook my head, thinking. "Maybe . . . maybe we look for the middle man who sells to Brent. He might have a lead on Lance."

"You mean the Little Dick? That's what Brent calls him. I have no idea where he is. Or what he looks like."

"Spike must have mentioned *something* about him. Anything you can remember will help."

She bit her lip slightly, seemed to be sorting through her mental archives. "All Brent ever said was that 'the Little Dick is in Rifle.' The guys Brent would send to him were supposed to meet him by King's Crown. I guess *they* knew what it was, but I don't have any idea."

"You ever see the guy?"

"Hell no. I haven't been to Rifle since I was a kid. And the Little Dick never goes to Junction. Brent always has to send someone. This guy probably has his own crew and has some pull if he's the one who never has to drive, right?"

"Right. We need to find the Crown."

"It must be a place. Give me a second." She pulled out her phone, swiped her finger against the screen for ten seconds and said, "Got it. Trailer park on the north side of town."

"How'd you do that?" I asked, amazed. I'd been in the backwoods for too long; technology had obviously advanced while I was overseas and in prison.

She explained the Google Maps thing, showed me a picture of the map, and yawned. Then she told me to wake her when we hit Rifle, that she'd had a long night.

After that I stopped only once, in a two-horse town called De Beque to gas up and grab burgers and drinks. My mood was definitely improving. It felt good to have a destination. Maybe when we got to Rife I could pressure this Little Dick guy and learn where Jen was being held. I was actually humming to myself when I checked my rearview mirror and noticed two black SUVs that I'd seen following us prior to our stop in De Beque. No way it was just a coincidence that they were behind us again. The vehicles were close enough to ID them as Tahoes, but they were keeping a set distance. Whoever was driving them seemed content to trail behind us and see where we took them.

I wondered where that would be.

CHAPTER SEVEN

andy escarpments rose up on the left and forested mesas hugged the right until we dropped off a hill and headed into the Rifle valley. The river was wider here, with waves shimmering white in the sun. What were once hay fields in the flat floodplains were now natural gas pads, pipe yards, compressor stations, and gas plants. One of the latter spewed a flame sixty feet into the air. Closer to town, the cattle pastures I'd known as a kid were buried forever under asphalt and pavement, with houses and apartment complexes built on top.

I jerked the truck off I-70 and into west Rifle. The Tahoes followed.

"Who are they?" Allie asked. She was awake now and looking in the side mirror. Her question was clinical, her face deadpan.

"Don't know," I said, reaching for the binoculars under my seat. I handed them to Allie. "What's on the license plate?"

She turned and steadied her elbows on the back of the bench. "US government. J dash four two seven."

"Great," I said. "It's not just the dealers who're looking for Lance. Only J plates I've seen have been DEA, ATF, or FBI."

Allie's eyes widened as she turned back in her seat and buckled in. "How do you know that?"

"Zebras don't like spots," I said, navigating the narrow two-lane through an industrial section of town.

"What?"

"Never mind. They've been following us for a while."

She continued looking at the Tahoes in the side mirror, then dug into the bag of burgers I'd picked up earlier. "You want yours now?" she asked.

I shook my head. "I'll have mine later. Right now I want to see if we can shake these government boys. You pack a coat in that bag?"

She gave me a quizzical look. "Barr, does that backpack look like it could fit a heavy coat?"

"A sweatshirt, then? Something warm?"

"Yeah, but—"

"I'll explain later," I said, steering the truck north through downtown Rifle. It wasn't more than a few blocks long, but contained all of the elements of civilization: library, fast food joints, car washes, bars, pawnshops, and yes, even marijuana dispensaries. When had pot become a staple of modern life?

Allie looked at the Feds again through the side mirror. "Are you going to let them pull you over so you can beat them up?" she asked. I couldn't tell whether she was serious or not.

"Not a good strategy," I said.

She smiled. "So there *are* other skills in your repertoire. Good to know."

As we turned right onto another two-lane road marked "Forest Access," both Tahoes followed conspicuously behind. Allie looked over at me, slurping a soda. "Have you actually done this before, or do you just watch a lot of movies?"

"There haven't been a lot of movies where I've been the past few years. I read a lot of books, though."

"So you learned how to shake a tail from a book?"

"Books. And experience, unfortunately. I've been chased a few times."

Soon we were clear of houses, passing a reservoir, a fish hatchery, and a campground. The Tahoes were still the only vehicles behind us. "You're not very good at this," Allie said.

"I know what I'm doing, trust me. The pavement ends soon and we'll lose them."

"How do you know?" she asked, swallowing the last of her burger.

"That mountain ahead?" I pointed to the large mesa in front of us. "I've camped there a couple times."

Her face remained blank but in her eyes I could see the wheels turning. *What have I signed up for?* they seemed to say.

As the canyon narrowed even further, with cliffs on both sides, a creek meandered back and forth. We crossed it several times, splashing and bobbing, bursting out to dry land, then splashing back again. There were very few trees down along the creek—there wasn't enough light—but the few that grew there grabbed at the sides of the truck, branches screeching along the paint, occasionally smacking the side mirrors. I pushed the reluctant truck up to fifty. We leaped over every bump and bottomed out in every little dip.

For a few seconds it looked like we were going to be boxed in. There were cliffs on both sides of the road, and the bulk of the mountain loomed in front of us. "Barr, are we lost?" Allie asked.

"No. Look up. There's a cut in the hillside, up in those trees. This road climbs out." And it *would* eventually, but it switchbacked the whole way. It was a south-facing slope, in the spring, so it would be muddy and icy, and in the shadows snow-packed.

I slowed, then ground the transfer case into four-wheel drive, turning left and pointing the nose of the truck seemingly straight up. As we slopped and slewed our way up the first pitch, mud spun off the front tires and plastered the side windows.

"They still behind us?" I asked. I kept my focus on the road, both hands tight on the wheel, forearms popping, trying to stay straight and moving.

"I think so. They're headed up the first part of the hill. No . . . now they're not. One of them is sideways in the road, blocking it. Four guys are getting out and walking around. I think they're stuck."

"Gonna get their suits dirty," I said.

It was a fight for both the machine and me to make it up the next couple of turns. The road alternated between mud, ice, and snow, but finally we roared over the top and leveled out in a small clearing surrounded by tall green pines. The grass was short, barely visible between the mounds of pine needles. There were small patches of snow in the shade and large icy drifts against some of the trees.

I pulled to the side of the road and got out. I grabbed the binoculars from the seat and walked to the edge. The Feds had a towrope out, the Tahoe in the rear trying to wrestle the other back down the road. *Welcome to the mountains, boys.* I walked back to the truck and climbed in.

"Jesus," Allie said.

"Yeah." We drove on, further into the forest.

CHAPTER EIGHT

"**C**an I get that burger now?" I asked, holding my hand out to Allie. We'd been driving for about twenty minutes, in and out of clearings, winding our way farther up the mountain and away from Rifle. I'd left the main road, turning instead onto a series of two-tracks that led farther north into the trees. Allie had sat mostly in silence as we bounced and jostled up the narrow roads.

"Sure," she said, handing me the congealed lump. "It's cold."

I took it from her and finished it in three big bites.

"Why are we still driving?" Allie asked.

"In case they kept following us somehow. If they make it as far as we're going, they won't be able to get back off the mountain. They didn't stop anywhere to get gas."

"Oh." The sun was much lower now. The lengthening shadows from the trees stretched across the road and into the open areas on the right. "Are we going back to town now?"

"Nope. Thought we'd camp up here for the night. Give everyone a chance to cool down."

"Camping?" She frowned. "You're serious, aren't you?"

"You *have* camped before, right?" I asked.

"I grew up in Mack, Barr. Camping was the only thing to do on the weekends after we finished chores. That and drinking."

I smiled and found the spot I was looking for. Stopped the truck in a narrow part of the road, jammed it into reverse, and backed into a clearing. The tailgate battered its way through branches until we were in the middle of a sunny, early-flower-filled park. I pulled underneath a tall ponderosa pine at the edge of the clearing and shut off the truck. Once I'd climbed out of the cab, I put my outstretched hand below the sun, thumb up, fingers parallel with the horizon, index finger sitting directly below the sun. There was room for another hand, so at least two hours until sunset. Fifteen minutes per finger, one hour per hand.

Allie got out, grabbed her backpack, and set it on the ground next to the mud-encrusted tires. She rummaged inside, found a hooded sweatshirt, and put it on.

"Aren't your legs cold?" I asked, as she zipped up her pack and slung it on her back.

"No. I'm fine."

I opened the back of the truck and pulled out one of the camping bags. "I've got extra pants, extra long johns, even a couple of coats if you want, though they'll be big on you."

She stared out from her hood, sour-faced. "Stop fussing over me. I'm fine."

I felt the cool breeze blowing off the snow-topped mountains, looked at the falling sun. "It'll drop twenty, thirty degrees tonight. You'll need pants."

"Not if you start a fire and give me something to do. I'll stay warm. Really, Barr, I'm not an idiot. I've done this before."

I shook my head. There was no arguing. If she got cold,

she'd shiver and suffer before she asked for any help. "Okay." I pulled the tent from the bag and tossed it to her. "Here. If you're such an expert, set this up."

She caught the small bag filled with the flimsy fabric, twirled it around, and opened the drawstring.

As I started walking away into the forest, I called back, "I'm getting firewood. See if you can figure that out before I get back."

Before I was more than a couple feet into the trees, I heard the poles hit the ground, then Allie responding, "It's not rocket science, Barr. Try not to get lost."

Deeper into the forest, I could hear occasional swearing from Allie as she attempted to set up the crazy configuration of tent poles inside the tent. I smiled as the clean spring wind blew by me and rattled the aspen leaves. I picked up fallen limbs until I had a good armload, then headed back, my boots sinking deep into the black loamy soil.

As I retraced my steps, my mind started drifting to Jen and what kind of trouble she might be in. Did it help or hurt that my nosing around had probably alerted Lance that I was coming? I hoped the former. Maybe word would get back to Jen, give her hope. But I forced myself to push those thoughts away, focusing instead on this new traveling companion I'd acquired and how I was going to get rid of her. Allie was tough, smart, and resilient, but I was trying not to fall into the old habits. I feared the danger I'd put her in if we stayed together.

"Took you long enough," Allie said as I finally returned to our campsite. The tent was set up, the fluffy sleeping bags were laid out, and the camp chairs and coolers were set in a semicircle around a freshly dug pit. "Right there," she said, pointing at the hole.

I nodded, impressed. Not to be outdone, I dropped the pile by the hole and went back to the truck. I reached into one of the duffels, found a small leather bag, and brought it over to the pit. After pulling out the contents and placing them by the firewood, I jogged into the clearing to strip a big sagebrush of its outer bark. Once I had a bird's-nest-size ball, I loped back into camp, made a tepee and log cabin with the firewood in the pit, and put the kit together. Allie sat down in one of the camp chairs and watched, amused.

A small, split branch of cottonwood with holes on the top and notches on the side went on the ground. Underneath this I put a small, flat piece of bark below a notch. A foot-long round cottonwood stick went into the hole with the notch and bark below. With what looked like a small, three-foot bow, I wrapped string around the round stick. After that I picked up a shot-glass-size piece of wood and rubbed it on my hair, making sure that the grease from the long day would lubricate the socket.

Then it was all just basic movements: kneel down, place a foot on the split cottonwood, stick the socket on top of the round stick to hold it in place and apply pressure, then use the bow like a crosscut saw, spinning the stick like a drill. In less than ten sweaty minutes, I had smoke. I kept going a few minutes longer and had a coal, which I dumped onto the little piece of bark and carefully moved to the bird's nest. Then I blew, soft at first, then longer and harder until the nest burst into flames. I placed those into the prepared firewood and pampered my baby until the flames were right.

Normally, with a Bic and dry wood, I could get a fire roaring in a minute or two. This took a little longer, but I hoped it would be more impressive.

"Not bad," Allie said.

I shrugged, secretly very proud of myself. The sun had started to set by the time my fire took hold, its flames waving frantically up toward a sky the same red-and-orange color.

From my big bag I pulled out some cans and the small zip-lock containing spices. When the fire burned down enough to add more wood, I put a little Dutch oven onto the coals and built the fire up behind it. Then I threw into the oven some pumpkin puree, chicken stock, and a little thyme as Allie sat in a chair across from me and watched intently. She looked relaxed, her chin in her hands, elbows on her knees. The fire turned her bare legs the color of Cheetos. "What are we having?" she asked, her nose wrinkled.

"Pumpkin soup." I looked into the cooler, grabbed out two bottles. "You want wine or whiskey?"

"I'm not a slam-back-the-hard-stuff type," she said, her gaze lost in the flames.

"Wine it is, then," I said, digging in the bags for my long-lost wine tool. I found it, opened the bottle, and poured some into a plastic cup. I poured whiskey into mine. *Why not*, I thought. I really should cut down on the stuff myself, but this didn't seem like the time. I handed Allie her cup, which she accepted with a smile, then I stirred the soup and added dried onions. We both sat and sipped quietly for a while, watching the fire and listening to the birds sing and the air swish through the pines.

We ate the soup as the moon rose in the east. Then we both finished our drinks. There were no sounds except the crackling and popping of the fire.

"Lance won't like that you're looking for him," Allie said, watching sparks drift into the dark sky. "He'll be even madder when you lead the Feds to him. *If* we even find him."

"About this 'we' . . ."

"You need me, Barr."

"I need to find my sister. You're not going to help me do that. You're just going to give me one more person to worry about."

Allie stopped poking the fire and gave me one of those *stop treating me like a child* looks. "I can handle myself, Barr."

"Uh-huh."

We both stared at each other, two equally stubborn people agreeing on a stalemate. A few seconds passed, then Allie broke the silence: "What did your sister say to you anyway? To make you so worried?"

I looked up from the flames. "She made me promise to come get her. Said some guy was trying to kill her. When she's high she can say anything, but she didn't *sound* high. Anyway, the call ended before I could find out more."

"And you're pretty sure it's Lance who has her?"

"Either he has her or he knows who has her. Same difference."

"We'll find him," she said. "We know where to start."

I grunted. There it was again, more "we."

Allie seemed to sense my skepticism. "I know what Lance looks like. Most people don't. That's why he uses so many middle men. If you find him without me, and he has Jen hidden somewhere, how are you going to know you've got the right guy?"

I nodded, took another slug. "Point for you," I said. "But what happens when this gets nasty, like I'm afraid it's going to? People will get hurt. A *lot* of people if they keep getting between me and my sister. Are you okay with that?"

She sipped her wine and waited a long time before answering. The flames were down to half their original size when she said, "I'm okay with it. Brent and Lance are assholes. I've known a lot of assholes in my life. Too many. They always seem to get away with it. Except this time I have a feeling they won't. I'm coming with you. It's final."

I didn't put up any more resistance. We sat in silence for another hour, each lost in our thoughts, listening to the crickets and the night wind. I was about to pour another cup when I looked over at Allie and finally saw her shivering. Without thinking, I rose, took off my coat, and put it gently over her legs. For the first time that day, she didn't argue. Instead, she looked at me closely—eyes scrunched, the way I'd scan the sky for weather.

A few minutes later she rose abruptly from her camp chair and I smelled wine and pumpkin on her sweet breath. "I'm going to sleep, Barr. We'll talk in the morning." I heard her rearranging things in the tent; then she tossed my sleeping bag out the door and into the brush. After that, the tent's zipper closed tight.

CHAPTER NINE

The robins woke me up at false dawn. I slithered out of the sleeping bag, found fresh clothes, and changed in the pale morning light, under the trees. I assumed Allie was still sleeping and knew that it would be in my best interest to let her stay that way. I packed the bag, grabbed my rifle, and went on a little patrol that mimicked one I'd done last night before turning in. I didn't think there was any chance of a new threat; I just wanted to smell the piney air and think.

Gawain, Perceval, Lancelot, and all the other knights I'd read about as a kid would have been proud of me. I'd defended the beautiful maiden, hadn't taken advantage of her, even made her a partner of sorts. What could go wrong?

Making my way back to camp, I remembered the answer to that question. *Everything.* Everything could go wrong. Like when Jen and I were little, after Dad had run away, and Deb was living in Aspen and Angie was in college. It was bad enough Dad was gone, leaving Mom to try and take care of us by herself. It was worse when Mom started dating again. The first couple of guys weren't too bad. Just drunk.

The third guy, whom we called Ski because we couldn't pronounce his last name, was worse. He and Mom would go to the bar and leave Jen and me to cook and clean and put ourselves to bed. Later that night they'd come home and the inevitable fight would start; they'd knock over pans, break glasses, wake the neighbors. I sneaked out of my room after one of their fights and have regretted it ever since.

Mom was facedown on the kitchen table, her bruised and bleeding eyebrows dripping onto the Formica. Her shirt was torn and hung off one of her arms, revealing her large breasts. Behind her, Ski stood with his pants down, yelling that she was a slut.

At the time I was a scrawny eleven-year-old. So when I raced across the room and started pounding on Ski—who must have weighed 250 pounds—with my little fists, it took only a backhand from him to knock me into the wall and unconscious.

In the morning Mom was bandaged and cleaned up and trying to make breakfast while still drunk. She said that nothing had happened—that I'd had a bad dream. But bad dreams don't leave huge knots on skulls. And two weeks later Jen told me about *her* bad dreams. In hers, Ski was visiting her in the night and touching her.

I pushed the memories back into the badger hole in my brain and went back to the tent.

Allie was up when I returned, sitting in a camp chair next to a small fire. She'd found a box of Pop-Tarts and had put a couple in a frying pan to warm over the flames. She'd changed into blue jeans and a pink sweatshirt. Her hair was loose and mussy, but her face was glowing in the bright sun as she looked up at me and asked, "Hungry?"

"Famished," I said. I stared at the crosshatch of branches blazing in the fire pit. "Nice fire."

She grinned. "I discovered this thing called matches. You should try them sometime."

"Maybe I will," I said, realizing that I actually liked it when she needled me.

As I flopped into a chair next to her, she handed me one of the warm pastries. I was still licking the lemony goo off my hands when I saw her expression darken.

"Do you think we're in trouble, Barr?"

"For what?"

"For running from the Feds. Isn't that some kind of felony?"

"I doubt it," I said. "I don't think we're the ones they're interested in, or they would have pulled me over a long time before. We were supposed to lead them to Lance."

"You sure?"

"No." And I wasn't. I was just working on educated guesses.

We were loaded up and on the road in less than an hour. I was impressed with Allie's packing skills. We worked as a wordless team, putting everything back in its proper place in the bags and into the truck. She smiled a little more today, as if our partnership was the beginning of something great. I hoped it would be.

She sat in the passenger seat enjoying the view as the truck rumbled down the gravel road on its way off the mountain. We rambled to a flat intersection where the drainage we'd been following connected with a larger creek that led back to Rifle. I pulled over at a wide spot and shut off the truck, then called Juan in Riverside. He wasn't too happy about helping again, but he told me about some of his connections in Rifle. He also said that he'd send Chopo my way.

"Now I need *you* to make a phone call," I told Allie.

"To whom?"

"Spike. Tell him I dropped you off in Rifle, and you want your job back. You're sorry, you're scared, and you don't know what to do."

"Why?"

"Neither of us knows what the Rifle boys look like. I figure Spike will recruit a few to come pick you up. We'll set up a meeting place. Once the welcome wagon arrives, I persuade one or two to talk."

Allie shook her head. "I could call Brent, make that little speech, but he won't buy it. It'll work better if you call, tell him you're sick of me and you're going to dump me out in Rifle if he wants to come collect me. Frame it as a double cross, as me believing I'm waiting for you to get back but actually I'm an offering to him to get the heat off you."

I laughed. "You have a devious mind, Ms. Martin."

She smiled. "The only motivations that Brent trusts are selfish ones. And anyway, he knows I'm unwilling to put up with his crap anymore." She handed me her cell phone.

When I got Brent on the line, he reacted predictably—threatening me with every kind of slow death his little mind could come up with. It wasn't a very long list.

"What'd he say?" Allie asked, smiling.

"Just the usual pleasantries. But he's going to send someone." I took the keys and handed them to her. "You think you can drive this pickup?"

"Of course. Anything with wheels. Why?"

"From now on we'll be improvising a lot. I may need you to drive. It's good for you to get some experience with this heap."

She shrugged, agreeing.

"Okay. Just remember, this truck is tricky. The steering is twisted, the shocks are shot, and both the throttle and the brakes are on their way out. Can you handle that?"

"Switch with me, and I'll prove it." So I did. Once we were back in and buckled, she proved it. She had to adjust the seat first, pull it closer to the wheel, but after that she was almost as good as anyone I'd ridden with. In fact, she raced down a couple of the dirt roads so fast I found myself pulling my seat belt tighter.

"Scared?" she asked.

"Not for me," I said. "For the truck. You're going to wear it out before we can get back to town."

She laughed—a little snicker that sounded younger and more feminine than her usual persona—then turned us back toward the pavement. I gave her the directions that would take us to Rifle. She switched from racing mode to casual and we hit the highway and headed south.

We passed a few old homesteads, and then Allie looked at me and asked, "How long has it been since you've seen Jen?"

"Too long."

"How long since you've *talked* to her?"

"Before that last call? Way too long."

"Why?"

"I was busy helping a lot of other people," I said.

"Did you work at a hospital or something?"

I *had* worked in one for a while, the same one that had patched me up in the Mtabila camp in Tanzania, but I didn't tell her that.

"Mostly I just helped to sort out the good guys from the bad—in Africa, South and Central America, then Mexico," I said.

"What do you mean by 'sort'?"

"I mean, there's always someone who wants to play the bully—in those places especially." I didn't like where this conversation was going, so I told her to pay attention to the road.

WE'D JUST CRESTED A HILL and started our long descent into the Rifle area when the truck suddenly swung into a sideways slide. I'd been zoned out, adrift in memories of Africa, when Allie gave a shout. I looked at the road ahead and saw two large cow elk standing on the center line, their heads staring straight ahead as the passenger side of the truck screeched toward them. They seemed bewildered and unable to move as the truck slammed into them.

One of the animals was thrown off its feet and launched into the bar ditch, where she lay flopping and kicking. The other's head connected solidly with my window, shattering the glass on impact, her body crumpling the door and side panel before disappearing underneath the truck. I brushed blue glass off my chest and told Allie to pull over. She jerked and lurched the mangled pickup to a grinding halt, far off the pavement.

"Damn it, I didn't see them. I couldn't stop." She stared straight ahead, hands gripping the steering wheel so tightly I could see the bones. Her eyes were red but she didn't cry.

"It happens," I said, more worried about what needed to be done than what had just happened. I grabbed the pistol out of the small bag in between us.

"Jesus," she said, eyes huge and following the pistol. "You going to shoot me for denting your piece-of-crap truck?"

"It's for them," I said. I pointed through the crumpled window at the two massive creatures wallowing next to the road. One was well into its death throes, feebly kicking the air. The other was trying to get up on broken legs, making small animal cries with every attempt, head thrashing, mouth foaming. Allie looked away as I got out.

I took ten steps and stood away from the legs to avoid getting kicked. Then I pulled the trigger twice, sending 180-grain bullets into the animals' skulls. Both elk lay still, their broken, mostly headless bodies nothing more than heaps of bloody hide on the pavement's edge.

When I got back into the truck, Allie's face looked flushed. I pulled the magazine, replaced the two spent cartridges, then slammed it back in place with my palm.

"Why?" she asked.

"You mean why did I shoot them? I didn't want to see them suffer—simple as that." I looked at her closely, concerned by how she was taking this. "You going to be okay?"

She nodded but continued starting straight ahead. Then she turned to me. "Tell me something, Barr. When you do what you do—you know, this fighting and killing thing—does it ever get to you?"

For a second, as I thought about how to respond, I flashed back to when I was twenty years old and came across my first scene of carnage, in the upper Congo—a carnage I had partly caused. So many bloody bodies, piled high in the noonday sun. Birds picking at torn camouflage fatigues. Flies buzzing. A meaty stench in the nostrils.

I looked over at Allie and met her eyes. "Every day," I said.

CHAPTER TEN

Twenty minutes later we were navigating through Rifle with me at the wheel, the wind roaring in through the mangled passenger-side door. Allie's hair whipped in the wind as I looked warily out my side window. Some part of me felt as though I was in enemy territory. We pulled into a housing complex north of the King's Crown trailer park and stopped in an underused lot littered with fast food wrappers and aluminum cans.

I could see the grassy park to the south that Allie had told me about. It was empty, save for two plump women speaking Spanish and pushing strollers around the cracked concrete walking path. The three-story apartment buildings were well behind us, angled in such a way that only a few had windows overlooking the park. This seemed the best spot to observe the grass unnoticed. I hopped onto the hood. Allie joined me. We went over our small plan again.

"Whoever Spike recruits from Little Dick's crew to 'collect you'—or whatever their real intention is—will be at this park in a few hours. You'll go to the junkyard that one of Juan's cousins owns and park my truck. Stay there, get our bags ready. Things may get nasty here. I'll take a car from whoever shows up at the park and pick you up after this is over. Hopefully by then I'll have gotten one of these errand boys to give us Little Dick's address. Chopo should be meeting me here soon to provide backup. If those Feds somehow get involved again, I'll walk back to the junkyard. Anything I forgot?"

"Why are we leaving the truck at the yard?"

"It needs to be fixed. And the Feds have my plates. Juan said his cousin has a car we can use. I'll trade him the car I'll be taking from Little Dick's crew. While we're gone Juan said someone would fix my truck. Make sense?"

Allie nodded. We hopped off the truck. As I watched her settle into the front seat, she turned and called out through the open window. "Hey, Barr."

"Yeah."

"I know this is just business as usual for you, but don't get yourself killed and leave me alone in a junkyard, okay?"

"I'll see you soon," I said confidently.

My smile faded when the truck rumbled out of sight. I didn't like this situation. And the incident with the elk had rattled me. It was getting harder and harder to run headlong into violent, potentially illegal situations. When people were being spit on, I could separate the work from myself, like I had in Africa and South America. When people killed others for no reason, it was easy to side with the underdog and help. That was simple. But in those situations I hadn't been *personally* involved. Sure, the outcomes of those little tussles could have put me in the ground, but I'd never worried about that.

But now I had a legitimate reason to care about the outcome. I had a family member who was counting on me—a sister who, when we were little, had been my best friend and confidant. A sister who'd been in trouble before when I was the only one around to help. I thought back to the week after Ski had knocked me out and Jen had told me he was starting to touch her.

SHE'D GONE MUTE FOR THE week. Mom must have known why, on some level, but she wouldn't admit that either she or Ski had anything to do with it. I knew better. And I was going to make sure it never happened again.

Two days after I was knocked unconscious, Ski and Mom had a rowdy night and were still in bed, both snoring with hangovers at 10:00 a.m. That morning, I soaked a rag in gasoline, sneaked out to Ski's Trans Am, and jammed it into the gas tank. Then I went back inside and washed my hands, listening to make sure Ski and Mom weren't awake. No change in the buzz saws. I checked Jen's room, but the door wouldn't open. I found out later that she'd pushed her dresser against the door.

Hurrying, I stole a Pall Mall from Ski's pants in the broken kitchen, grabbed a pack of firecrackers, and went back outside. Carefully, I cut a small hole in the rag and made a foot-long string of fuse pulled from the firecrackers. I wrapped one end around the cigarette and one end through the hole and around the rag, making sure it would stay, and put a Bic to the Pall Mall. The breeze was light, and puffed the red end enough to keep it lit. I went back inside.

I'd practiced using this type of fuse with Juan, blazing gas cans when we were up in the hills the summer before, and I knew that I had about ten minutes. So I used anger to push away the fear and opened Mom's door. I ignored the naked bodies on the bed, and said, loud enough to wake them, "Mom, I'm hungry."

Ski came off the bed first, threw a right into my teeth that sent me into the closet door, kicked me when I fell, then threw his pants on and left. Over his shoulder he yelled, "You need to control your shitty brats. I'm out." Mom cried, but was either too drunk or too broken to come to my aid. I was a fast healer, and I wasn't too worried about the beating. I was, however, worried about my miscalculation.

I'd planned for Ski to stay awhile, see his car on fire, wonder how I could do it when I was still inside, and run away scared. Instead, I read in the paper the next day that a man with a hard-to-pronounce last name had suffered severe burns on half his body when his Pontiac had burst into flames while slowing for a speed bump in a trailer park. Ski never returned, and Jen and I thought that our troubles were over.

That's when Mom started seeing a man named Jimmy Paxton. And things got much, much worse.

A CAR CRUNCHED TO a stop next to me, shaking me out of my reminiscing. It was a black Camaro—according to the writing on the side—with a big trunk and a bigger engine, made in a time when vehicles were built with steel. I put my hand in my jacket pocket, my fingers curling around the pistol, as a very muscled man unfolded himself from the car.

He had black bushy hair and a thin mustache and wore a crisp polo shirt and jeans. Tattoos ran from his hands, up his large arms, and into the short sleeves. His boots were ostrich or something else fancy. He moved lightly for a man his size, waltzing up to me. The strong scent of cologne waltzed up with him.

"Hey, Chopo," I said, taking my hand out of the coat.

"*Qué pasó*, Barr?" He spread his feet wide and folded his

arms, showing off his massive biceps. Chopo worked as a free-lance shooter and fixer for the cartels. He had a reputation for carrying out assignments without complications, so he was usually busy on the border. "Juan called. Said you might need a hand with some punks."

"I appreciate it."

"No problem, man, I owe you," he said, calmly scanning left to right. I'd ridden with him down to Mexico once, a simple matter of moving his mom from her little thatched house out in the country to a bigger, brick one in the city. He wanted her closer so he could take care of her. It wasn't dangerous work, but helping family meant a lot to Chopo.

"Rifle boys are coming, huh?" Chopo asked.

I nodded, said, "They think they're picking up a bartender from the Cellar—a woman on their shit list. I need them to lead me to their boss, a guy named the Little Dick."

"Jefe?"

"Same guy?"

"Yeah, his *real* name is Jeff. He just calls himself Jefe because he thinks he's one of us bangers."

"Jefe might know where the number one guy, Lance Alvis, is cooking. My sister's with him."

Chopo spit on the ground. "Hell, man, everyone's looking for Mr. Alvis. He cut off the cheap local stuff. You want my advice, I'd steer clear of him. The dude had three dealers nailed up on crosses in Albuquerque. Just like Jesus."

"Damn," I said. This was the second indication that I might have underestimated Lance. "Well, it's not like I've got choices here, you know. I've got to get my sister away from him. And I may not have much time." I told Chopo the rest of my plan.

"I got my end, bro," he said. He pointed at a .50-caliber

Desert Eagle wedged into his belt. Most people couldn't *hold* one of those, let alone shoot it more than once with any accuracy. In Chopo's hands, however, it looked as small as my own .40.

Chopo noticed my interest. "Like it?" he said. "I found it on the ground." Then he gave me that type of sinister grin that told me I really didn't want to know where he'd found it.

CHAPTER ELEVEN

We sat in the car and watched the park. The sun was warm and the air smelled of dry grass and Dumpster garbage. Families came and ate small lunches in the gazebo, their little kids playing in the clumpy brown grass. More mothers came and went, some walking fast and swinging flabby arms for exercise, others slowly shuffling with strollers. Ravens came and searched the sidewalks for food.

Finally, at about six o'clock, the park cleared out. The neighborhood must have an unwritten schedule stating that toward dark, it's gang business hours. A newly washed and waxed red Mustang slowly drove past, then swung back around and drove by us again before disappearing down the street. "Little Dick's fetch-it boys are here," Chopo said.

"Okay, so let's do what we discussed. You tell 'em you're from another crew. Say you've got the girl and want to get paid a few bucks to hand her over. Point them around the corner to that alley. Once they're there, I'll put my pistol to the driver's head and force them out of the car. You really have to sell your offer, though. Let them know you're not greedy, just looking to make a little green."

Chopo nodded. "I'll make it easy for them."

The Mustang cruised at a walking pace into the main parking lot and stopped. Two men got out and leaned against the car. Tall, dirty white boys with long hair, wearing leather jackets and black jeans.

As Chopo began sauntering in their direction, I positioned myself next to a Dumpster in the alley and kept my pistol's safety off. I scanned up and down the street, occasionally checking the buildings behind me. I couldn't hear what Chopo was saying; the traffic noise was starting to get loud and was interspersed with sirens. The two men appeared to be laughing. Chopo wasn't. He took a step back, his hand twitching by his side.

Three pairs of hands flew and three pistols appeared. Two shots rang out. Chopo was already on the move, running back toward me as the other men's bodies crumpled to the ground. I had my pistol aimed at the bodies, watching Chopo crouch and run below my sights. *Bad. This is bad.*

It got worse. "Get in the damned car, Barr!" Chopo yelled as he ran past me and yanked the driver's door open. "Your plan was shit."

I reached for my door as a second car roared around the corner toward the park. A man in the passenger seat pointed a shotgun out the window. A shot boomed and steel pellets rang off our hood, shredding paint and cracking glass. I squeezed the trigger three times, aiming at the receding taillights of the shotgun car.

The back window shattered, then the car was out of sight. I wallowed in the passenger side as Chopo slammed his car in reverse and tore off, wheels spitting rocks and trash. Chopo yanked the wheel, the front end spinning 180 degrees, before he threw it into drive and headed east through town.

Son of a bitch. My hands shook as I put the pistol on my

lap. The barrel was warm and the car reeked of burnt powder. "What the hell just happened?"

"Word came down from Mr. Alvis. You and the bartender are dead. They couldn't figure my angle at first; then one of them recognized me and put me with Alejandro. They drew down, saying that us Mexicans will never get it back. I dropped them."

"The second car?"

"Who knows? You sure as hell aren't very popular, Barr." I could tell he was mad at the situation, but other than that he didn't seem fazed at all. Another day at work.

"If Alvis is gunning for us, then we need to get Allie. Now."

"For sure. My cousin's junkyard on Antlers Lane?"

"Yeah."

We headed east out of town, driving a reasonable speed on back roads. Once we got on US 6 we picked up speed, watching for cops. Our car was missing a lot of paint and would be pulled over on sight. Horses and cows stood listlessly in fields to our left, nibbling on the short, sweet green grass. Chopo's car smelled strongly of a different kind of grass and expensive cologne. It was clean though, not a piece of typical car trash anywhere.

How I could be so stupid? All along I'd underestimated Alvis. It made sense that once I told Brent I was in Rifle, the troops would be called in. Somehow in a matter of days, I'd gotten involved with multiple drug-dealing gangs, Feds, and a girl who was starting to mean something. To me and everyone else. So much for the quiet life in the Yukon.

A train rumbled down the tracks on our right, a long one carrying heaping piles of coal. It belched gray smoke as it clanked away in the opposite direction. Up ahead lay the junkyard; I could already see the tall wooden privacy fence that from here looked like a thin brown line, seeming to stretch forever. As we got closer, however, I began to see smoke. Thick black columns swirled steadily into the dimming blue sky.

"See that?" Chopo asked. He was steady and professional now; his right hand relaxed on the wheel while his chiseled left arm pointed out the window toward the junkyard. He aimed the car toward it and picked up speed.

I nodded. The smoke came from the center of the yard, where the office should be. I could make out some of the flames in the diminishing light, dancing like dervishes above the fence. Allie was in there.

As we pulled into the yard it became abundantly clear that everything was wrong. Cars spewed flames from their shattered windows, the gate sprawled in a splintered wreck, and bodies lay on the ground near the burning office. I jumped out, pulled my pistol from my jacket, and sprinted toward the flames. Chopo hopped out and covered me, his pistol resting on the office's open door. No shots. The bodies didn't move, and I prayed that none belonged to Allie. I reached the office and stopped, crouching near the bodies. Then I waved Chopo over. There were three men: two facedown in bloody pools on blackened soil, and one moaning in the fetal position near an oversize truck tire.

"You know any of these guys?" I asked Chopo when he came huffing over.

He walked slowly by each one, then knelt next to one of the dead men. "This is my cousin." He ran his large hand down the bloody cheek. "The other dead guy was a shooter, by the look of his threads. For Jefe or Alvis, most likely. And the *güero* crying must be the new guy my cousin hired. He must have ratted us out to Jefe or Alvis."

Holding my pistol toward the ground, I marched over to the white boy. "Chopo," I called back, "my truck's junky, white, with a camper shell. Find it and look for Allie. See if she packed a couple bags. They should be near the truck, out of sight." Chopo patted his dead cousin's shoulder, then stood up, his eyes cold slits, and nodded. He walked off, fists clenching, and I was alone with the man by the tire.

The man—a young boy, really; not yet out of his teens— had caught lead in his stomach. His blue denim shirt had turned dark black, and he held both hands tightly against it, eyes screwed shut, moaning. I stood over him and stomped a booted foot down on his messy guts. He screamed and opened his eyes. I crouched beside him.

"Where is she?" I asked.

"I . . . who . . . ?" His words gurgled out, accompanied by little rivulets of blood.

"I don't have time for this," I said. "There was a girl here. Brunette. Ponytail. Drove a white truck. Where is she? Did you call Jefe?"

He didn't answer fast enough, so I put the muzzle of my pistol into the dark, round bullet hole in his belly. Then twisted.

He shouted in tongues, writhing underneath me.

I pushed deeper into the hole. "Where *is* she?"

"Okay . . . make it stop!"

I eased the pistol out. It dripped blood out of the muzzle. "Where?"

"Okay, okay," he said, spitting up red. "Jefe—Jeff—he's my girlfriend's dad. He sells the good stuff. He said you were try- ing to wreck the business, said you were running with some bitch. I was supposed to call him if either of you showed up. César fought back, though." More blood trickled from his mouth. "Come on, dude, am I gonna die here?" His skin had turned ashen.

"You're *not* answering my question. Where's the girl? Does Jefe have her?"

The boy coughed up more blood. "Yeah . . . they took her to him. Help me out, please . . ."

"Where is Jefe?"

"You gotta help—"

I said, "*Where* is Jefe? Where does he live?"

The boy was fading now. I turned his head back toward me, got close to his face, almost eyeball to eyeball. *"Where?"*

"Big house . . . on Fir Court . . ." He coughed out an address.

I stood up and scanned for Chopo. When I looked back down, I saw that the boy's eyes had closed and his body was limp.

CHAPTER TWELVE

We were in a newly acquired vehicle and headed on a looping route north, away from the junkyard, then back east toward Rifle via the large, looming hills of the Hogback. I was in the driver's seat, Chopo on the passenger side. We passed by hobby ranches, with their token horses and cows, then into narrow canyons filled with both luxury and ramshackle cabins. Chopo's car was too big a target, so we'd borrowed a run-of-the-mill white Jeep Cherokee from César's lot. We left just before the sirens of fire trucks, police cars, and ambulances caught up with us at the junkyard.

"Sorry about your truck, man," Chopo said, finally breaking the strained silence.

He'd found the truck burning. Hot metal warping and popping, flames ten feet in the air—and the heat coming off it was enough to keep even Chopo from getting too close. He located the two overstuffed, backpack-type packs and the little bag hidden away from the truck, and it took almost all of his immense strength to drag them back to the Jeep. I wondered how Allie had managed to move them.

"It wasn't much of a truck," I said. I was more remorseful about the things inside it: almost all of my new, warm gear, the accessories for my retirement plan. I would guess that other people feel the same sense of loss when their houses go up in flames, or the stock market drops and they lose money in their 401(k).

"You got enough junk in those bags, *cabrón*?" Chopo asked.

"Maybe," I said. "Thanks for that. No sign of Allie?"

"None. That white boy who ratted us out said Jefe's guys took her, right?"

"That's what he said. I hoped he was lying."

"Hombre ain't gonna lie when he's bleeding out on the ground."

"You saw that, huh?"

Chopo nodded. "You can be a cold *pendejo* sometimes."

I shrugged. "I've got two women depending on me." Inside, though, I wondered if every time I took it that far I gave up a little piece of who I was.

We rolled into Rifle on a network of small, gravel back roads. We had an address but no idea where it was. I found myself wishing I had Allie's fancy phone with that map gizmo, and then I remembered taking a phone off the dead kid who'd given me the address. I fished it out of my pocket and saw that it was one of the newer models. "Hey, Chopo," I said, handing him the phone. "You know how to bring up a map on one of these things?"

Chopo smiled. "It's called an app, Barr." He started pushing buttons. "Okay," he said a minute later. "I got Fir Court. Keep going straight, then take your next right." He kept directing me until we were on a county road that ran north of Jefe's neighborhood. The road ran east and west directly below a hill to the south. Fir Court and a bunch of other tree-named streets were on top of the hill. A gully ran straight south across from a dilapidated ranch house and would run directly underneath Jefe's backyard, if the address the kid had given me was correct.

It was almost full dark now, the streetlights looking like halos on the top of the hill. We backed next to the run-down ranch house and killed the headlights. The hill between us and Fir Court was covered with tall sagebrush and a few dying cotton-woods in the gully. The ranch house, the hill, and the gully were the only open land left in the area that hadn't been gobbled up by developers or smacked into modernity with renovations.

Chopo stayed in the Jeep while I used the failing light and dark shadows as cover to quietly check the house. No cars. No animals. The fences were all down and the last tracks in the dirt drive were those of deer and a few kids on bikes. A sign hung in one of the cracked windows, and I read it before going back to the Jeep.

"Anyone home?" Chopo asked.

"All clear."

"How you know?"

"Well, I checked the tracks, listened for any noise, and used a couple of skills I picked up in the wild."

Chopo rolled his eyes.

"That," I said, "and the sign in the window says the build-ing is condemned and is the property of the town of Rifle."

Chopo smiled. "You gonna make a run at Jefe, huh?"

"Through his daughter," I said, getting out of the Jeep.

"How we gonna do this?"

"I figure we coax the daughter out of the house and one of us grabs her. The other covers from somewhere on that hill over there with a rifle. We bring her back here and call for a switch."

"You think it'll work?"

"Probably not. But that's all I can come up with."

"It's kidnapping, you know. . . . Just saying."

"Yeah, but they started it." How many of history's stupid acts had been justified with *that* explanation?

Chopo nodded. He seemed reconciled to all my schemes being kind of crazy-ass. "So how we gonna get her out of the house?"

I thought for a moment. "I could figure out which car in the driveway is hers and set off the alarm?"

Chopo shook his head. "She might just use the fob, and who knows if she even *has* a car." I didn't know what a fob was—there was *so much* about technology I didn't know now that I was back—but I decided not to say anything. "So you got a better idea, Mr. Criminal Mastermind?"

Chopo thought for a second, then said, "We'll use that kid's phone." He pulled out the phone with the map app. "The kid said he was the daughter's boyfriend, right? So we'll just send her a text from his phone, tell her to secretly meet him out in the backyard."

A *text*? I hated texting.

Chopo saw my reluctance. "Jesus, Barr—you're like a brother from another planet. People send text messages from their phone."

"I know that, I just don't do it. Show me," I said.

He shook his head and gave me a quick refresher class.

Chopo volunteered to make the snatch while I covered him with my rifle, so I went into my gun bag and debated for a second whether to use my big gun—the .375 H&H—or my .22. The H&H was for shooting large African game—or a particularly hard-to-stop human—so I selected the lighter weapon. After zipping up the case, I strung my binoculars around my neck. Then I picked up the kid's phone and looked at Chopo. He shoved his pistol in his waistband.

"Ready?" I asked.

He nodded.

We crossed the road and headed into the gully, moving low and quiet. I stopped about fifty yards from the target house near a pair of large sagebrush. "I'll be here," I whispered.

Chopo nodded, then continued slowly up the hill until he was at the foot of Jeff's privacy fence. I settled down onto the ground, lying prone with the rifle nestled tightly against my shoulder. Through the scope I watched Chopo pull his pistol. The crickets chirped loudly in my ear; far away I heard someone's sprinkler come on. Without taking my eye off the crosshairs, I slowly pulled out the phone and pressed Send, firing off the text I'd written earlier. I waited a couple minutes and pressed call and was rewarded when I saw Chopo stir against the fence.

As hoped, Jeff's daughter had come out into the backyard. I didn't have any contingency plans if she hadn't.

The rest happened in a blur. Chopo was up and over the fence, the back gate crashing open, the lock splintering off with a massive kick, and then he was running down the hill, a thin white girl thrown over his shoulder. He loped, lugging his prisoner down a serpentine course through the brush toward me.

Two large men in sweats burst out of the gate in pursuit. I watched them through the scope, saw them raise carbine rifles, so I fired three quick shots. One man immediately went down to his knees, red spraying from his chest, so I centered the crosshairs on the second. I pulled the trigger three more times right after a few shots rang from his rifle. He fell onto his face and rolled down the hill in a writhing heap. By then Chopo was past me, the girl kicking and squirming on his shoulder. I watched the gate a little longer, and when no one else came out, I hopped up and followed Chopo into the darkness.

As we moved through the head-high cut in the dirt at the bottom of the gulch, I wondered what the hell I was thinking. I was ramping this up too fast, escalating it to the point of no return. This wasn't the Congo or Chile or even Mexico. This was kidnapping and possibly murder in the eyes of the law. In *my* eyes, though, it was retribution and a means to an end. So I stayed low in the gulch and scrambled to catch up with Chopo, noticing the lights of Jefe's neighbors come on one by one.

Chopo took the girl into the abandoned ranch house. I followed them in and laid my rifle on the old kitchen table. The windows were dirty enough to be opaque, and the place smelled of mildew and mouse droppings. The only light came from Chopo's penlight. The girl sat in a rickety chair, her mouth and hands bound in duct tape. I couldn't look at her.

"We can't stay here," I said. "Neighbors are calling the cops. Jeff's probably calling in reinforcements."

Chopo nodded. "I know a *chica*, runs a safe house here for some of the guys out of Mexico."

"Let's go, then." I finally looked at the girl, her brown eyes wide and starting to tear up. She couldn't have been older than sixteen. I tried to smile at her. "Listen, kid. We're not going to hurt you. I need you for a trade. Your daddy has a friend of mine. When I get her back, you go home safe and sound. Okay? Nod if you understand." She jerked her head up and down, her shoulders slumped.

We grabbed our stuff, led the girl out, and put her in the backseat, then we threw our gear in the back. We drove slowly away, following back roads again until we arrived at a trailer park full of low-riders and short-bed pickups with tinted windows. Chopo hopped out and went up onto the porch of one of the trailers. He pounded on the thin wooden door until a very large, round, brown woman in a floral-print housedress emerged. She and Chopo talked for a few seconds, and then she waved us into the house. As I got out, the woman shut off her porch light to hide us in the darkness.

"Not a sound, kid," I whispered into the girl's ear as I led her up to the house. "This will all be over soon." She nodded, tears streaming down her pale cheeks.

The woman met us at the door, putting her large, flabby arm around the girl's shoulders. She had a round face, with fleshy jowls rolling over her collar, and her smile seemed warm. Her eyes, though, were deadly serious and blazed with matronly concern.

"I'm sorry about this, ma'am, really," I said. "Thank you for taking us in on short notice. You can watch her for the night?"

"Yes," she said, her husky voice filling the house. "It is nothing. I like visitors. You're welcome to stay in one of the rooms. I will keep the girl in the other. My son Julio will move your car to somewhere safe, and if you need it, he'll bring it back. Julio!"

A thin boy, maybe seventeen, ran into the room. He had a chunk of plastic in his hands, headphones around his neck. His mom yelled at him in rapid Spanish and he rushed out the door. "I'll take her now. You two stay and talk here." She led the girl down a narrow hall away from the kitchen, her massive arm draped over the girl's shoulders like a cellulite shawl. Talking quietly and in an endearing, earnest way, she said, "It's okay, dear, this is just some stupid men's thing. They don't know any better. I'm going to put you in a special room." Her voice faded as she walked away. "It'll be locked, but you'll have everything you need. . . ."

Chopo and I sat down at the small wooden kitchen table. The trailer was well worn, with paint missing in the usual spots, but clean and taken care of. Everything in the kitchen was recently washed, the dishes were all put away, and the table was bare. A fluffy yellow cat came out from somewhere and rubbed against my leg, purring loudly. I reached down to pet it as I asked Chopo, "Who is she?"

"The cat? I don't know. The lady, her name is Nita. She's an aunt of a friend. She helps hide people, sometimes us guys from the crews, sometimes whole families from Immigration. She's very good at it."

I nodded. Julio came back in then and sat down on the single couch in the living room across from a big-screen TV. He picked up a controller and started to play a video game, oblivious to us sitting in the kitchen. Nita came out shortly afterward, closing a door and locking it quietly.

"She is very scared but I talked to her and she'll be okay. You want me to cook something? You boys look hungry."

I was going to say yes. I'd taken my hat off and hung it on the back of the chair. But Chopo said, "No thanks."

"Okay, let me know. Your room will be the first on the left down the hall. You need to smoke, go out the back in the yard, okay? You need anything out of your car, tell me, and Julio will get it, okay?"

We both nodded and she went into the living room, plopped next to her son on the sofa, picked up a magazine, and started flipping pages. I stood up and zipped up my jacket, gestured to the door.

Outside, Chopo asked, "You only want Alvis, right?" He lit his cigarette and took a deep drag.

"Right. We'll make the trade, then I'm going to have to find him another way. But I'll find him. I *have* to. He has my sister."

"Then I can have Jefe."

It wasn't a question.

"All yours," I said. "I won't get any leads from him now." I really wanted a cigarette, so I allowed myself one. Just one. Tomorrow I'd quit.

"They killed César, man. Add that to the list of shit they've done since they took the game from Alejandro, and the war is on."

"I understand. Just let me get Allie back first, okay? Then you can do whatever."

"That *chica* means something to you, doesn't she?"

She did, of course. But I hadn't thought of her in the way Chopo was insinuating. Well, maybe I'd *kind* of thought of her in that way. I mean, sometimes I found myself looking at her and it was hard to turn away.

"She does," Chopo said, not needing a confirmation.

I changed the subject. "Listen, Chopo, you put your ass on the line a couple times for me today. I won't forget that. Once we make the switch tomorrow, I'll be out of your hair, and you've got a marker you can cash in with me. I just want you to know that."

Chopo nodded. He was starting to ask me about the game plan for tomorrow when Nita creaked onto the porch, ending our conversation. "Everything all right?"

We said yes. She waddled back inside as we finished our smokes. Then we went in and settled down for the night.

We both slept in the spare bedroom on a floor of thread-bare carpet, surrounded by walls covered in peeling Superman wallpaper. I felt worthless for involving the girl and swore I'd make it right the next day.

Sometimes the universe has other plans.

CHAPTER THIRTEEN

I awoke on the floor in the dark, thrashing, half-covered in blankets that were too small. Nothing looked familiar. I heard someone snoring next to me and it sent me back to the dark rooms, waking up next to men I barely knew, all of us forced to inhabit, indefinitely, a Mexican hotel with iron doors. The first year I was locked up, before I got moved out to the "village," I was held inside the towers, in a small cell with four others.

It was a place where time meant nothing. I could still smell the sweat and fear that permeated the hole, could still feel the hollow lump in my stomach that came with the thought of another day stuck in that spot, with the only break in the monotony coming from a trip to the yard that would inevitably lead to random violence and pecking-order maintenance.

I could hear the taunts and jeers echoing off the walls, the catcalls and the agonizing screams of loneliness and abandonment. I screwed my eyes shut and shook my head, hoping it would go away.

It did, when Nita started singing in the other room. Some Spanish song—one of Shakira's, it sounded like—and it brought me immediately back to the present. I got dressed, stepped over Chopo, and headed into the kitchen.

Nita had made coffee and breakfast. She handed me a steaming mug of the black elixir and shoveled eggs onto a tortilla. I sat at the table and sipped the coffee. The kitchen smelled fantastic, and until then I hadn't realized how famished I was. I'd eaten three fresh tortillas slathered in hot sauce by the time Chopo came to join me.

"The girl sleep?" he asked.

"Yes," Nita said, "but not much. She needs to go, you know?"

"We know. Barr?" He raised his eyebrows over the top of his coffee cup.

"Right," I said. "After I finish this coffee, we'll all be out of your hair. You're a wonderful host, Nita. You ever need anything, give me a call." I wrote my number on the back of one of her magazines, finished my coffee, and went outside. I fumbled around in my jacket pockets for the right cell phone. I had three: mine, the boyfriend's, and the girl's. The girl's phone contact list contained a number for Jeff. I highlighted it and pushed Send.

"Katy?" a voice asked after one ring.

"Hello, Jeff," I said.

"Who is this? Where's Katy? You the one who took her? If so—"

"Yeah, I have her. She's safe, she's not hurt. You have a friend of mine. We need to make a trade."

"We do, huh? I think if you don't let Katy go, I'm gonna put your dick in the dirt."

"Now that just isn't very nice, Jeff," I said. "And it isn't much of an incentive for me to hand her over. I get Allie back, you get Katy. Simple. Let's just do some business."

"Business? This ain't about business. You done screwed my business. You got Spike running around crying like a little pussy. And you done pissed me and my guys off. I'm down four. Spike's down more than that. And now I'm just supposed to hand you the little bitch?"

"*Only*," I said, getting very tired of talking on the phone, "if you want to see your daughter again. I have a guy here, a very bad man out of Mexico, who would gladly do very bad things to Katy. I don't want that to happen. I want Allie, then I go away. How about that?"

I could hear Jeff breathing heavily, thinking this through, trying to find a way to get his daughter and jam me up at the same time. Finally he said, "If I don't get her back, the wife will cut my nuts off. So, fine. Screw it. How you want to do this?"

I told him we'd be at the rest stop by the interstate at noon. There'd be cameras there, and plenty of people, so neither of us could pull anything. I'd let Katy out and send her to the bathrooms. He'd do the same with Allie. Simple. I liked things simple.

"Fine," he said. "Done. But if Katy's hurt, I'll never stop hunting you. I'll kill you and everyone you know and love. Your mom, dad, sisters, brothers, friends, the librarian that checked out your first goddamned book."

I believed him, so I gave him an inch. "I'll drop Katy off first. But if I don't see Allie within thirty seconds of letting your kid out, she'll get one in the back. Deal?"

"Deal. You son of a bitch." He hung up.

Nita and Chopo were at the table sipping coffee, talking amiably in Spanish, when I came back in. They stopped when they saw me.

"Thanks again, Nita. Showtime, Chopo."

WE PULLED INTO THE REST area for the first time at eleven o'clock. Drove the paved loop that circled the concrete restrooms and info center, and then drove out and got on the interstate. Nothing looked out of place, and no one followed us. We repeated this three times, then finally stopped and parked under a canopy of cottonwoods at the far end of the passenger-car parking lot. I peered into the backseat. We'd taken the tape off Katy's mouth. She sat there looking quiet and forlorn but not angry or upset as I would have expected. She stared out the side window into the spaces between the tall trees.

"Chopo, you want to cover all this from over there by that pond? It should give you a good line of sight to the bathrooms. You can cover her and Allie, if Jeff keeps his end of the deal. My hunting bag is in the back. Use the twenty-two, and leave me the big gun."

"No problem, *patrón*." He got out quickly, rummaged in the back, and then headed off into the tall grass next to the large stagnant pond. I pulled my pistol from the small bag I'd moved to the front seat, chambered a round, and looked back at Katy.

"I'm sorry it's gotta go down like this, kid. But if your dad plays this right, no one is going to get hurt. You should be home by lunch."

"I hate him," she said faintly, as if she were talking to herself.

"What?" I asked, turning around in the seat.

"I hate him," she said, louder this time. "Jeff is an asshole. He isn't my real dad. My stupid whore mother likes money and Jeff has it. I don't want to go back. Drop me off somewhere else, okay? Max, my boyfriend, can come and pick me up. How did you guys get his phone anyway?"

This was going to be awkward. "We picked it up at the junkyard," I said.

"What do you mean?"

I wished Chopo hadn't left the car. Maybe he'd be able to think of the right reply. I waited a moment, sighed, and just let it out: "I'm sorry to have to tell you this, Katy, but Max is dead."

She inhaled sharply. "No . . . I saw him yesterday. He can't be—"

"He did an errand for Jeff," I said, simplifying. "I'm afraid it backfired. He was pretty shot up when we found him." Watching Katy's face from the front seat, some part of me was thinking back to the people I'd buried when I was real young. One corpse would have been too many, but there were a few. Kids shouldn't have to learn about death this early in life.

For a long moment there was silence from Katy. Then, "Jeff killed Max." She said it deadpan, no emotion, matter-of-fact. "I knew it might happen, eventually. My other boyfriends—they all got run off or beat up. Not by Jeff himself—he's too much of a weasel. But his guys always took care of them. I'm not allowed to be happy."

She broke down then, tears streaming down her cheeks, her back heaving with every sob. She pounded a fist against the window and the seat, crying out Max's name every time it connected.

Damn. I turned back around in the seat, looked vacantly through the windshield. Now I was stuck. The girl didn't want to go, and I didn't want to send her back into that mess. *You can't help them all*, I told myself. I'd started out blindly searching for Jen, had discovered and lost Allie, and now I had this bawling teenager to deal with. Could it get any worse?

For Katy it could. That was pretty clear.

"Please," she said, slowing to a stop mid-weep. "Get me out. You kind of owe me, anyway, for kidnapping me."

I wasn't sure about that logic, but I knew right then that I wasn't going to say no. I ran a hand through my hair and exhaled. It was time for another crazy-ass plan. After thinking on it for half a minute I laid out a sequence of steps that most likely wouldn't work but was worth a shot. Sometimes when you're knee deep in horse manure, you just have to keep slogging forward.

"We get out of this," I said, "you can't stick with me for long. You got anyplace else to go?"

"My real dad. He lives in Reno. He calls sometimes. Said I could come visit."

"Okay, then. I'll put you on a bus. *If* we make it."

CHAPTER FOURTEEN

As we sat and waited, I heard a muffled sob from Katy every once in a while, no doubt spurred by memories of her boyfriend. Me, I was on edge, wanting desperately to see Allie, to make sure she was okay, but also because I was thinking of Jen. Had word gotten back to Jen that her brother was looking for her? Had her situation deteriorated? How much time did I really have to find her? There were too many unanswerable questions, so I decided to concentrate on the "swap" that was taking place.

It was almost noon. We were the only passenger vehicle in the lot, but there were five tractor-trailers idling just north of us. I doubted Jeff would send a crew in one of them—fuel was too expensive. Jeff's boys would come in from the east because that was the only road in. It came off the cloverleaf exit on I-70, wound for a quarter mile through willows and trees, following the river until it looped around the restrooms and tourist info building, then connected back into itself.

I drew a map of the place in my head. The parking lot was on the west side of the buildings, and the pond was west of that. North of us was the Colorado River, and south was the interstate. There were at least three cameras mounted on the light poles, and I'd made sure to park outside of their line of sight.

My guess was that the crew would come in and park one car, presumably the one that contained Allie, leaving another car back on the quarter-mile stretch. They'd let the trade go down, then leave. We were supposed to wait and then go out the main road, where we'd get popped by whoever was waiting for us. If they took up positions on both sides of the road, we'd get mowed down.

It was a classic ambush technique—one I'd first learned from the books I'd buried my nose in as a kid, and then re-learned in places like Cabinda and Freetown and Khartoum.

The sun shone almost directly overhead, glaring down on the Jeep, heating it like a can of soup on a fire. I rolled my window down as a blue BMW sedan pulled into the lot, then backed into a parking space across from us. I glanced to the left and slightly behind our Jeep, out at the six-foot-tall river grass surrounding the pond.

Chopo would be lying in there somewhere, watching the lot and the restrooms through the scope of my little semi-auto .22. The rifle held twenty-five rounds per magazine, was reasonably quiet, and could handle multiple targets as long as they weren't too far away.

I still had my pistol, though if everything went right I wouldn't have to use it. If things went real bad, I had the big .375 in the back. It held only three rounds, but it could stop a moose in its tracks.

"They're here," I said. "Get ready." Katy unbuckled her seat belt, wiped her eyes, and retied her shoelaces.

"These shoes are horrible for running," she said, sniffing.

Her cell phone buzzed in my jacket so I handed it back to her. She answered and said, "Okay."

"Remember our plan."

"I hope you know what you're doing," she said, then got out. She walked to the bathrooms and stopped with her back against the gray concrete. I started counting. I'd made it to twenty when the back passenger door on the BMW opened and Allie got out. Her clothes were ruffled and her cheek sported a fresh bruise, but other than that she looked good. She made her way to the restrooms quickly, trying not to run. Both girls nodded at each other, and then crossed toward their designated vehicles.

Allie made it to the Jeep first, shuffling quickly and hopping into the passenger seat. Katy took her time, like I'd suggested. When she was within a couple yards of the Beemer, she turned and ran back toward the restrooms, crouching and running, zigging and zagging. Two men immediately got out of the car; one pulled a pistol from a shoulder holster, and the other started to sprint after Katy.

I took aim at the sprinter, but before I could squeeze the trigger, Chopo opened fire with the little .22. He was much closer to us than I'd thought he'd be, maybe twenty yards from the Jeep, shooting at men maybe fifty yards away. And he was pulling the trigger as fast as possible, the staccato popping sounds hesitating only when he switched magazines. The sprinter went down, rolled into a ball, and lay still. Katy changed direction in the grass and ran across the pavement toward my Jeep.

The man with the holster returned fire, aiming at the grass. The second burst from Chopo found him, and his face disappeared in a blur. His body fell onto the Beemer's hood. Katy made it to the Jeep and clambered in.

"What's he *doing*?" she shouted. "I thought we weren't going to kill anyone?" For a second there was only the sound of both girls panting.

"It's what he does, can't stop him now," I said.

Chopo had stopped firing and the lot became quiet again—or mostly quiet. Truckers were coming out of the restroom, out of their cabs, yelling, talking, wondering what the hell just happened. An elderly black woman hurried out of the tourist info office, talking into a phone.

Time to go. I jumped out of the Jeep, telling the girls to stay put. Chopo should have been hauling ass back to the Jeep by now. He wasn't. So I put the pistol back in my jacket and headed into the tall grass. The thick reeds towered above me, making it difficult to see. Shoving the thick grass aside, I made my way toward the area where I'd heard the shots, and saw a boot.

Chopo's fancy boot. I moved closer and saw his jeans sticking out into an open, muddy spot. They weren't moving. I ran as fast as my sore leg would allow and crouched beside him.

He was facedown in the mud, my .22 rifle lying inches from open hands that were stretched above his head. He looked like he was jumping up to catch it, frozen in mid-jump. But he wasn't jumping. A puddle formed underneath his neck, and when I moved closer I could see the source of the blood.

A large, neat hole had been drilled in the front of his neck, and another, larger one, from the exit-wound two inches down from the base of his skull. He must have caught a random round from the man with the holster just as his own shots connected. *Damn.* Another pointless death that was entirely my fault.

I stood up. The only way I could rationalize his death was by remembering that he was a soldier, and this was bound to happen one day. Live by the gun, and eventually this would be the result. I'd arrive there, too.

I left him dead on the ground, left the .22, said good-bye.

Then I walked slowly back to the Jeep, trying not to attract attention.

As I settled back behind the wheel, I heard the wail of sirens coming closer. I put the Jeep in gear and headed west out of the lot on a dirt service road that skirted the edge of the pond. Once on the backside of the pond, we drove up the steep, grassy shoulder of the interstate and onto the paved westbound lanes, slipping unnoticed into the flow of traffic headed toward Grand Junction and places farther west.

"Who's your friend?" Allie asked, tilting her head back at Katy.

"The daughter of the man who took you. I kidnapped her, was going to trade her for you, but she didn't want to go back. So here we are."

"That's *great*, Barr—now we're kidnappers."

I looked at Allie, saw that she was trying to play it tough but was still shook up from her overnight with Jeff. She kept looking out the windows to her right and left, probably wondering where the next lethal threat was coming from.

"Relax," I said softly. "You're okay now."

She rocked back and forth slightly, looking as if she were trying to convince herself that was the case.

"What happened to the other guy?" Katy said from the backseat.

I put the Jeep on cruise control at a speed five miles over the speed limit. An eighteen-wheeler blew past. "He's dead. Caught one in the neck."

"What do we do now?" Katy said, sounding almost excited.

"We get off the interstate, just in case they set up roadblocks. Just in case, but I don't think they will. This will look like a big drug deal gone wrong, or some gang shoot-out. I hope."

Allie stopped rocking. She seemed alert now, focused on the situation at hand. "What if someone at the rest stop gives the police a description of us? Aren't there cameras there?"

I was already brooding on that. "They probably have footage of you two girls. You'll be persons of interest," I conceded.

"Wonderful," Allie said.

"Listen, I did what I did to save your ass. And for all they know, you were just scared rest stop patrons."

Allie looked like she was going to argue, but then her face softened. "Yeah, well, I appreciate your coming to collect me."

We continued down the road for another ten miles, at which point Allie said, "Pull over."

"Why?"

"You're shaky," she told me. "And I'm the better driver. Give me some directions."

She was right. I hadn't noticed that my own adrenaline hadn't worn off, and truth was, I *wasn't* that great of a driver. So I got out, Allie got out, and I told Katy to take the front seat. I'd ride in back and stretch out. When Katy got in the passenger seat and closed the door, Allie leaned toward me as she passed and whispered.

"We go to Leadville," she said.

"Why?"

"That's where Lance cooks. I got one of those idiots in the Beemer to tell me. The guy says he's been there. Somewhere in the woods outside Leadville—a little fortress hidden in the mountains."

I felt like a hound striking a scent, realizing this was my chance to find Jen. "Good job," I said. When Allie's face didn't brighten as much as I expected, I asked, "Hey, you okay?" I didn't ask *how* she'd gotten the man to tell her.

"Yeah," she said, opening the driver's door. "They smacked

me a couple of times. No broken bones, though. I knocked one of them to the ground at the junkyard before I got clobbered on the head. See." She showed me the scabs on her knuckles.

"Nice," I said, and stuffed myself into the back of the Jeep.

"Where are we going?" Katy asked.

"Barr?" Allie said, putting the Jeep in gear.

I didn't want to go to Leadville just yet. "Head north. We'll make a big loop through the mountains, let this thing die down a little, get Katy on a bus, and then head to the place you were telling me about."

Allie nodded and eased us back into the work traffic of heavy trucks and white pickups. As the Jeep began eating up the miles, Allie looked over at Katy. "So you got to meet the famous Clyde Barr, huh?"

CHAPTER FIFTEEN

And so it began. Their conversation became more friendly and intimate with each passing minute, and soon it sounded like they'd known each other their whole lives. Allie traded in her tough-girl persona for that of a protective older sister. It was a side I hadn't seen, but it looked good on her.

We continued north on the narrow two-lane state highway.

I tried to pay attention to the road and the surrounding scenery as the young ladies carried on, sisters now due to shared calamity. Though the subjects were varied, the conversations revolved around a central theme: men.

It was apparently an inexhaustible topic: problems with men, men they were trying to get away from, the stupidity of men, the horror and brutality of men. Sitting in the backseat, I felt like a human sacrifice, burnt on the pyres of gender. Although I resisted their blanket condemnation, a part of me had to concede their point: men tend to make a mess of things.

As the ladies' diatribe continued, the Jeep worked hard to pull us up the incline that would summit at Rio Blanco Hill. In front of us in every direction was rough, wild, and empty country—my favorite kind. The mountains outside the window, the Hogback and the Roan, brought me back to my early teens. At thirteen I'd started driving around Junction's surrounding mountains and deserts to put meat on the table. Mom worked as a waitress, but between deadbeat boyfriends and her kids, the money didn't go very far. So I supplemented by hunting. It was illegal, of course—both my driving and the constant poaching—but we needed to eat. It was the beginning of my professional hunting career.

It was rough in the beginning: being alone in the mountains, figuring out the art of wilderness survival all by myself. Lightning, rock slides, poor driving, and a fledgling sense of direction had all come close to ending it for me.

Looking back on it now, I had to admit that those years in the hills were about more than obtaining food; they were also a way to escape. I was a big reader even then and my heroes were mountain men like Hugh Glass, Jim Baker, Liver-eating Johnson, and John Colter. They belonged to a different age. I guess I did too.

I broke away from my reminiscing in time to hear Allie and Katy conversing about the basics of vehicular locomotion. Allie was saying what she'd do if she were to fix the hundreds of problems with the Jeep. Katy was taking it all in and telling Allie that she was planning on becoming a chef when she grew up.

I stretched out in the back, trying to sleep, but ended up thinking about Jen.

WHEN I TURNED TEN, DAD met a seventeen-year-old lot lizard while he was driving his Peterbilt to Nevada, and called Mom to tell her he wouldn't be coming home. Mom started dating random drunks, then Ski. Deb and Angie were both gone, one marrying rich and the other getting her accounting degree. After the Ski debacle, there was what Jen and I called "The Year of Paxton"—the worst year of our lives.

Jimmy Paxton was a concrete contractor who ran a crew of ten illegals. They poured and formed foundations for the new subdivisions in town. When Paxton was working, he made decent money and was usually reasonable. He was working when Mom met him at the breakfast place where she slung plates. A month after they met, the housing market crashed and he was unemployed. He became a different person then—an absolute psychopath, bent on control and violence.

Mom wasn't allowed to work. Paxton had a little savings and thought he'd be back to work soon, so there was no need to have her out of the house where other men could look at her. Even though we were living on less money than before, it didn't matter. The market was coming back, he said. Soon Mom wasn't allowed to leave the house at all. Ever. Then she wasn't allowed to wear her favorite clothes. Paxton bought clothes for her, and if she wore something else, he'd break a rib.

He broke a lot of ribs. He'd taken to using a chopped-off piece of rebar from his never-moved work truck as the rod that would not be spared. When he moved in with us, after his big house was foreclosed on, there were rules that we all had to follow to keep our bones together. Mom couldn't voice any opinions. Jen and I couldn't talk in front of him. Any resistance was answered with precision strikes of steel. While Paxton was out looking for work, all of us went to the hospital with injuries that we said were the result of doors and stairs.

I was older then, and stronger, and had been hunting to supplement the meager meals that Paxton's savings allowed, but I still was no match for the man. I tried twice: once when he knocked a good book out of my hand, and the second when he called Jen a slut. Ski had been big, but what Paxton lacked in size he made up for in work-hardened muscles and rage. Both times I tried to stand up to the man, I was pummeled into putty. These were times that Mom was sleeping off a drunk. Paxton never hit us when she was awake. After the second futile attempt, I gave up and tried to follow the rules.

Jen didn't. She was older and a hell of a lot more rebellious. When I was away, and Mom was passed out, Jen got the losing end of the rebar. Two of the times were bad enough for hospital stays and visits from child welfare. Mom and Paxton covered it up well enough to keep us together. Now I wish they hadn't.

Because on a night in November, after I'd turned sixteen, Paxton destroyed our family. I came down from the mountain with deer meat and found Jen cowering in the living room corner. Paxton was beyond drunk, well into black-out mode, trying to suck the last drops out of the second empty vodka bottle on the table. Mom was asleep. We thought.

Jen had told Paxton that he should either go to sleep or leave. He told her that she was an uppity little bitch. Jen threw a vase of dead flowers, which bounced off Paxton's wide jaw. I swung my rifle at his head, which he caught with one iron hand and took from me, then slid the bolt out and tossed it on the couch.

I tried to kick him in the crotch, but he twisted and caught the boot on his leg. He took the boot and tossed it toward the moldy ceiling, sprawling me on my back. He grabbed the rebar from the center of the coffee table and started stumbling toward Jen.

That's when Mom came out.

She was red-eyed and slurry, saying she needed one more cigarette. And for the first time, she saw Paxton hurt her daughter.

The rest happened in a hazy blur. For years I've been alternately trying to remember and forget what happened next.

Mom screamed and lunged at Paxton. Jen blocked one swing of iron with her arm, scratched at his face, drew blood, and caught a second swing of rebar on the skull. She dropped.

As I was getting to my feet, Mom was tearing and slashing and slapping at Jimmy. Jimmy tried to smile but was too drunk. I picked up the rifle, grabbed it by the barrel, and got in a lucky swing that connected with his neck and made him stagger against the coatrack.

But I didn't get lucky twice. The adrenaline in Jimmy's system must have overridden the alcohol and he came right at me, no stagger this time, and laid into me like he'd never done before. I didn't last more than a few seconds. The world went black.

I came to the next morning with a headache that has yet to be rivaled. From my spot on the floor I could see Jen, still out, her face caked with dried blood. She was lying beneath a skull-size hole in the paneled wall. Scanning the rest of the room, I saw Mom by the door.

I wished I hadn't.

There was a little linoleum section just inside the door, where we took off our shoes. The uncarpeted area was once yellow but had turned black. Completely covered by the blood that had leaked out of Mom's crushed skull. The walls and ceiling of the kitchen and the front door were covered in crimson splotches. The house smelled of piss and shit, vomit and blood. I puked harder and longer than I have on any drunk night since.

When I finally was able to get to my feet, I checked Jen's pulse. She was still alive. There was no reason to check Mom's. No one can live when their head looks like it was trampled by buffalo. After the shock, and the tears, I called 911. Then I searched the house for Paxton.

He was gone.

THe Jeep sToPPed and woke me up.

"Where are we?" I asked, sitting up and adjusting my hat.

"Meeker, according to the sign," Allie said. "Katy and I are starving. You got any money?"

I pulled out my money roll and peeled off a couple of twenties, handed them to the women, then scanned my surroundings. We were in a tiny parking lot in a tiny town, at one of the apparently rare convenience stores.

Inside the store were aisles of junk and crap food. Nutrient-free jerky, chips, cupcakes, and candy bars, all full of modern chemicals. I read the ingredients on a few food-like items. Tertiary butylhydroquinone, hydroxytoluene, and sodium benzoate. I couldn't pronounce them out loud, and had no idea what they did. I wasn't sure the people who put them in there knew either. I wouldn't have been surprised if in another twenty years a new wave of cancer was attributed to one or more of these unpronounceable things. I wanted a fresh hunk of elk meat and mountain spring water. I settled for jerky, a big cup of coffee, and a pickled egg. I prepaid for gas, then stood by the door to wait for the girls.

There were a couple of clean tables next to the coffeepots.

Wrinkled old men wearing hats sat at the tables talking, cussing, and discussing, their loud elderly voices drifting across the store. They didn't notice me or the girls. It was a common sight almost everywhere I'd been. Old men gather, separate from the women, letting the wives do all the work. Other places, these men would be a central part of society and would be revered. Their stories were important, because it's only through stories that we truly learn. Here, they set up shop in a gas station and are ignored. I tipped my hat to them as I passed.

Allie led Katy up, down, and around the store and ended up with armloads of junk food. I had to fish another couple singles out of my pocket to pay for the crap they lugged to the counter. We trudged outside, gassed the Jeep, and headed back out on the road. Meeker seemed calm, peaceful. There were only a few vehicles on the road, mostly beat-up ranch pickups pulling gooseneck trailers full of livestock. There were no pedestrians.

Once upon a time, I'd read somewhere, this area had been a meeting place for the Ute, a hardy mountain people that roamed from the Rockies to the Uinta Mountains. Then the government had tried to settle them, had started an Indian agency here and tried to get the aggressive hunters to start plowing and farming.

They'd responded by brutally killing the chief agent, Meeker, kidnapping his wife and daughter, then fighting and killing some of the army troops who were sent to put down the uprising. I couldn't blame them. Now the valley was full of ranches and farms, big buildings, and paved roads. The town even had one of those fancy health clubs, full of treadmills and weights, in a place where most people spent their time chasing sheep and lifting hay. Made me wish I'd seen the place before Meeker arrived.

An hour of nothing but deer and empty gray valleys and winding roads ensued, and then we were in Craig. It was a bigger town, big enough to have a Kmart and a Walmart, but small enough to drive all the way through in ten minutes. On the other side of town I had Allie swing the Jeep into a seemingly abandoned parking lot and shut off the engine. I made a quick phone call to order a bus ticket while Allie and Katy got out to continue their conversation. Allie was dispensing life advice, and Katy was all ears.

Twenty minutes later it was hugs and tears and then Katy stepped into a Greyhound and headed west, hopefully toward something brighter. I tried not to think about it, tried to focus on the fact that she'd asked me to take her away and I had. If it turned out that where she was heading was worse than where she'd been, well, I'd done my best. You control what you can control.

Allie opened her Jeep door and leaned on the cab. "Please tell me that was the first time you ever kidnapped a girl."

I shrugged and climbed in. She didn't *really* want to know.

After Allie put the Jeep in gear, I saw her reach down and pluck a marshmallow-type thing from her snack horde and begin absentmindedly nibbling on it. I looked outside my window at the sun's position above the mountains. It would be getting dark in a few hours. "How about we head east," I said. "Maybe we can find some real food."

CHAPTER SIXTEEN

We careened up the Yampa River Valley, through another town full of irrigated fields and fat cattle, and then pulled into Steamboat Springs. It felt good to be out of the high desert, which was predominately brown, and back in the mountains, which were nice and green. The ski season was mostly over, and the summer season full of mountain bikers, hot air balloon riders, and rafters hadn't started yet.

I suggested we stop at McDonald's.

Allie sneered. "That's your idea of *real* food, Barr? You scorn my chemical-laced convenience store crap but yearn for the Golden Arches?"

I told her that when I'd been overseas, I was in places where they didn't have fast-food restaurants. To me, a double quarter pounder was an exotic delicacy.

"We're *not* going to McDonald's," she said, ending the debate. "A place like this ought to have something better than that."

We were rolling down Main Street when she started scowling again. That's when I felt the Jeep surge and heard clicking in the engine compartment. The digital clock on the dash flickered; then the numbers disappeared.

"Problem," she said.

"What?" As I said it, the engine died and we coasted into a lot. "Oh."

Allie muscled the Jeep into the middle of a shopping complex parking lot. She popped the hood, and we got out and looked at the engine. The snake-pit of cables, lines, and modern accoutrements under the hood baffled me. I'd worked on old Rovers, and Toyotas and Nissans, but nothing this new.

"Most likely the alternator," she said. "I can fix it." She pulled her phone out and flicked around on the screen for a while, then said, "But not today. All the parts stores are closed."

"Then we ditch it and get a new horse," I said.

"We can't steal a car, Barr. The cops are probably looking for us, because of your little shootout, and we don't need to add grand theft auto to the reasons to lock us up."

Her comment reminded me that she was continuing to take a risk by playing Bonnie to my Clyde. "Why *are* you partnering with me anyway?" I asked. "Why didn't you grab a bus ticket back in Craig and head west with Katy, or go back to see your mother or something?"

"So you want me to do that?"

I looked down. "Well, no, it's just . . ."

"Look, Barr. If I could explain this 'partnership,' as you call it, I would. Maybe I like that a brother would do this for his sister, try to rescue her from the Big Bad Wolf. I never had a brother—or a sister for that matter. And Jen, the little I knew of her—she seemed like good people. Maybe I think there's ultimately some money in this. Lance has a lot. And you seem like a determined guy. Hell, maybe I just find you . . . *interesting*. I've been bored for a long time."

"So what you're saying is, you like me," I said, trying not to smile.

"Let's not go that far, Barr. You're pretty unevolved. Let's just say I'm interested in seeing how the Clyde Barr movie ends."

"Yeah, me too," I said with some dread.

"Anyway, I won't let you steal another car, and the one we have is dead. Suggestions?"

I turned around slowly, taking in the layout of the town. "I say we walk to the motel across the road and rest. Take a shower. We might even find a place to eat better than McDonald's."

"You think?" She agreed to the plan.

Once in our room, Allie immediately took her bag into the bathroom. While she was showering I took a quick walk around the hotel, checking for potential threats. There weren't any, of course—this wasn't Juárez, Mexico; it was Steamboat, USA—but old habits die hard.

When I came back into the room, I was presented with a brand-new Allie. Somewhere in her bag, she'd found a small, silky black dress that ended halfway down her shapely, tanned thighs. The neckline plunged down her breasts in a naughty V. Her hair rested neatly on her shoulder in a tight braid.

"Nice," I said. I was trying my best not to stare but doing a terrible job of it. I wondered why she'd pack something impractical like that. Is an evening dress something that every woman throws in their backpack? I thought about it some more, and maybe it made sense. On her, this dress was a weapon.

"You should shower," she said. "The water pressure's great. And you stink."

In the shower I scrubbed hard to get flecks of Chopo's

blood off me and thought about family, which led to remembering the morning a month after we buried Mom.

LIKE USUAL, I'D MADE BREAKFAST for Jen and me: coffee, eggs, and leftover poached meat from dinner. I ate alone at the Formica table, reading a library book, and waited for my sister to roll out of her disastrously messy room and join me. She didn't. I finished the page I was reading, scoffed down the rest of my breakfast, and then went to wake her. She wasn't in her room.

Instead, a yellow note lay half-crumpled on the unmade bed. I read it, understood, grabbed my pack, and went to track her down. This was after the police had given up looking for Paxton. White-trash cases fetch only minimally more interest than minority ones. Jen and I had been in court a couple of times, when they'd tried to put us into the system, but eventually they deemed us old enough to live on our own.

Jen's note said that she thought she'd found Paxton and was going to watch the place all night to see if he showed. She left the address. I walked the two miles and found her little Toyota in a dusty alley behind a house built in the sixties. Twenty minutes later, the ugly son of a bitch walked into the backyard and lit a cigarette.

"It's his mom's house. He's living with his mom," Jen whispered as we crouched beneath the dash of her car. "Do we call the cops?"

"No," I said, and laid out my plan. A plan that would change our lives again.

FIFTEEN MINUTES LATER I'D FINISHED showering and toweling off and was trying to get Allie's fit body out of my mind as I dressed in a pearl-snap shirt and jeans, then ran a comb through my unruly beard and mussy hair.

All this time Allie apparently had been reclining on the bed, reading. She pulled herself into a sitting position as I came limping out.

"My, my. You almost look like a human, Barr." She had a Haggard book in her hands—one of the novels I'd read twenty times.

"Ha," I said. "What's with that dress anyway?"

"We're back in civilization. This is how you dress, Barr, especially if you're eating somewhere besides McDonald's."

AFTER a LENGTHY DEBATE, WE decided on a grill with a view of the river. She wanted Mexican, but after I'd explained where I'd been the last three years, and the food I'd forced down my gullet, we agreed on the grill. We walked and stretched car-cramped muscles. Within the first block, she noticed my now-more-pronounced limp.

"You going to make it?"

"I'm fine." I tried to walk normally, but the badly healed tendons around my knee wouldn't let me until they had a mile or two to limber up.

"That happen today, when you were kidnapping and shooting people?" she asked. She tried to hide it, but I could see the faintest hint of worry. It was the first time I could remember her showing concern for me.

"It's an old thing. Gets tight if I sit for too long."

"How did it happen?" she asked as we turned a corner and hit the walking path that followed the river. The roaring water and the chirping swallows and the moss-scented air brightened my mood, so I decided to answer honestly.

"I was in Africa, guiding hunts. A wounded Cape buffalo

hooked me in the leg, the clients split, and I was left unconscious for a day. That night a hyena started gnawing on the leg, until I woke up and shot him. A couple of villagers found me the next day, and the local nurse sewed me up and stopped the infection. I got lucky."

"It doesn't sound lucky." She was still staring at me with concern, but also something else. Interest? We were nearing the restaurant, and the fragrance of grilled meat and seasonings made me salivate.

"Well, I still have the leg," I said, forcing a smile.

Inside the little place, which was all mirrors and wood, I ordered the biggest, rarest steak on the menu. Allie ordered a tofu noodle bowl. Whatever that was.

By tacit agreement we both kept the conversation light, playing a game of imagining what the people in the room around us did for a living. Allie was better at it. She noticed small things about people's jewelry or dress or the way they held their napkin, and she created unique histories for them based on it.

"You win," I said. "I like your stories better, and you notice things Sherlock Holmes would miss."

"You've been in rough country for a long time, Barr," she reminded. "You're easily entertained."

"The opposite, actually. I'm pretty particular." The words hung there for a moment, and then I pulled a fifty out of my pocket and tossed it on the table.

"What, no dessert?" Allie asked, mock offended.

"Nah. We need to go. Get a good sleep, wake up fresh, hit the road. Jen's in the mountains, and I need to break her out of wherever she is."

"*Oh my God,*" Allie said suddenly. Her eyes squinted as if she was staring into her own thoughts.

"What?"

"Something just came to me, a memory . . . of when I was being held in the junkyard."

"I thought you said they knocked you over the head and temporarily put you in a self-storage unit."

"They did. I was really woozy and couldn't hear much. The unit had a metal roller gate. But I heard a couple guys talking outside. One was running his mouth about Mr. Alvis. He said something about this one girl he had drugged up, that he needed her for something—a break-in."

"Why didn't you tell me this before?"

"It didn't seem real until just now. I probably had a concussion at the time, but I'll swear that's what he said. When you mentioned 'breaking her out,' it made me remember the 'break-in' comment."

"You sure he was talking about Jen?"

"Of course not. But it fits, doesn't it? And I think it could be good news?"

"How do you figure?"

"If Lance needs Jen, she's okay—for a while at least."

"But for how long?" I felt my fist clenching and unclenching. I wanted to *do* something. Allie reached over and touched me lightly on the arm. "Barr, there's nothing to be done tonight. In the morning I'll fix the Jeep and we'll head to Leadville. In the meantime, I could use a drink."

"I don't know . . ." I had half a mind to steal a car and drive to Leadville right then.

"C'mon, Barr. One drink. Then we turn in, get a good sleep, okay?"

My eyes kept going to the thin straps that kept that tiny black dress on her shoulders. They seemed pretty precarious there, as though if she twisted quickly, the dress might fall off. "Okay," I said, "but just one drink."

CHAPTER SEVENTEEN

We paid, then followed the walking path to the next big bar. I was still jumpy, preoccupied with how to proceed once we got to Leadville, but Allie was right. I was too worked up to sleep anyway. The river behind us gurgled loudly and smelled clean and fresh. The willows and the cattails along the water swayed with the wind.

The building was old, but the bar had been decorated with new, cheap junk to make it look older. Fake antique signs, and factory-weathered skis and oars hung on the wooden walls. There were maybe twenty people inside, all young and good-looking. And in a corner, a band setting up.

"What should we drink?" Allie asked.

"Beer?"

"Beer it is." She swung off to the bar, talked to a couple of the kids who could have been fashion models, then ordered. The bartender's face lit up when Allie talked to him. She came back a while later carrying a pitcher of beer and two glasses.

"So much for one drink," I said.

"Well, one *pitcher*," she replied, smiling.

I filled her glass, then mine. I bent to take a sip and then gagged. "What the hell is this?" My tongue felt glued to the roof of my mouth.

"Microbrew. The bartender recommended it. It's called blueberry ale. A world traveler like you is always up for a new experience, right?"

"It'll do," I said, trying not to hurt her feelings. Actually, the brew tasted like bear dung, but it must have been pretty high in alcohol content, because halfway through the pitcher I was pretty buzzed.

It was at that point that I noticed that the number of people in the bar had tripled and that most people were on the dance floor, thrashing to a song with a thumping beat. Allie looked over at me and put her glass down.

"How about it, Barr. Do you dance?"

"Only when I have half a pitcher of beer in me."

"Then I'd say you're prequalified. C'mon." She rose from the table and motioned to the dance floor.

We hopped around to a couple fast songs, arms swinging and heads bobbing like we were spastic marionettes. During the slow songs we assumed the middle-school dance position: Allie's arms around my neck and mine around her waist. She smiled at my discomfort.

Then the band took a break between sets and Allie announced that she had to pee.

"Good idea," I said. We made our way to separate bathrooms and disappeared inside. After minimal eye contact with a bunch of cologne-smeared guys inside, I stepped back into the hallway and waited for Allie to come out. As usual, the number of women waiting to do their business was long so I struck up a conversation with two dark-skinned guys in cowboy hats who were standing next to me, also doing sentry duty. The other guys spoke Spanish, so I did, too, trading friendly comments with them about the beaches in Baja.

Allie came out then, engrossed in a conversation with her own new friends: two tall blond women, all angles and cheekbones. Allie saw me, waved, then pointed outside, and walked out the door with the women.

That left me with my buddies. We talked about playing pool, until I mentioned darts. They seemed up for it, so we made our way over to the dartboards. For me, there isn't a better bar game than darts. Unlike pool, which requires a geometry degree, darts is all about muscle memory and instinct. It's a game that appeals to the lizard part of the brain. My kind of contest.

I won the first round. Eduardo the second. I scanned the room for Allie, wondering why she hadn't found me, and saw her dancing again—with her new friends and a couple of men. I felt a pang of jealousy, but pushed it away, knowing I had no right to be jealous.

We were about to play a third game when a man at a table next to us stood up and started talking to us. He had his arm around a nice-looking redhead. He wore a fresh shirt, but it was stretched to the breaking point by the gym-grown physique beneath. His arms couldn't rest against his sides because of the giant lumps of muscle in the way. He had no neck, had close-cropped hair, and carried himself straight and tall, chin up. Probably ex-military or ex-cop.

At first we ignored him. But when my brain switched back to English, I started hearing words like *beaners*, *wetbacks*, and *spics*. Jaime and Eduardo heard the words, too, I'm sure, because they pulled their hats down and stared at their boots.

I put my darts down and took a step toward the loudmouth's table. "What's your problem?" I asked. In Spanish.

"Learn our language, assholes," he said, laughing and checking to make sure his girlfriend had heard. She had but didn't look very impressed.

I took another step toward him and his girlfriend. "What's *our* language, smart guy?" I asked in English.

He laughed, a little uneasy because he was laughing alone. "American," he said, then corrected himself. "English."

"Wrong." I took another step. "This country doesn't have an official language."

He didn't have an answer to that. So he puffed up his massive muscles like a cat lifts its fur and said, "It's people like your friends who are ruining this country."

"Wrong again," I said, shifting a little weight to my back foot. "It's loudmouthed, ignorant assholes like you who are ruining this country."

The loud guy smiled. "Did you just call me an asshole?" This is what he wanted, to provoke someone into a physical showdown, trounce them, make himself look like a prime male specimen in the eyes of his fair lady.

"*And* ignorant," I said.

He was a massive guy—over 250 and at least six five—and he'd likely seen combat. But I would have bet money I'd seen worse. He stood his ground, looked around, and didn't see anyone watching. Other than his girlfriend, who looked bored. Either he wanted an audience or he was afraid that someone might have seen something that would damage his reputation and ego. Seeing neither, he told me where I could go and what I could do to myself, then sat back down.

His girlfriend stared at me like I was the devil incarnate, then leaned over and whispered something into the big man's ear. Whatever was going to happen next would be her fault. Luckily, all the big man did was fume and swig beer. I left

Eduardo to set up the next round of darts and went to the bar, where I ordered a lemon water.

When I returned, things had gotten Western.

The big guy had Jaime against the wall, two meaty fists wrapped in Jaime's fancy shirt. He was yelling something about stealing jobs and how he was going to throw the trash out of the bar. Eduardo had disappeared. Redheaded girl-friend was smiling, happy to see her man take action.

I checked the bar, couldn't see Allie.

I should have gone to look for her. That would have been the smart thing to do. The rational thing. Walk away, let the big guy and my friend work out their differences on their own and leave quietly. The civilized part of my brain—the part you use when you play pool—was screaming at me to do just that.

But I'm a dart player.

I grabbed a pool cue from the nearest table, walked over, and stood directly behind the loudmouth. "Let him go," I said.

"I'm gonna teach your little friend a lesson first," he shouted back, "then it's you and me."

I didn't want to wait my turn.

I tossed the lemon water on the back of the big guy's head, watched the water run down his shirt. He let go of Jaime and whirled around, snarling, showing me his perfect teeth.

I watched his eyes flick as he made a microsecond assess-ment. He saw the pool cue, and the way I was standing, and planned accordingly. His training, or experience, told him he needed to hit first, to get inside the swing of the pool cue. So without a word, he rushed.

He was fast and knew what he was doing. If I hadn't been ready, he probably would have beaten me to a pulp. But in-stead of swinging, I lifted the cue up and stuck the heavy end in the bull's-eye of his throat, right below his Adam's apple. I braced myself the same way a Masai would against a lion charge, and let the man's momentum hurt him.

The impact rattled the stick and sent shock waves through my arms and legs. I stayed braced until the man fell back and went down, coughing and gagging, grabbing his throat. Part of me saw the wounded man and wanted to finish him off— wanted to deliver three or four good thumps to his head, to make sure he stayed down. Maybe kick him a couple of times for good measure.

But I didn't. This wasn't the savanna; it was a public place in the middle of a busy town. When the big guy's girlfriend started racing toward us, I dropped the cue and walked away, trying to disappear into the gathering crowd.

I found Allie two rows back. She'd been watching.

"Let's go," I said.

"You think?"

We hauled ass along the walking path, too busy worrying about the police showing up to stare at the river or take in its cool scents. Allie hustled in front of me, looking back with reproach. "You're an idiot, Barr," she said.

"The guy insulted my friends. Deserved it."

"Does the zoo keeper know you're missing?"

I didn't answer, just tried to keep up with her frantic pace.

We made it back to the motel. No one followed. As I paused to light a cigarette outside our door, Allie whirled on me.

"Jesus, Barr. Just tell me one thing: Why do you keep doing things that could get you killed? Do you have a death wish? Don't you care about what will happen to you?"

I sucked in the nicotine and thought about it. I didn't have a death wish. It's just that when you spend enough time in places with horrors, you lose yourself. You lose any ego. When people need help, you say "Why not? What do I have to lose compared to others?" And when you don't care, it lets you operate at a higher and faster level. Ironically, not caring was one of the things that kept me alive.

"I don't know," I said, shrugging.

"Jackass," she said, then sighed and went into our room.

I finished my smoke, went inside, and fell onto the empty bed by the door. Crawling under the cold covers, I somehow felt lonelier than I had in years.

CHAPTER EIGHTEEN

My cell phone woke me up with a tinny electric song as the sun started to curl around the edge of the dingy curtains. I muted the phone by throwing it into the wall, furious that it had pulled me out of my snoring slumber and a strange lack of dreams. The dull intellect and ragged emotions that present themselves after a night on the sauce were there in full force, leaving me unable to feel much more than pissed and horny.

I looked over at the other bed. Allie lay sprawled on the half-drawn-down bedsheets, still in her black dress, her arms stretched above her head, her legs straight and wide apart. It looked as if she were trying to make snow angels in her sleep. I pulled her dress back down, so that I wouldn't be tempted to wake her up. Then I showered, threw on clothes, coat, and hat, and opened the door.

Outside, the sun had just crawled above the horizon, and the town was just starting to move. I sat down at a concrete table and watched the birds flit and play in the surrounding trees. Ravens, crows, and starlings fought for the few scraps ringing people's overstuffed trash cans. And on the phone lines, squirrels were performing miraculous acrobatic feats despite their obesity. The smell of still-wet leaves piled under the trees lingered in the early morning air. I was surrounded by enough of the natural world, even in a touristy town, to keep from going crazy, but I still longed to get away from the buildings and the vehicles and the people. *Soon enough*, I thought.

I pulled out the phone and checked the missed call. It read "unavailable," but whoever it was would call back if it was important. I hoped it was Jen.

I fought the urge to smoke and tried to remember last night. I recalled dancing, and a little spat with a racist jerk, and Allie. Tried to remember everything we had done.

The phone vibrated on the concrete table, buzzing and dancing in tight little circles. I looked at the ID. Unavailable. *What the hell*, I thought, and flipped the phone open. "This is Barr."

"Mr. Barr, this is Lance Alvis. Let me just say this: you need to stop looking for me and your sister."

Well, well—the man himself. "And why is that?"

"Because, Clyde, you are interfering with my business. At this point in time, I need my operation secret and removed from those who would exploit its location."

"I made a promise to Jen," I said.

"She agrees with me that you should stop looking for us. She's worried about you, Clyde."

"You don't say. Well, put her on the line then so we can clear up this misunderstanding."

"She isn't here with me, but I assure you she is fine."

"You haven't hurt her? Because if you *have*—"

"I haven't hurt her. But I will, if you keep coming. Ask around, and you'll hear that I can be very creative in expressing my displeasure."

"Really? Well, I guess that means we have something in common."

"Let me *reiterate*: I'm only calling because your sister has asked me to tell you to stop. For your own good."

He sounded slick, which could easily be confused with sincere. His pitch made me pause, though. If there was a shred of truth to what he was saying, I might be tilting at the proverbial windmill. I was willing to bet that he was lying, though. And I *had* given Jen my word.

"Sorry, I made a promise to Jen. It's sort of a thing with me. Like Scout's honor. You were probably in the Boy Scouts, Lance. You know what I'm talking about."

"Promises can kill, Mr. Barr. In this case, fulfilling your promise will force me to kill Jennifer, as well as the rest of your family. Have you visited sisters Deborah and Angela since you've returned to the area? I can supply their addresses if you like."

"I'm sure the Feds would love you to get near my sisters, Alvis," I said, lying through my teeth. Bullshitting was a survival technique I'd mastered over the years.

Alvis didn't say anything immediately, then sputtered, "What—what are you talking about?"

"The Feds actually think I work for you, Alvis. That's pretty rich, eh? It's a bit of confusion having to do with my taking out some of your brother's people. You see, they have this theory that your brother is trying to make a move against you, and they've ID'd me as your chief tidy upper. They've been tailing me and watching my family ever since." Some of this tall tale I'd previously concocted, figuring Lance might go down the "I'm going to terrorize your family" path. Some of it I was making up on the fly.

"Mr. Barr, you are truly an irritant."

"Sorry you feel that way, Alvis. I hoped we could be chums."

"You're heading into a hell you can't imagine." Alvis was seething.

"And I look forward to seeing you there."

We were both blowing smoke at each other, of course, trying to convince the other that behind the black clouds was a raging inferno. I had no doubt that Alvis was exceedingly dangerous, but the situation being what it was, I figured my best play was to dispel the idea that his knowledge of my family's whereabouts constituted leverage. I had to convince him that going after them risked full-on exposure and that I wasn't about to be stopped anyway—that I was full-on crazy.

Maybe I was.

Alvis hung up the phone before I could beat him to it.

I was getting very sick of the phone and wanted to smash it against a tree or drive the Jeep over it a couple of times. But I still had another call to make. I autodialed Juan.

There was no small talk. "Chopo's dead," I said.

"Yeah. I heard."

"I tried to keep him alive, Juan. I really did."

"No one's blaming you, Clyde. He went out the way he wanted. The way he said he would."

"Still . . . I should have done more. Or I should have gone alone."

"You couldn't have done either. It's okay. Alejandro has already made a call to California."

"That's what I was calling about."

"They're on the way. Chopo will be avenged. Big-time."

"Just one thing, Juan. Tell Alejandro he can do whatever he wants with Jefe and his boys, but Alvis is mine, okay?"

Juan sighed. "You at the head of some army I don't know about, Clyde?"

"I've got one enlistee and there may be more help where I'm going."

"You're going to get yourself killed, Clyde—you know that, right?"

"Maybe, but I've got to play out this hand."

After I hung up I went into the lobby and filled a Styrofoam cup with coffee that smelled like a parking lot puddle. It was horrible but hot. I took a couple long sips, then reached for my phone. I had one more call to make—if I could remember the devil's number.

CHAPTER NINETEEN

"**Z**eke?" I asked.

"Maybe. Who the hell is this?"

"It's Barr."

Silence. Then, "Clyde, man. You out?"

"Yeah. Less than a month ago. You head the way you said you would?"

"Yup. Up in Leadville. Doin' my thing. What the hell you up to?"

"Someone called me, asked for help, and I couldn't say no."

"You never could, Barr. If you weren't a mean bastard, that little failing of yours might have made you someone's punk. So why the hell you calling me again? Thought we weren't doing that unless it was big."

"It's big enough. My sister needs help. She's the one who called. Now I need yours."

He laughed. I could picture him smiling his big, condescending grin. "My help, huh? You still owe me from last time."

"I know. Double in your debt if you do this. It's for my sister."

"Which one? They're all fine little pieces, but the nicest—"

"Careful," I said. "We talked about this."

"Come on, man. We talked about everything. Three long years in Mexico and those pictures you painted in my mind kept me going. I still think about them. Maybe if I help this sister of yours, she'll be grateful, huh? I mean, like BJ kind of grateful?"

He was testing my patience. "Actually, I was thinking that you'd get another IOU from me. That enough or do I hang up now?"

Silence again. Then the sound of Zeke spitting tobacco juice onto the ground. "Is there any money in this? I mean, if I'm gonna help, I'll need *something*."

"Plenty of green. The guy who has her, he's rolling in it. We get her, collect some scalps, take home the spoils." A part of me balked at having to talk like this again.

"Sounds like fun. You coming here, or I gotta go somewhere?"

"I'm on my way there now. My sister's supposedly up in your mountains. We'll meet in town."

"Okay, brother. Meet me at the opera house, just inside of town, can't miss it. Call me when you're a half hour out."

I hung up and lit a cigarette. The tar and nicotine reminded me of prison.

Three years in that hot hellhole. The first year I kept my head down, but I hadn't been able to turn down a request for help during the second. I got in a little over my head, and Zeke intervened. We roamed the dusty yard together after that, making some friends, more enemies, and avoided joining any gangs. Most of the men in that Juárez madhouse avoided us; they called us the loco mountain men. We weren't necessarily harder or tougher than the other inmates, but we had a rep of sheer lunacy.

As emotionally opposite as we were, we did share one thing: our love of the lonely places and our passion for the mountains. We agreed after we got out that we'd go back into them—the Yukon for me, Colorado for Zeke.

The last year in that hellhole was especially bad. Zeke lost any interest in the human race and ended up killing two men with his bare hands and a guard with a shoelace garrote. He was never caught, because I was the only witness. I thought not snitching would make us even, but Zeke didn't. He said I'd still owe him after we were out. I thought I'd never see him again, and now I needed help from the scariest man I'd ever met.

Damn it, Jen, you're going to owe me.

I went back into the room and discovered that Allie had left. I walked across the street and saw her under the hood of the Jeep. A new set of tools sat on the ground next to a tire. She was swearing, but as I got closer I could see her expertly cranking off bolts and removing parts.

She saw me, asked for a 9/16 socket. I handed it to her, after a long search, and she said, "Almost got it. Give me another thirty and we'll be on the road."

"Where the hell did you learn all this mechanical stuff?" I asked.

She still wasn't looking directly at me, sending a message that she remained pissed about last night. "Remember I told you that I dated a guy seriously at one point—the relationship that went bad? He liked the fact that I was pretty handy, from fixing tractors on the farm. He put me to work in his garage."

"How romantic," I said.

She reached deeper into the engine to push back a wire. "Yeah, well, for a while it paid good money. Then stuff . . . happened."

I lingered for a while, trying to feel useful, but it was clear Allie didn't need me, so I decided to walk back to our room and gather up our stuff. I needed to think about how I'd handle Zeke, so I sat down and cleaned my pistol and .375 while I waited for Allie to finish. The sharp smell of the Hoppes gun oil acted as aromatherapy; my muscles relaxed, and my breathing became regular.

I finished oiling both weapons, rubbing the cold metal until it shined, then reloaded them and started sharpening my knife. The rhythmic scraping sounds of the blade on the whetstone helped me focus. I jammed the knife into its sheath and stuffed the stone into my bag, then grabbed everything and went to check out.

Back at the Jeep, Allie was slamming the hood shut and putting away tools. "Breakfast?" she asked.

"No time. There's still jerky."

"But no chips."

"We'll get some for lunch."

"Fine. But you drive for a while, okay? I've got a massive headache, and I banged the hell out of my knuckles getting those rusty nuts off."

I gave her my best smile. "What happened to that girl in the black dress I met last night?"

"She lost her sense of humor."

CHAPTER TWENTY

I drove.

The temperature dropped as we climbed out of Steamboat, winding east and then south along the western edge of the Rockies. I tried to focus on the road as we followed the paths that water had cut aeons ago through the hard rock and rubble, but instead found myself looking over at Allie.

Banged knuckles aside, she looked pretty damn good.

Her hair was pulled back in a tight ponytail and had been thoroughly brushed. She wore tight blue jeans, a gray sweater, and a flannel. She put both her feet on the dash and hugged her legs, her worn-out sneakers leaving dusty footprints on the shiny plastic. Her clothes were cotton and her shoes had small holes on the creases. Which only reminded me: we needed to stop and outfit ourselves for the kind of country we were headed into.

I stopped sneaking looks at her after she'd drifted off and was snoring quietly with her head resting on the side window. I alternated between handling the curves in the road and looking out at the scenery. These weren't the same mountains I'd hunted in when I was a kid; they were bigger, lonelier, standing like gods against an azure sky.

I reached for my pack of smokes but hesitated, and then rolled the window down instead. The sharp, crisp smells of pine and wildflowers and creek water flooded the cab and helped ease the growing anxiety that squeezed my chest. If I could just stop here, maybe pull over and make a small fire along a babbling waterway, maybe sleep for a night or two under the bright stars, maybe I could start to forget the things I'd done and the things I'd seen. Maybe I could forget that now all three of my sisters were likely in jeopardy.

I thought about calling Deb and Angie and warning them, but what would I say? "Hi, Sis, a vicious drug lord has your home address and may ring your doorbell one of these days"? Every time I rehearsed the calls in my mind, I pictured my sisters cursing me. And how would they respond once they hurled down the phone? Likely they'd do nothing more than inform the police, who were completely incapable of stopping Alvis if he had a mind to make trouble.

The Jeep dropped down out of one range of mountains and hit the interstate. As we merged into the wide rumbling pavement with its mass of indifferent motorists, I glanced over at Allie again. She was still asleep, her head at an awkward angle against the door panel, her rear at the edge of her seat, a small thin line of drool oozing out of the corner of her mouth. I envied that kind of sleep, the kind children enjoy when they're tucked next to loving parents. It was the kind of sleep I'd rarely had in the last ten years. Most mornings I woke up in the throes of some nightmare.

And the images followed me into the day: bodies piled along roads, beautiful large animals I'd killed for rich clients, tattooed half-naked men shoving knives at me, villagers on two continents being run over and shot and burned and raped while I shot at the men who did these things, often being forced to run and disappear into the bush when they came after me. Every night was a kaleidoscope of killing and violence.

I fought my way through the thick traffic, slowing, speeding, weaving around cars headed every which way. The diverging lines of cars reminded me of wildebeest herds running, then splitting up in multiple directions to avoid a predator. We stopped in some ski town with too many roundabouts, and I found a sporting goods store.

It had been a long time since I'd shopped in a place that wasn't full of pickpockets and children selling candy and trinkets. Here the only shysters and criminals were the ones licensed by the state.

Inside the giant sporting goods warehouse, I felt like a village kid in a grocery store. The place was stacked to the ceiling with camping gear, ammo, weapons, fishing poles, sturdy clothing and shoes—the kind of stuff that millions of people around the world had never seen and, if they had, would kill to get. Allie seemed unimpressed.

I spent most of my remaining cash buying stuff for Allie: a sleeping bag, pack, coat, hat, boots, and long underwear. On the way to the cashier, I saw something I couldn't resist—a recurve bow that broke down into three parts. Perfect for my pack. I threw it in my cart along with a six-pack of metal arrows and compatible broadhead points.

The total almost bankrupted me. After I paid, I had maybe one hundred dollars in cash left out of what had been my life's savings. I'd packed the cash around with me across three continents, spending and replenishing, until I'd been locked up. Even then I had a cousin of Chopo's watch the cash and send lumps of it inside to make life in the hellhole a tad more comfortable.

BACK IN THE JEEP, AFTER Allie and I left the interstate and started winding up the continental divide, I settled into my seat and brooded on what was ahead of us.

"You look like you're worried, Barr," Allie said, glancing at me briefly, and then returning her gaze to the side window. In the breakdown lane, an old man was pulling a mule. "What are you worried about?"

I stalled for a few moments, then looked at her. "Well, *you* for one thing. I still can't figure why you've signed up for this. Like you said last night, I'm a jackass."

She flashed a thin smile but then stared straight ahead. A few seconds passed. "Because that's where we're at," she said finally.

"What the hell does that mean?"

"Means that the things that happened the last couple of days have led to this. It's where we are now and what we're doing. Can't change what happened or what will happen next."

I still didn't understand. "You don't *have* to be here. This is my deal."

"You helped me, now I'm helping you. That's just the way it is. Look, Barr, ever since I was a kid, I've taken life one day at a time. When you grow up on a farm, you have to. The dullness will eat you alive if you don't. If you look too far into the future all you'll see is plowing and planting every year until you die, and it'll make you go crazy. If you look back and see that all you've done with your life is grow stuff and cut it down, you'll get depressed. So I don't waste time with the past or the future."

I nodded. Made sense, but it still didn't really explain why she was willing to risk her life to help me. I said as much.

"I want to be here. That's all that matters. Whatever happens, happens. Now shut up and drive, and let me get a little more sleep."

I shook my head. No use arguing with her.

We climbed up the narrow two-lane, whipped around hairpin turns, and then flattened out in a small, level valley. There was a historical monument sign and a parking area. I stopped the Jeep in the gravel on the wrong side of the road, got out, and read the sign. Years ago, it said, this spot had been the training ground for the 10th Mountain Division, whose ski troops had prepared to kill Hitler by slicing down the mountains on sticks. An elderly couple was standing off to the side, taking pictures. I heard the man, who looked old enough to have fought in World War II, say that this spot had also been an internment camp and then a CIA training ground. Proof that mountains everywhere hid secrets.

Allie was awake when I walked back to the Jeep after taking a piss on the scrub brush. I got in and turned the key. Our previous conversation was still bothering me.

"So there's nothing in your past that you can't let go of?" I asked.

"I never said that, Barr. I said I didn't waste time with it."

"Nothing at all?"

"Well, if you're going to be a dick about it," she said, "there *is* one big thing. My daughter."

I didn't say anything, but the look of surprise must have been obvious.

"I haven't seen her since she was born. That guy I dated, the one who owned the garage—he dumped me when he found out I was pregnant. Mom had her stroke when I was in my third trimester." She stopped, looked through her window at the waving trees, wiped her cheek.

I put a hand on her shoulder. She didn't shake it off.

"I was alone," she continued. "There wasn't any way I could take care of myself and my mom *and* a baby. So . . ." She coughed. "Shit, I'm getting all wimpy here. Nice job, Barr. But it does feel good to talk about it. I've never told anyone about my baby before."

I wished I could tell someone about *my* past. A few strands of hair escaped Allie's ponytail and fell in her eyes. I gently gathered them and brushed them behind her ear.

"So I gave her up. I was going to go to the agency, but I kept stalling and couldn't make myself go. I stayed on our farm. Didn't have the money to go anywhere else. Anyway, I was crying on the porch one morning and the Ottermans, who raised goats two places down, they stopped by. The wife, she held me and made me come over for dinner. At dinner she told me about her history, that she couldn't have kids, and made a proposal. I took it. They're raising my daughter."

"You've never visited?"

"No. I tried to forget. Never really could, but I was doing okay until you had to be an asshole and bring it up."

I apologized.

"But I'm *going* to visit," she said. "When things are better for me, I'm going to visit. I don't want her back, it's been too long, and the Ottermans are good people. But I want to look her in the eyes, see a little piece of me in someone else."

I nodded again. Rubbed her shoulder. She sniffed and changed the subject. "That's why we're going to get Jen. You need to see her again."

I tried to meet her eyes. "It'll be rough."

Allie grabbed my thigh, hard, and said, "That's why we

do this together. Two is always better than one, right?" She looked at me hard, her eyes searching, hoping, waiting for me to answer correctly.

"You stay with me, neither one of us might make it out," I said.

"In the long run, Barr, no one ever does."

I put the Jeep in gear. "One day at a time, right?"

"Exactly." We pulled back onto the highway, into the warm rays of the sun, pretending to be prepared.

CHAPTER TWENTY-ONE

Leadville was dirty and old, and we drove straight to the opera house, parked, and got out to admire the scenery. It was a good kind of dirty, and a good kind of old; a living ghost town. The buildings were all either massive Victorian, false-fronted wood, or impressive square blocks of brick. Most had been converted into office or apartment buildings, but you could still feel the history.

You could almost smell the gunpowder and booze wafting in the thin air, could almost hear the old miners whispering in the cool wind. Remnants of a time when thirty thousand people stumbled up and down these streets. Now there were only a couple thousand.

The town sat in a relatively low spot, surrounded in every direction by some of the state's tallest peaks. Snow still dominated the tops of the mountains, and down where Allie and I stood the grass had barely begun to sneak up between the cracks in the pavement. Most of the lots were empty, filled with nothing but sprouting wildflowers. Ours wasn't.

An old, beat-up, primer-gray pickup sat at the far end of the lot. No other cars. Out of habit I scanned the top of the opera house and the surrounding buildings and streets for shooters. Nothing but ravens and magpies. I looked back over at the pickup, saw a cloud of smoke rising from the driver's side window, drifting slowly into the air.

Allie moved beside me as a man emerged from the pickup and walked slowly into view. He was taller than me by a few inches, pushing six foot six, wearing a large-brimmed cowboy hat. His dirty denim shirt was tucked neatly into his dirty denim pants. As he walked toward us, we could see the large drooping mustache above a tight mouth with a loosely held cigar. His face was wrinkled and tanned, one eye puckered with a wide scar starting at his brow and ending at his ear. I regretted not grabbing the pistol out of the Jeep.

"Barr," the man said as he came over to us, stopping close enough for me to smell the horse sweat on his clothes.

"Zeke."

He threw his fat cigar into the parking lot, locked his eyes on mine. I whispered to Allie, "Don't scream, don't yell, no matter what happens. Just get in the Jeep. Zeke has an odd way of saying hello." She knitted her brow as if to say *Now what crazy thing are you about to do?* Then she slowly backed away toward the Jeep.

Zeke rolled up his sleeves, walked back to the middle of the lot, and stamped both booted feet hard on the ground. Then he started pawing the pavement with his right boot, snorting as he did it. The snorting quickly became throaty bellowing, and I took a step back, bracing myself. I took my hat off and put it on the Jeep's hood.

We both started running toward each other at the same time and collided hard in the middle of the lot, our combined speed and body weight making the impact substantial; it jarred every bone in my body and made my teeth rattle in their sockets, and it felt like the muscles in my arms and legs were about to tear away from the bones.

Zeke had me in a bear hug before I could steady myself. I'm not light, but he managed to pick me up off my feet with alarming speed and ease. I got one of my arms out of his python grip and shoved my hand in his face, hoping to hit an eye with one of my fingers. He turned his face away with a chuckle. "Come on, Barr, you can do better than that."

I kept my hand by his face and slashed that elbow at his head, connecting hard on his ear. "Oh, here we go . . ." Zeke said. His grip loosened a little, but he didn't let go. So I hit him three more times on the ear, then head-butted his head as it turned. My forehead landed on his cheek bone and he dropped me, clutching the side of his face, giving me an opening. I grabbed the front of his shirt, whipped him around, and tripped him over my foot. He hit the pavement hard, grunting, but rolled and shot up, standing in a cloud of dust.

"Been a while, Zeke, you getting rusty?" I asked. We charged at each other again but didn't collide. Zeke ran past me, somehow managing to land a good left hook that rocked me, dimming my vision and causing me to stumble. I landed on the blacktop, thumping my knee and skidding hard.

Zeke ran back over to me while I fell and kicked me hard in the gut as I was trying to get up. I acted more hurt than I was and he tried to kick me again. I rolled and grabbed his pointy boot with both hands. Twisted hard and Zeke slammed to the ground, saying, "Dammit, Barr. Okay, okay, that's enough." I let go and started to get up, and he kicked me hard in the thigh. "Well, now it's enough," he said, and got up slowly, dusting himself off.

I got up, too, feeling a little sore, but not bad, thanks to my old friend adrenaline. Zeke stuck his hand out and I took it reluctantly, but he just shook it and said, "Goddamn, it's good to see you again, you crazy son of a bitch."

"Good to see you, too."

We walked back over to the Jeep, where Allie was sitting behind the wheel, her window down and left elbow on the door.

"You boys have fun?" she asked.

"Well, well, well, Barr. Who's this little piece of ass?"

"Careful," I growled.

"Sorry, who is this little lady?"

"This is Allie. Allie, Zeke."

Allie smiled her best man-melting smile, said, "Pleased to meet you, Zeke. You gonna help us find Jen?"

I hadn't mentioned Jen's name previously. Zeke stroked his chin, winked at me. "So it's Jen our boy wants to help. Sure. What you gonna do for me?"

He walked up close to the Jeep's driver-side panel and leered at Allie through the window. I grabbed him by the back of his collar, yanked him away, and whispered in his ear, "Leave it alone. She's with me." Zeke swatted my hand away, smiling. "Sure, sure, just kiddin' with the girl. Let's get going. You got gas?" I nodded. "Good," he said. "I live way up there." He pointed toward the looming peaks in the distance.

CHAPTER TWENTY-TWO

I motioned Allie back into the passenger seat and we followed Zeke's pickup, quickly leaving the town and the pavement behind us and heading up into the skinny forest of pines and aspens. Zeke drove like he did everything else, fast and wild. I had to push the Jeep hard to keep up and was worried we'd break down again.

"How do you know Zeke?" Allie asked.

"We were friends," I said. I didn't tell her about prison.

"Did you meet him in an insane asylum or something?"

"Something like that."

"What does he do? Does he know where Jen is?"

"He prospects. Lives in a cabin and looks for gold in the streams, sometimes digs a little in all of the abandoned mines around here. In the fall he guides hunters, and occasionally he does some other, shadier stuff. He might not know exactly where Jen is, but he knows these mountains, and if Lance is cooking somewhere up here, Zeke can tell us where to look."

I didn't tell her what Zeke *used* to do. How he used to run drugs out of Mexico, hidden in the floorboards of stock trailers full of Mexican cattle that he sold in the states for triple what he paid. Or how he screwed a bunch of cartel guys out of a lot of money and then ran and hid in Arizona. Until a little guy found him and Zeke shot him, way out in the Cabeza Prieta. Zeke buried the body, and then, ironically, got popped back in Mexico for speeding. He beat the tar out of the traffic guy, knocking out an eye. No one ever connected him to the Arizona body, but he was given ten years in a Mexican border prison for the cop.

"What happens if Lance isn't at the cook house? What if Jeff's guys were lying?"

I looked over, tried to hide my worry. "I doubt they were lying," I said. "They were planning on killing you, after all."

Allie chose not to say anything after that. She rubbed her temples and put her seat back, her eyelids falling low.

Zeke's pickup wandered up the little gravel road, then turned off onto an unmarked two-track and continued farther up, past little crystal-clear ponds, streams, and creeks. I spotted two beavers swimming in one of the ponds. My mind started to wander, although I knew I should be paying closer attention to the route. I couldn't stop trying to figure why I continued to push Allie's and my luck with the search for a sister I hadn't seen in years.

It really came down to selfishness. At some level we're all selfish. It's a survival mechanism, meant to propagate the species by keeping individuals alive long enough to mate. But there are layers of selfishness. Food, clothing, and shelter is the base layer, the only real selfishness that is necessary for survival. After that we need social mechanisms to thrive as a group. I say that helping family is for *them*, that I care for my family and if they need help, I give it. The truth was, I was helping Jen mostly out of guilt. I felt guilty for not being there in the past when she really needed me.

I saw two red eyes ahead of me and my mind was jerked

into the present, just before almost crashing into Zeke as he slammed on the brakes. He'd jerked his rig to the left and into a narrow open lane between clumps of aspens. I followed, almost rolling the top-heavy Jeep. The short lane led us past a barbed wire gate with a cattle guard and into a glade filled with horses and wooden buildings.

I nudged Allie, told her we'd arrived.

"Where?" she asked, slowly shaking off the excessive sleep.

"Zeke's spread."

"They still say *spread* nowadays?"

"Zeke does. Be careful around him. Hand me my bag."

She tossed it to me as we parked next to his truck in front of a large, rebuilt log cabin that sat nestled against the mountain to the north. It must be the main house, I thought, since it was the largest building in the compound and the only one with windows. There were old barns, corrals, tack and grain sheds, all surrounded by three strands of barbed wire fencing that sagged in places between rotting fence posts. Horses grazed in a far meadow on the short grass in between snow patches. I grabbed my knife out of the bag and handed it to Allie. "Take this. Hide it on you. Use it on Zeke if he gets frisky. Don't threaten him with it, just stab. Like this." I jerked my arm, mimicking a stabbing motion. "Got it?"

"I know how to use a knife. And I won't have a problem using it. This dude gives me the creeps."

I nodded and grabbed the pistol out of my bag, shoving it in the front pocket of my Carhartt jacket. "You have no idea," I said. We watched Zeke get out of his truck; then we followed behind as he led us up onto the wooden porch and into the cabin.

The place was a simple two-room affair. The main room was spacious, containing a large, square wooden table and a few chairs. There was an old wood stove in the corner, a cabinet containing dishes and cookware, and a wash basin next to it. An overloaded bookshelf sat at the far wall next to a dusty, holey recliner. To the right was a narrow opening that led into a room with a single bed and a trunk. The only modern things visible in the house were the cell phone lying in the middle of the table and the scoped rifles in a rack by the door.

Zeke pulled out two chairs from the table and said, "Sit down, take a load off. Goddamn, Barr, you know how long it's been since I've had visitors? Hell, I ain't seen no one except in town for more than a year. Sit down, shoot the breeze with me. We can't do nothin' till tomorrow anyway. Be getting dark pretty soon. Those big-boy mountains hide the sun pretty good and we got months until real summer."

The whole situation made my heart rate go from a trot to a gallop; every rational, wary bone in my body screamed to get out of the cabin, but I sat down, keeping my right hand in my pocket. Allie sat down next to me. She smiled up at us both and kept her hands under the table.

I stared out of the western window, saw the immense forest surrounding the cabin, watched the sun slowly touch the top of what I guessed was Mount Massive. I should have paid better attention on the drive. Thousands of acres of wilderness between us and Lance, and I wasn't sure where either was.

"So," Zeke said, leaning back in his chair, "where you two lovebirds first meet?" I hadn't thought of Allie and me as that, not really—more as the jackass and his sidekick, or the idiot and his accomplice.

"He helped me out of a jam," Allie said, derailing my train of thought.

Zeke laughed. "Damn, Barr. How much trouble you gonna get yourself in helpin' people? But I got to say, you picked a really fine one to help." He smirked at Allie. She smiled back, her hands working under the table.

"One more, Zeke. One more. After that . . ." I let my voice trail off and put up my hands in a *who knows?* gesture.

"Sure, sure. Just foolin', Barr. Damn, you always were the sensitive one. Carin' about people's feelings. And always the one to look after the little guy or girl. Defender of the help-less. Read a lot about people like you since I been out." He pointed at the bookshelf. "Yup, knights, cowboys in them Westerns, lotsa people who look after others. Funny thing is, you know what always happens to those guys in the end?"

"I have a feeling you're going to tell us," I said.

"They end up dead. It makes for a better story. Martyrs and such—readers like those kinds of heroes, folks who give up their own life for someone else. People like me? There aren't as many stories about us. 'Cause we look after our-selves and prosper. We're the majority, Barr. You guys will die off." He chuckled again and got up; came back with a bottle of rye and three glasses. "You have to. There ain't no living heroes. The best ones are buried." He poured the whiskey into the glasses, mirth showing in his eyes. "Not insultin', don't get me wrong. Just the way the world works. You know that. Otherwise you wouldn't have called me. Wouldn't have needed my help. Our kind has its place."

I sipped my rye slowly. I'd heard this speech every day when we were inside. Zeke was one of the rare sociopaths who could defend his malady and he did it well. Allie drank her glass fast, then sucked air quickly through her teeth.

"So, back to business," I said. "You know this Alvis guy?"

Zeke refilled his glass. "Don't know him, no. I don't *know* all that many people. Rub them the wrong way, I guess." He took another sip. "Heard of him, though. Cookin' and runnin' crystal out of my mountains. Didn't ask for my permission to move in, either. Heard he's a ruthless son of a bitch. There's a story that a dealer shorted him once, some guy out in Kansas. Mr. Alvis drove over there himself and used a spoon to pop the dealer's eyes out."

Jesus. "How hard will it be to find him?"

"Oh, easy. These are my mountains. Pretty sure I know where he is already. Maybe twenty miles from here. Up in a little canyon, there's a new place. It smells like they're burning bodies. The crank smells so bad it scares my horses. It's a pretty big operation. They're runnin' the stuff out in big trucks. I've seen a few guys up there drivin' fancy SUVs and one guy in a big ol' Land Rover. Sound like your guy?"

"Could be," I said. I took another sip of the rye. It was pretty tasty and getting better. "So you've been close to this place?"

"Hell yes. Come on, Barr. You think I'm making this up to make you happy? I was just up there not more than a week ago. Flippin' rocks and diggin' in a hole maybe a mile up the mountain from their compound. And it *is* a compound. Ten-foot fence, wire, one main gate on the south side. They have two roads to the main gate, kind of a loop road, one comin' up the mountain and one going down. But"—he finished his glass and reached for the now half-empty bottle—"they don't have much security to speak of. Just some tweakers at the gate and a few wandering the grounds with guns. The whole backside of the place is open, and it butts up to the forest on that side." He smiled. "Easy."

"So," I said. "Our plan is to go over on horseback, keep away from the roads. They probably have security on the roads, especially close to town. We spend one night up in the hills, hit the place early. Sound about right?" Zeke nodded. "Do you know if my sister is there? Alvis could have a place in town."

Zeke shrugged. "All depends. You said your sister's not with Alvis of her own accord, right? She's some kind of prisoner or something? If that's the case, I doubt Alvis would be hiding her from the housekeepers at whatever fancy place he has. Come to think of it, there's a big trailer in the compound— I've seen the Rover parked next to it a few times. Your sister could be there. But who the hell knows."

It sounded sketchy to me. She *could* be there. But maybe not. Was it worth busting through whatever security existed to find out? I wrestled with whether this whole operation made sense, but my gut said that whatever I found in the compound was likely to move me closer to finding Jen.

I finished my glass and said, "I think it's worth a shot. We hit them hard, look for Jen, and ride out."

Zeke smiled. "And don't forget, I get paid for services rendered. You think ol' Alvis is keeping a pile of cash there?"

"Either that or a lot of product. Same thing." Just what the world needed, I thought: Zeke with a couple hundred doses of crank to lure desperate women with. I had no intention of paying him, but I'd cross that bridge when we came to it.

Zeke's smile widened as he noticed Allie's eyelids drooping. "If you're getting sleepy, baby doll, you can go ahead and crash on that bed in the back. I'll meet you there later." He winked at her, and she looked at me.

I launched out of the chair and backhanded Zeke, trying to wipe his smile off. The force was enough to knock him backward, chair and all, and he crashed hard on the wooden floor against the wall. The smile didn't disappear, though. He sprang up, grinning, walked toward me, then stopped suddenly when he saw my pistol.

"Good boy, Barr," he said, still smiling. His eyes flickered toward the gun pointed at his belly, then met mine. There was mirth in his look, but also menace. It said he'd eventually get his payback, whatever it took. "Glad you came with a leadslinger. Mind putting it away?"

"Sure," I said. I placed the gun back in my pocket. "You keep pushing me, though, and I'll put you down." I sat back down and sipped the rye, my hands a little shaky. "I think we all should be getting to bed. Big day tomorrow. The bed's all yours, Zeke. Allie and I will sleep outside."

Zeke nodded, pulled his chair off the floor, and settled into it. Poured himself another drink as we went out the door.

INSIDE OUR TENT, NESTLED INTO layers of double-zipped sleeping bags, Allie asked, "Were you serious in there? You'd kill Zeke?"

The bags were warm, made warmer by Allie's clothed body next to mine. "If he makes me do it, yeah, I will. He wouldn't hesitate to kill either of us, wouldn't lose any sleep. The man's a complete sociopath, but we need him and his horses. He knows these mountains better than anyone, and the horses will take us where we can be sure we won't run into any of Alvis's boys."

"I think you might *have* to kill him," Allie said, snuggling closer. "The guy really scares me."

"Me too," I said, inching closer to her warmth.

We'd set up the tent between the cabin and the barn in a grassy spot surrounded by rabbit brush and dry thistle stalks that rattled in the evening breeze. Allie helped, and it went up quickly. She glared at me when I'd asked if she'd prefer to sleep in the Jeep, so I zipped our two sleeping bags together and both of us settled into the tent, pulling most of our new gear in with us, just in case. The dry thistles would shake an early warning if Zeke came too close. And if I heard that, I'd be ready. I kept the loaded pistol by my pillow; Allie kept the knife by hers. I also had the loaded .375 by my side.

When the sun had gone down, it had dragged the temperature with it. We could see our breath floating like smoke inside the nylon bubble that protected us from the elements.

"Hey, Barr?" Allie asked. She rolled over, facing me, her breath hot on my face.

"Yeah?"

"I don't think I can sleep."

"Me neither. We should though, long day tomorrow."

"But I don't really want to, not yet."

"Yeah, why is that?"

"There might be bears. Or . . ."

"Or what?"

"When we were dancing, in Steamboat, did you think about kissing me?"

I moved closer to her. "Maybe."

"Wanna kiss me now?"

"I do."

"Then do it."

So I did. I put a hand gently on her neck and pulled her to me, then kissed her lightly. She pushed me away.

"What was that, Barr? Are we in grade school?" She squirmed closer and grabbed my shoulders. "This is a kiss," she said, and firmly planted her soft lips on mine. Then she proceeded to show me how it was really done.

Five minutes later, we caught our breath and stared at each other in the faint light. That stare was all it took. Clothes were tugged off, pants jerkily pulled down—hard to do without standing or leaving the sleeping bag. Smooth, silky skin met hairy, scarred flesh. Cold lips touched, hot breath mingled, the long day and the night before were forgotten.

It all went so well that we decided to do it twice. Afterward, we lay back exhausted, holding each other like survivors on a life raft, our tent a floating refuge in a sea of violent madness. We found the sleeping bag, somehow, and snuggled deep into its warm nylon folds. Somehow, we also located the weapons and returned them to their previous places. That's when we heard the laughter.

It drifted on the cold air, like the night sounds of hyenas, becoming louder and louder, until we heard, "'Night, lovers!" After that there was the sound of boots on wooden planks and a door slammed shut.

I pulled Allie's warm naked body closer to mine and held the pistol in my hand as we reluctantly drifted to sleep.

CHAPTER TWENTY-THREE

I woke in the predawn murkiness to the sound of Zeke leading a horse slowly past our tent. The sound of boots and hooves stopped, followed by a soft, "Barr, you up?"

"Yeah," I replied softly, trying not to disturb the sleeping Allie.

"Then get your ass out here and help me saddle the goddamned horses."

"Yeah, sunshine, give me a minute."

I heard him grunt, then walk away mumbling something about being up for hours, with no sleep, people humping in the bushes, horses don't saddle themselves, and on and on until he was out of earshot. I found my clothes and quickly pulled them on, put the pistol in a holster, and strapped it to my belt. No need to hide it anymore.

Before I left the tent, I took a long, lingering look at Allie. Her face looked innocent in sleep, but her naked body belied such virtuousness. There were small puckered scars on her back, the results of hot embers or hot metal. On one forearm were multiple small horizontal scars that reminded me of the lines used to mark the years on prison walls. She must have needed to feel pain at some point, and cut herself to prove she was living. There were other marks and tattoos I hadn't noticed before. Evidence of how little I knew about her; proof of how much alike we really were.

She stirred under my gaze, looked up, and smiled. "Morning," she said, and pulled my head down for an affectionate kiss.

"We need to get going," I reminded.

"I know. I'll only be a few."

I began unzipping the tent door.

"Hey, Barr?"

"Yeah."

"One thing. I don't know how to ride a horse."

"Great," I said. I threw my rifle over my shoulder and hunched out of the tent, heading toward Zeke in the crisp morning air.

He saw me approaching as he finished pulling the cinch tight on the last of the four horses standing tied to the hitching rail. He glanced at the pistol, then the rifle, saw the hole in the end of the rifle barrel big enough to stick a finger in. "What the hell, Barr, you expect to run into an elephant?"

"If I did, I'd have brought a bigger gun," I said. "What kind of string did you fix us up with?" I asked, pointing to the horses.

Zeke finished tying the latigo, then hitched up his belt. I noticed the large revolver slung low on his hip. He wasn't hiding anything today, either. He patted the horse next to him on the neck. Thick puffs of dust rose off the hide into the now lightening sky. "This here is Nebulus. My horse. Stallion. Best of the Chimney line. Worth pert near fifteen K. Next to it"—he pointed at a paint mare—"is Sheila. That'll be your girlfriend's horse."

"She gentle?" I asked.

"Who, the horse, or your girlfriend? The horse is. She packs kids around when I guide. She'll follow the others; Allie won't even have to ride, just hold on." I shuddered, imagining Zeke around children. "The next one, that dappled gray mare, is Jess. We'll lead her, pack a few of our things on her; then when we grab Jen, she can ride her back."

"That one mine, then?" I asked, pointing to the last of the line. The black horse shook his head and pawed at the ground, his back bowed up underneath the saddle, froth dripping off his lips.

"Yup. Name's Popcorn. Hope you remember how to ride." Zeke chuckled and lit a cigar. "Your woman out of bed yet?" He was much friendlier this morning, but he still had that crazy edge to his voice and his hand never drifted far from his gun. I told him I'd go get her, pack up, and be ready to leave in half an hour. "Only bring your bedding and saddlebags," Zeke commanded. "There's not much room and we travel light and fast." I nodded and headed back over to the tent as the sun started its climb over the jagged eastern mountains.

Allie was dressed in jeans and a Western long-sleeve shirt, had already packed the bags, and was starting to take the tent down by the time I got back over to her. I helped her load all but the essentials into the Jeep; then we headed back over to the horses.

Zeke and I packed the bedding into the panniers on Jess, and then I tied the saddlebags onto the back of what would be my saddle. I double-checked my rifle, then slung it over my back so that both of my hands would be free. Zeke swung onto his horse and rode away from us, leading Jess. "Let's go, lovers," he said.

Quickly I gave Allie a boiled-down riding lesson. Showed her how to mount: two hands on the horn, reins in one, swing over. Demonstrated the basics: kick means go, pull reins and "Whoa" for stop. Press your ass into the seat by pushing down on the stirrups with your feet. Told her to keep her horse behind mine and she should be fine. Helped her onto Sheila, noting as I did her grace and athleticism.

Allie eeked like a little kid at first, terrified, until I led Sheila around in circles. Then she smiled, eventually beaming as she felt more comfortable. When I left her to get Popcorn, Sheila was playing tug-of-war with Allie, trying to pull the reins out of her hands so that she could nibble on the sweet grass.

Popcorn glared at me as I approached, then chuffed as I untied him. I led him in a couple of small circles, watching him walk stiff-legged, before I tried to get on. I pulled my hat down tight, put my boot in the stirrup, and swung on.

I didn't get a chance to put my other foot in the stirrup before Popcorn exploded in massive leaps and bounds, bucking, spinning, snorting, trying all of his tricks to dump me. I held tight to the horn, somehow managed to get my other foot in the stirrup, then pulled hard on the left rein, forcing him to buck in smaller circles. He slowed to mere crow hops, and I gave him his head and let him run. He sprang forward, running full tilt, then threw his head down and really started bucking. But I was ready and matched his leaps with the proper leans until he started to tire. Then I let him buck in circles for a little longer and was starting to enjoy the ride until I heard Allie scream behind me.

I turned to see her wide-eyed, gripping the horn with white knuckles, breasts bouncing. Sheila was following closely as my horse bucked along the fence, past the buildings, looping back around.

Looking back turned out to be a mistake, as it made me

off balance, and Popcorn saw his chance and jumped high, then twisted and landed stiff-legged. I flipped ass over elbows and landed hard on my back, the rifle digging into my kidneys and deflating my lungs like a whoopee cushion. I heard Allie squeaking, so I achingly managed to pull myself up in time to see Popcorn run past Zeke and out the gate he'd just opened.

"What the hell, Allie?" I asked, my voice barely a croak.

She was busy yelling, "Whoa, whoa, whoa," and jerking on Sheila's reins. I hobbled over to Allie, who was still sitting astride Sheila, and asked again what the heck she was doing.

"You told me to follow, so I did," she said.

I couldn't help but laugh, glad that she hadn't followed my running horse out of the gate.

"Don't laugh at me, dammit. It's not funny. I told you I didn't know how to ride."

"It kind of is," I said, smiling, and led her and Sheila over to Zeke. Allie fumed and glared at me.

"Screw you, Barr."

It took an extra ten minutes for Zeke to run down Popcorn, corner him, and lead him back to us while I held Jess and Sheila. "Forgot how to ride?" Zeke asked as he handed me the reins to my reluctant horse. He looked disappointed I was still breathing.

"Nope," I said. "I remembered how to fall." I swung back onto Popcorn, spun him in a circle, and sat ready for another round of rodeo or whatever else Zeke had planned.

If he wanted to get rid of me, he'd have to try harder than that.

CHAPTER TWENTY-FOUR

Two hours later, in the warm morning sun, we'd settled into a nice little convoy. The horses had all calmed down and were walking with quiet purpose in an orderly single-file line. We followed a narrow trail, barely wide enough for the horses' hooves, as it wove alongside the contours of the mountain. The tall trees whispered and sang in the breeze, accompanied by the songs of magpies and jays. The wind smelled of crisp snow, fresh pines, and sagebrush. I turned in my hard leather saddle and looked at Allie. "I'm sorry," I said. She didn't answer, just looked away into the trees.

I turned back around. She'd gotten the hang of the riding thing in the last hour but was still a little sore that I'd laughed at her. She stayed mute, occasionally patting Sheila's neck, and stared adoringly at the scenery.

Ahead of me Zeke lit a cigar and turned in his seat to look back at us. "Comin' up is a fork. We stay to the left and follow the trail toward that compound. But to the right is a canyon that I work sometimes, looking for the yellow stuff. I swear, Barr, some of the roughest damned country on earth. Takes a man leading his horse hours just to work his way down into the bottom. Rough. Creeks with some of the whitest water you ever seen, granite boulders fallin' off the steep sides the size of houses. No old mines, mind you, just placer stuff. Me and my pan in the creek. Spent a week in there last season, never made it to the lakes at the end of the canyon. They call it Quartermoon Canyon. Like I said, I never made it to the lakes, but I came back to the assayer in town with about a grand's worth of gold."

Zeke turned back around, jerking his saddle hard left and right until it was centered perfectly on the back of his stallion. He gestured with his cigar, pointing to the vista of canyons and trees below us, smoke drifting up into the bright blue sky. "Yes, sir," he said, turning back around. "This here is God's country. Gets even better. Another couple miles and we're in the wilderness. Government designated. No motorized vehicles allowed. Gotta walk or come in on horseback. We'll spend the whole day crossing it. Probably not see another person this time of year. Later on all them granola backpackers will come in, stink up the place. After that it's hunters and outfitters like me—not much better. Either way it's too many people wandering in my mountains. But I understand why they come. I tell ya, you're gonna see some of the best country God ever made."

I had to laugh to myself. Zeke's mentioning God was a joke. No one sinned as well as he did. But he was right: it was some of the most breathtaking scenery I'd seen in a while. It felt good to suck in thin, clean mountain air, to be surrounded by trees and animals and rocks and rivers, and to be on horseback again, despite the considerable chaffing that was starting to wear on my inner thighs. A chipmunk shouted his high-pitched warning chirp to his neighbors as we passed beneath him. Below us a river churned and roared through the rocks, sending fine spray up toward the sky.

Zeke still talked. ". . . and after that we'll come up to a nice little pocket, nestled in a pretty gully, full of aspen and pines. We'll camp there tonight—a bare-bones camp but we'll have water. Fresh snowmelt water. Nothin' better but whiskey. It'll be damn cold though. Gets below freezing. We're up at about ten thousand five hundred feet now, but we'll be up to damn near eleven before we get to camp. We'll take a break here," he said, stopping us in a small meadow. "Horses have bigger lungs than us, but up here, even they have a hard time breathing."

I hadn't really noticed until he mentioned it, but we'd been climbing all morning. Now the trees were smaller, the air thinner, and the sun, despite the crisp air, seemed warmer. I put my jacket on when the wind started, the air coming off the snow chilling me to the bone.

"You okay?" I asked Allie as she gracelessly clambered off her horse. She glared, patted her rear, and said, "My ass is killing me." I shrugged. I'd ridden plenty but had always preferred to walk, carrying my stuff on my back like one of those dirty granola types. But in this country you couldn't beat traveling by horseback.

Zeke dismounted gracefully, looking every bit like the John Wayne he imagined himself to be. He shifted his gun belt and said, "You get used to it, cutie." He grabbed a sack full of jerky from his saddlebags. "You guys hungry yet?" I was starving, the mountain air amplifying my appetite, but waited for Zeke to eat a piece before accepting the bag. He noticed my hesitation, said, "What? You think I'm gonna poison one of my best friends? Or his good-looking girlfriend? Hell, Barr, who do you think I am? You're not still brooding on what happened last night, are you? I told you I was just messing around. Giving you hell, is all. Hadn't seen you for so long, thought you needed a little jabbin'. Forgive an old man?"

I nodded, took a piece, and handed the bag to Allie. It was hard, and I nearly broke a tooth trying to chew it, but it was tasty and I told Zeke so. He grinned. "Yep. Made it myself. Moose. There are still a bunch of those big guys around here. Gotta love 'em. Tasty, and enough meat to last a winter. Easy to hunt, too, if you're far enough away. With a rifle. 'Cause if you get too close, by God they're the meanest creatures on earth. Even the grizzlies stay away from 'em."

Zeke hitched up his belt, dug into his vest, and pulled out yet another cigar. The man was a nonstop smoker—as I suppose I was when my willpower was at a low ebb. He lit the stogie and said, "Almost there, folks. Couple of hours up over this hump, then another couple to drop down into a bowl. We'll camp there. From there it's just a little hop, skip, and a jump over another hump to drop down to the compound." He took a big drag, blew smoke toward his horse. "That compound, did I tell you? Used to be one of the biggest mines around here, back in the day. Late 1800s."

He kept talking, but I didn't pay much attention. These weren't humps. They were the tallest peaks in Colorado. It would be a tough day tomorrow, with the travel and the raid and the rescue. *If* Jen was there. If not maybe I'd get some clues as to where I could find her.

Zeke was still rambling. Allie had wandered off into the trees, hopefully only to squat in the bushes. Zeke turned around, saw that it was just the two of us, and stopped talking. His smile vanished. "I said we were just fooling around last night," he said, his voice cold and hard. "But you ever pull a gun on me again, you better pull the trigger." He stared at me with dead eyes, the ones I'd seen in Mexico, the ones that sent ice through my veins and made me sick to my stomach. "And that is your last warning."

I stood my ground, tried not to shake, tried to match his gaze, barely managed a maniacal smile, and was relieved when Allie came back and stood behind me. She didn't reach for my hand. Didn't put an arm around my waist. Only stood there, impatient, and said, "Ready?" Zeke put his smile back on immediately, as only a person who has guided before could, and said, "Mount up, folks. Long way to the campsite."

Zeke knew the trail, and in what I could only guess were a couple of hours we reached the place he'd described. A nice little niche in between the peaks with a small creek and plenty of trees. We went to work setting up camp and in no time had everything unloaded and set up and the horses picketed in the only grass around.

I showed Allie where to put our sleeping bags, underneath the biggest living pine with the most foliage, so that we'd have a roof for the night. Zeke built a little fire and put his bedroll next to it, then went and filled a couple of jugs of water from the ice-cold creek.

"Whistle pig for dinner?" he asked as he set the jugs by the fire.

"Sure," I said.

"What is that?" Allie asked as she appeared by the fire.

"Marmot. Little critter," Zeke said. "Tastes like guinea pig."

"Did you bring some?" she asked.

"No," he answered, laughing. "We're gonna go and kill us some."

"That compound, you think they'll hear the shots?" I asked.

"I hunt these slopes all the time; a few shots won't worry them any."

"Okay. Pistols," I said as I looked over at Zeke. "I'll go downstream, you go up. Thirty minutes. Come back here and see who has better luck."

Zeke nodded and walked away quickly, his eyes already searching for the creatures hidden in the rocks. I told Allie to gather some more firewood, keep the fire going, and that I'd be back soon. She told me not to tell her what to do. I reminded her that I didn't trust Zeke, so she should keep the rifle handy, in case he doubled back and tried anything. She said she'd be fine.

I heard a shot upstream, then another farther away. He was working away from the camp, and I was already losing the competition. I headed down to find some dinner.

CHAPTER TWENTY-FIVE

I came rambling back into camp twenty minutes later with four gutted and cleaned marmots. The sun had begun its final dive behind the peaks, meaning that we still had an hour of good light, but I didn't want Zeke to beat me back and be left alone with Allie.

While hunting I'd been remembering more bad times as a kid, worrying about Jen, and taking little mental trips back to Africa and South America. The wild places tend to do that; they have the ability to send you deeper into your mind than you'd go if you were in a more civilized place. It's what makes those of us who spend most of our lives in the wilderness go crazy.

Allie had dragged a log next to the fire and was sitting on it, feeding small sticks into the flames. She saw the look on my face and knew what I'd been thinking. "Having a hard time staying in the present, Barr?"

I shrugged and wriggled a marmot onto a stick. Then I sat down next to Allie on the log and shoved the dead critter into the fire.

"Tell me what you're thinking," she said.

"Just that I've seen a lot of bad things. And that we're about to see some more."

Allie nodded. "That's another reason to stay in the here and now. Look around you, Barr. Look at the trees and the birds and the horses. We're surrounded by beauty, but you can't really see it if you're stuck in the past or worried about tomorrow. You may never get a chance to see it again."

"You don't understand," I said. "I want to get this over with. Knock Alvis out of the way and get my sister home. The longer this takes, the greater the chance she won't make it."

"No sense worrying right now. Nothing to focus on but eating."

I shrugged again and thought about having a smoke. I pushed the thought away and turned the meat on the fire.

"It's funny," she said, breaking the mountain silence. "You and Lance aren't that different."

"That's *not* funny," I said, "or true."

"Okay, maybe not funny but interesting. What's true is that the two of you are both wrecking balls. Once you both put your mind to something, you go all out until it's done. And it doesn't matter who gets in the way. The only difference between you two is that Lance is stuck in the future, always thinking about how big he can make his empire. Killing and scheming his way to the top. And you, you're stuck in the past—always looking back."

She had a point. But there was more to it, in my mind. I was right, and Lance was wrong.

Allie saw my expression and said, "I'm not saying you're wrong for doing this, Barr. Sometimes, when someone's as mean as Lance is, it takes someone just as mean to take him down. That's you."

Zeke sauntered into the camp then, a string of six marmots on his shoulder. He laughed when he saw me on the log and counted the animals I'd brought in. "I win," he said, and hung the meat on a nearby branch. He rummaged in the panniers and pulled out his kitchen kit, started putting the rest of our dinner together. He grinned at me, said, "You still can't beat me at anything, can you, Barr?" I shrugged and put my arm around Allie's waist. She didn't scoot away.

We sat and ate our hearty meal as the daylight disappeared and the stars began glowing in the night sky. I put a bigger log on the fire to help warm us and to burn through most of the night.

Zeke said, "You feel better up here?"

I did, and grinned. The stars, the clean smell of the pines, the cool free air, pushed away my fears for tomorrow and my distrust of Zeke. I couldn't let my guard down, but he was right. "Beats the border."

Zeke spit at my feet, said, "What you done since you got out?"

I rubbed my greasy hands on my pants. "Only been out a couple of weeks. I got a ride across into Texas from Jasper, that coyote we knew from TJ. I bought his truck off him and wandered up north. I tried to get in touch with my sisters, but only Jen wanted anything to do with me. And you know the rest."

"You gonna keep going north? It's cold up there."

I nodded. "It'll be a nice change, after the jungle and that dust pit we were in."

"You looking for something to do?" Zeke asked, rubbing grease into his mustache, trying to get it to curl at the ends.

I shook my head. "I'm going to try and stay away from the citizens for a while. Maybe try trapping, wear a coat, put on a little weight. Don't want to get pulled into any more nasty conflicts, other than this one. My wild days are numbered."

"Too bad. I could get you some work around here."

"Those kinds of jobs are too risky. I'm not going back inside, and you should think about that, too, unless you liked it behind those walls."

"Careful, Barr. I do whatever the hell I want. No one tells me what I should do. Not even you."

I didn't like where this was going. "It was a suggestion. Let it lie."

Zeke's eye twitched. I moved my hand to my coat. Allie said, "Hey, boys, play nice." Silence. Nothing but the popping of the campfire. Zeke relaxed and I moved my hand away.

"So, missy, what's your story? What do you see in this dirt-bag?" Zeke asked, spitting a long, mucousy stream of tobacco juice into the fire.

"He's not that bad, really," Allie said.

"Thanks," I said.

"For an asshole," she said.

"Thanks," I said again, with less zeal.

Zeke laughed. This one sounded real, coming from his belly, not his usual affected psychopathic har-har. "You didn't answer my question. Why this guy?"

"I told you before. He helped me out of a jam. I needed a lift out of town, Barr was going, I hopped in, and here we are."

"Sure, sure, honey," Zeke said. "I bet good money it wasn't that simple. Well, if you don't want to share during story time, then let me tell you how I met this man, this here Clyde Barr." Zeke stood, made a *just wait a second* gesture with a finger, wandered off into the darkness, and came back with a bottle of rye. He took a swig, then passed the bottle to Allie, who declined and passed it to me. I took a big slug, not wanting him to talk about me, but wanting even less to try and stop him. I handed the bottle back to Zeke.

"Just south of the border, south of Juárez, there's this big prison. I'd been wallowing in there for a couple of years, just minding my own business, you know, then one day I hear a huge hubbub in the central court. It's not really a yard, like in American prisons—this one is like the main street in Juárez with little shops and stalls. There's always commotion, always something going on that's pretty rowdy, but this one day, it's just noisier than all get-out.

"So I stop reading my Bible and head on down to see what all the fuss is. I get down there, elbow my way past beaners crowded close around a bunch of guys beating the piss out of each other. I mean, they're laying into each other like it's the Olympics and the goddamned gold medal's on the line. Three huge Mexicans, the kind who don't do nothing but lift iron and pose in the mirror, are fighting this dirty bearded guy.

"They think they got him, and he's backed into a corner of the fence, but then he just flies off the handle. I mean, Jesus, girl, you should have been there. It was all white elbows and fists and knees and stomping. Like a monkey on crank and someone's just stole all his bananas. Like a bearded tornado. Just like that, those three guys are down on the ground and moaning like cows in labor. It was quite a sight.

"And then maybe ten more guys go after Mr. Beard. And these guys have knives. So I was doing good, just admiring the gringo and minding my own, but I thought that maybe us Anglos should stick together. So I pull the two shivs out of my boots and wade in there, prodding and poking. I throw the bearded guy a shiv and he's right with me, back-to-back, poking and stroking, you know? Until there's a bunch of bleeding beaners on the ground, and even more trying to join the fun. Then the Federales break it all up with their shields and whopping sticks. Beard and I get stuck in a cage for a night, don't say anything, just nod at each other and try to sleep.

"But the night they let us out, we go back to Beard's cell. He's got a little apartment, with a cot and books and real booze. We drink a bottle of mescal to celebrate being alive, and I finally ask him what that was all about. You know what he says?" Zeke took another long pull from the bottle, an inebriated twinkle in his eye as he looked from me to Allie.

Allie shook her head. She leaned forward, her eyes wide, focused. She was truly interested.

"He says he was trying to help out Lefty! I mean, Lefty? Goddamned Lefty was this crippled kid who everyone pushed around. The kid was used to it. *Everyone* did it. But this dumbass here, this guy who called himself Barr, he decides to stand up against the whole damned prison to help out this one dumb cripple who don't really care if he gets beat on. He's used to it, you know?" Zeke took another long pull.

"So I ask him why in the hell he'd do something so stupid. And Clyde here, he's drunk. He dumps the worm from the bottom of bottle into his mouth, chews it up, and starts in on these stories about Africa. How he's seen kids and women treated like dirt for so long that he starts to help them out, how he gets involved in all these civil wars, just 'cause there's people who are getting picked on. I'm drunk, too, and at first I'm confused.

"Like, why was he so worried about a bunch of niggers? But after a while I can't believe some of the stuff he's telling me. It's too messed up. I ask him how he made it out of there alive, and he tells me he's lucky. Hell yes, I say." Zeke paused, caught his breath, then took another long drink. He looked at Allie. "This here fella you're riding with? He has to be the luckiest and dumbest man I ever met."

"I'd have to agree," Allie said.

"Thanks," I said.

We all stared into the fire, quiet then, each lost in his or her own thoughts. Zeke continued to drink, staring at the stars. Allie looked up at me again. This time I thought I saw something close to admiration. But it might have been the kind you feel when you see a three-legged dog running around town. I scooted a little closer to her on the log. She didn't leave. We all sat quietly around the crackling fire, underneath a ceiling of stars, and listened to the wind rustle the aspen leaves until the siren call of our beds couldn't be ignored.

CHAPTER TWENTY-SIX

An hour before the sun was to break over the eastern sky, Zeke and I were standing behind a gray granite boulder, elbows resting on the cold rock, looking down through binoculars at the meth cooking compound. The stars and the moon and the gray light in the east allowed us to make out most of the place.

It was a few acres of bench land, fenced with razored chain link. In the center sat one large tan Quonset hut, surrounded by construction-site office trailers parked along the fence. And between us and the Quonset was a larger green trailer, with a window that glowed. A couple of white box trucks were parked back-to-back by the main gate. Everything looked as alien and ugly as the mines that once dotted the landscape. Nothing grew inside the fence.

It was quiet now, but a while ago it had been a whirl of activity. Ten men in tactical dress, armed with black rifles, had stood by the gate while six straight trucks passed through it into the compound. Once they'd loaded up at the dock, six of the guards left with the trucks. Now only four were left to wander and protect the grounds.

We stood silent, watching. I pointed at the glow from the dirty window of the green trailer. Zeke nodded.

We'd been busy that morning. The three of us had pulled on our clothes in the dark, saddled the horses, and made our way down the trail in the cold moonlight. After an hour we'd arrived at this little perch, situated perfectly on a bench above and to the north of the compound. Zeke said this was where he'd sat before and that we couldn't be seen from below. Allie sat above us, in the trees, watching the horses.

"You miss it, don't you?" Zeke whispered.

I put the binoculars down, hitched the rifle sling higher on my shoulder, and smiled. The cool wind rustled my beard as I stood up straight and nodded. "A little," I said.

It was something I'd started thinking about last night as I lay underneath the pines in the fresh night air. In the decade and a half that I'd knocked about, how many times had I woken and grabbed a rifle, ready to head into some sort of danger? The thrill of the hunt never got old. What I *didn't* miss, what I was trying to get away from, was what happened at the end of a hunt. Those things still gave me nightmares.

"Thought so," Zeke said. "I could hook you up with a couple of jobs, get you back in the action."

I nodded and said what he wanted to hear: "I'll think about it." Then I picked up my binoculars again and focused on the men moving inside the fence. Two were walking the front gate. One hugged the back perimeter. One went inside the Quonset. All carried themselves like they were military. Probably these were some of Lance's buddies from Iraq. Zeke's info had been wrong. The place was heavily secured; this wasn't going to be as easy as we'd thought.

"We got our work cut out for us," I said.

Zeke shrugged. "I seen the place a moon or two ago. They

know you're hunting your sister, so they're bound to up the folks guarding it. We can still do it, though, you and me. You just need to find something in there that's going to make it worth my while."

I nodded matter-of-factly, as if helping Zeke's financial circumstances was an implicit part of the plan. Anyway, it looked like I'd need a few extra toys for this one. I told Zeke to keep an eye on the place and headed up the hill to get my bag.

Allie had kind of freaked out earlier that morning when we'd woken and I'd told her my plan, which was really not much of a plan at all. Somehow, she'd thought that I had a lower-risk way to get Jen out. I wasn't sure where she'd gotten that impression. After trying and failing to talk me out of directly entering the compound, Allie agreed to stay back and watch the horses, them being, in her words, "the only sane and rational creatures on the mountain." I sat my .375 by her, told her to use it if Zeke and I were killed and the men down there ran up the hill. When I said the word *killed* she called me a dumbass, then went over to talk to the horses. I grabbed my bag and headed back to Zeke.

On the way down, I heard a vehicle roar to life, heard the clanking of the front gate, and saw a brief brake light flash on the main road.

"Who was that?" I asked when I reached Zeke.

"The Rover lit out. Hopefully it was just Alvis but he might have taken your sister, too. No telling till we get down there."

"No *we*," I said, setting down my pack and rummaging inside. "Can you pick off any of those guys from up here, in the dark?"

Zeke laughed quietly as I locked the three pieces of my

new bow together. "Son," he said, "I've been to the store less times than I've taken meat in the dark."

"Good," I said, strapping the new quiver of arrows to my belt. I stuck the pistol in my holster, took out a small set of lock tools, and threw the pack on my back. "This needs to be a quiet in-and-out. The men down there are pros. So I'll sneak in and get Jen, if she's there, and then we're out of here. I just need you to overwatch the egress."

"What the hell does that mean?"

"Cover my ass while I'm running up the hill. Hopefully with Jen."

Zeke nodded, grunting. "That I can do. You sure you can take out mercs with your Injin gear?"

"As long as you don't shoot me by accident," I said, adjusting my belt and tightening my pack straps.

"If I shoot you," Zeke said, chuckling softly, "it won't be no accident."

Encouraging words, I thought, and headed down the hill.

With every careful step through the trees, I was conscious of being tracked in Zeke's scope. This would be a short trip if he decided to pull the trigger.

If he didn't, and I made it down to the fence without getting a bullet in the back or alerting a guard or falling and breaking my ankle, then the real challenge would begin.

It was four against one—at *least*. And I hadn't nocked an arrow in at least four years.

CHAPTER TWENTY-SEVEN

Moving toward the gate, I felt myself slip back into the comfortable role of hunter. The careful placement of feet, nose to the air, bow in hand, ears straining against the wind for the slightest sounds—all of it reminded me of what had kept me going all those years in the jungle and the desert, despite the horrors that resulted.

The tree line ended thirty yards from the fence. I stopped at a tree on the edge of the gap and listened. No sounds of alarm. Just the wind in the trees. Nothing to worry about.

I eased out into the gap between the trees and the fence, using the tree's moon shadows as cover. Here I'd have to go slow, careful of every step and sound. I took one step, listened, then another.

And almost fell into a pit.

I caught myself and fell back, landing hard on my ass, then waited until my eyes adjusted to the dimmer light to see what I'd almost fallen into.

The pit was maybe ten feet deep, twenty feet wide, and seventy-five feet long. Half-filled with propane tanks, Coleman fuel tins, boxes full of used matchsticks, rubbing alcohol bottles, broken glass, black trash bags, and what looked like salt. Lots and lots of salt. At first I thought it was the world's weirdest punji trap, until I realized it was their trash dump. Of course they wouldn't want the refuse in the compound, and burying it in the mountains made a lot more sense than having it trucked out to a landfill.

I carefully crawled around the hole, staying low and quiet, until I reached the chain link and was rewarded with a small, person-size gate that they must have put in for dump access. It saved them having to walk around the compound to throw away all the crap it takes to make poison.

The small gate was locked with a hefty chunk of chain and an American lock. A brand that was notoriously hard to pick. I was distracted, thinking about the lock, and also thinking that if Jen were in the compound I'd have to hurry and get her before Alvis got back. He probably had a few gunmen with him. It was that moment of distraction that almost ruined me.

I was reaching into my back pocket for my lock tools when the guard patrolling the back fence drifted into view. He turned my way and started walking along the fence, running his hand along the chain link. Just to hear the sound and for something to do, I guessed. It was enough to cover the sound of my stepping back away from the gate into a darker shadow.

I had been visualizing pins and tumblers and hadn't heard or seen the man as he appeared from behind the nearest trailer to my left. In front of me, just on the other side of the fence, was the green trailer, with the light on, and hopefully Jen.

But I wouldn't be able to just run in and get her, if I wanted to make it back to the horses alive. I'd have to take out all of the guards before Lance returned. And the one coming right at me had to be dealt with first.

He was twenty yards away. I eased my hand away from the pick set and grabbed an arrow.

Ten yards away. The man turned on a flashlight, waving its yellow beam in front of him and occasionally through the fence. The flashlight was a good sign. It meant there weren't security lights and that there was probably no outside power to the compound. Made sense. Lance couldn't be on the grid. He'd use generators to power whatever he needed. And I didn't hear any generators. Another good thing.

Bad thing was that the guard was now five yards away from the gate and was shining the light closer and closer to the thin shadow where I hid. This was my only chance. Any closer and he'd sound an alarm. There was a small opening to the left of the gate. If I could release the arrow perfectly, the arrow's tip wouldn't bounce off the chain link. I nocked the arrow, lifted the bow, sighted down the shaft, aimed for the man's chest, and . . . let go.

And missed.

The arrow shanked to the right and bounced off the fence. Confused, the man pivoted and jabbed the flashlight beam through the fence. It wavered and wobbled wildly, until it finally found me.

I let the next arrow go, and this time it hit its mark.

Sort of. Instead of piercing the man's chest, it flew through his throat, and he fell to his knees, clutching at the new hole in his windpipe. I ran to the gate and fumbled for my tools with shaking hands.

As I adjusted the tension wrench and started feeling and counting pins, I heard the door to the green trailer creak open. I saw a man dressed in Tyvek lab coveralls with a respirator hanging around his neck. He stepped into the dark, his eyes not yet adjusted. In a few seconds they would, and he'd see the dead man sprawled on the ground.

There was a brief moment when I thought about the bow, but I stopped when I saw that the man was unarmed. So I cupped my hands, turned my head toward the trees, and let loose with my best imitation of a coyote warning howl. The whoa-yip-bark-bark had the desired effect. The man hustled off toward some hole in the compound without taking in his surroundings, disturbed by the presence of another predator.

I listened hard, knowing that the call might have attracted attention, but after a few achingly long minutes, when no one else appeared, I went back to the lock.

And ten minutes later I had it open. At first the damned thing false set on me, and I had to microadjust individual pins, which isn't easy when your hands are shaking and your heart is pounding. I wondered if ER surgeons felt the same thing. Eventually it popped open with a satisfying click, and I unwound the chain and slipped through the gate.

One down. Which still left three. And I wasn't sure if they'd changed up their patrols since I started down the hill. No way to find out since I couldn't contact Zeke. I'd just have to wing it. As usual. I patted down the dead man's body and found a mike on his lapel, an earpiece in his ear, and a radio on his hip. I quickly ripped them off, shoved the radio and mike in my pocket, and screwed the earpiece into my ear. No radio traffic, which was good.

I dragged the body under the green trailer, kicked dirt over the blood, and readied my bow. Then I slid from shadow to shadow, easing my feet softly onto the hard-packed dirt. I worked my way along the backside of the Quonset, where I'd seen one of the men enter.

I squatted in a tire rut, readied the bow, and slapped the tin siding as hard as I could. The metal rang, hollow and loud, vibrating along the backside. My new radio crackled.

A steady, rough voice was saying, "Central, this is Parker. Status: Burke is not responding at the Alvis trailer. Request that you send Spencer over there to query. I'm beginning an investigation of noise on the north side of warehouse."

A female voice, sounding far away and lost in static, said, "Central to Burke, status." Then a few moments later, "Central to Burke, status."

The female voice waited another couple of seconds, said, "Ten-four, Parker. Spencer en route. Burke is still ten-seven. Proceed with caution."

You could hear a faint laugh when Parker responded, "Ten-four. Parker clear."

He was still laughing when he rounded the corner, shaking his watch-cap-covered head, probably thinking that no threat in these mountains could compare to what he'd previously gone up against. He stopped laughing when he almost ran right into the razor-sharp end of the broadhead that I had ready and waiting. I'd moved to a corner, listened for steps, and hearing none moved to the other and readied an arrow.

"Put the light down," I whispered. He shut it off and slowly bent toward the ground.

"No. Drop it."

He did. "On your knees," I said, waving the bow. My arms were starting to shake, the result of holding back sixty pounds of tension. "Hands behind your head."

He did it, reluctantly, looking up at me with a smart defiance that scared me. The man had a lethal edge to him and I should have put the arrow in his throat when he first arrived. Giving people the benefit of the doubt can get you killed.

My arm shook too bad to keep holding the bow drawn, so I relaxed the string and motioned to Parker's hands.

As he moved his hands up, I saw the shift of weight on his knees and knew what was coming. I pulled back the bowstring again and kicked out hard, trying to connect a heel to his jaw.

But he'd shifted the other way and jumped to his feet and out of range, leaving me with a leg up and off balance.

Which he used to his advantage as he rushed in, one hand on my leg, shoving it away, and the other hand reaching for his sidearm.

I knew if he got the pistol out, either I'd be dead or the game would be over. One shot and the place would look like a kicked anthill. Central would radio for backup. Zeke might be able to take a few out, but I'd never leave with Jen. So I shot the arrow, which flew up and over the guard, whistling into the dark. Then I reversed my grip on the bow and threw the bowstring over his head as I fell.

The hard cord caught the man in the eyes and pulled him down next to me. I shoved my shoulders forward, jerked the bow down, and pulled the string tight against his neck. Using my knee for leverage, I yanked the bow toward me with all the strength my shaking arms had left until I heard the wood crack.

The guard struggled for a few moments, unable to get his pistol out of his holster and unable to hit me, and then lay still. I caught my breath, shoved the broken bow away, and pulled myself up. I checked the man's pulse. His heart was still beating, slow and steady. He wasn't dead, but he'd definitely be out of it for a while. I listened to the sounds in the compound. Nothing out of the ordinary. Only a faint crackle from my earpiece.

"Central to Spencer and Flint. Be advised, silent alarm sent from Parker. Please follow protocol and secure the asset."

A new gravelly voice said, "Central, Flint. Currently at gate. Will remain as per procedure until situation demands otherwise." Then a hard-breathing voice: "Central, Spencer. Ten-four, on my way."

The race was on. Jen's trailer was the finish line, and my sister was the prize.

CHAPTER TWENTY-EIGHT

I couldn't just take off across the compound, full speed, without attracting the attention of the guy at the front gate. So I unslung my pack, crammed my hat in it, and replaced it with the guard's watch cap. I took his tactical vest and his rifle, too, hoping I'd be seen as Spencer if the fourth guard were to get in my way.

Then I took off running along the west-side trailers, the pack and rifle banging against my back and side. Soon the small glow of the green trailer became visible. I aimed toward it, my heart about to jump out of my ribs, my lungs aching, my legs jelly. I didn't think I'd be able to keep it up, until I saw Spencer run out from the east and cut in front of me.

I wasn't going to beat him. He was fifteen yards ahead and had perfect runner's form, arms reaching high, knees pumping. My first impulse was to stop and use the rifle, but I knew I couldn't if I was going to get Jen out. And I was so close now.

So I pushed harder, and when I'd closed the gap to twelve yards, I slowed and grabbed the first baseball-size rock I saw. Without completely stopping, I hopped and whanged the rock at the sprinter in front of me. And prayed.

As a kid, I never played catch with my father. Never played

baseball with friends. Never even watched a game, because it was boring. Nothing like boxing. But I'd spent countless hours whipping rocks at animals for food, or at holes and trees for fun. It was like a more primitive version of darts. You spend enough time doing it, and your body remembers the motions.

Everything seemed to slow as I watched the rock sail straight and true through the starlight. As Spencer turned toward the trailer the rock caught him on the base of the skull. There was a meaty smack and he fell forward, skidding in the dirt.

I ran to him, kicked him quick in the temple, and flew to the door.

I threw it open, pulled the pistol, and swung the sights in arcs, searching for more guards. There weren't any. The room was empty.

I closed the door quietly and took a closer look at the room. A small battery-operated Coleman lantern sat on an aluminum table, casting a yellow glow on the industrial carpet and freshly painted white walls. A half-played game of solitaire was laid out by the lamp. A camp chair sat on one side of the table, and resting against it was a Remington shotgun, black, with a flashlight attached to the barrel. Extra MP5 magazines were stacked neatly in a box beside the Remington.

No sign of Jen. Across from the camp chair, on the other side of the room, was a brand-new shiny black couch. I could smell the crisp leather from where I stood. A wool blanket was folded neatly at one end of the couch, but that was the only other thing in the room. There was, however, a door on the east side, hard to see because the paint matched the walls. If Jen was here, maybe she'd be on the other side.

Or maybe there'd be someone else.

I tried the door, found it locked—*of course*—and took a step back. It was time to find out what lay behind door number one. I jumped forward and stomped the flat of my boot against the door, near the jam. I imagined a point five feet on the other side of the door and tried to kick to it.

The door splintered but held. It took me one more try to bust through, and when I did, the door swung open so fast I nearly sprawled on the lush carpet.

Lush. The word didn't fit the place. But it was lush nonetheless. So was everything in the room, I found, once my eyes adjusted again and the light from the Coleman filtered in. The place looked like a posh hotel room: empty king-size bed with feather duvet, flat-screen TV on the wall, and a large framed picture of the mountains hanging crooked above the bed. A red-eyed alarm clock sat on a bedside table, next to two large pill bottles.

I stepped to examine the pill bottles: prescription with a doctor's name and the words *Ambien* and *Librium* in bold print. The names didn't mean anything to me. But the fact that Jen wasn't in the room did. It meant I'd risked my life for nothing. I'd have to get the hell out and regroup and come up with another plan. And I wasn't good at plans.

Two sounds kept me from leaving the room in a fury. Sounds that I wouldn't have heard if I hadn't spent years living in the wild relying on my senses to keep me alive. I heard very faint snoring, and the patter of footsteps outside the trailer.

The snoring came from the small crack between the bed and the wall opposite me. I crawled across the bed and peered down as the patter neared the trailer. Jen had fallen off the bed and was curled into the closest approximation of the fetal position you can achieve when you're in a crack. She looked thin and older—worn-out but peaceful.

The patter turned into creaking as the person outside the trailer mounted the metal steps.

I stood still, considered dragging Jen out and throwing her over my shoulder. Before I could think of another option, the person opened the trailer door and entered.

"Yo, Burke," a voice boomed. "We still on for—" A pause. "Burke?"

I put my pack on the bed, kept the MP5 rifle, the pistol, and the stolen black parts of the uniform. I took a breath and stepped out the door.

"Where's Burke? Who are you?"

I didn't answer, just affected a bored attitude and walked over to the camp chair and sat down. I grabbed an extra magazine for the MP out of the box and put it in my pocket. Then I sat pondering and moved the six of spades below the seven of diamonds. "Bumppo," I said, trying to find a five of hearts to go below the six. "Alvis brought me in late last night, because of the new threat."

"Oh." This was the man I'd seen earlier wearing the Tyvek coveralls. He went over and sprawled on the couch. He was one of those redheaded males who'd catch fire in the sunlight. The gene pool hadn't been kind to him in other departments, either: he wore glasses and had a keg belly. "Where they got Burke? We usually play poker."

I shrugged. "No idea. My orders are to watch the woman."

Geeky guy figured out he wasn't going to make a new best friend so he rose from the couch. "I'll leave you to it then."

"Uh-huh," I said, not looking up from my game of solitaire. "Catch you later."

He swung open the door and clomped down the steps.

Back in Jen's room, I gently maneuvered my sister out of the crack and onto the bed. She was wearing silk pajamas, dark purple, long-sleeved with pants. Other than the thin line of drool oozing out of her mouth, she looked healthy. No bruises. No cuts or scratches. No missing fingers or casts.

She was gaunt and pale, but no more so than some society woman who'd spent too much time on a veggie diet. Her pulse was good and her breathing regular. Something about the expression on her face—it reminded me of my childhood best friend and confidant, and for a moment I felt that aching loss you feel when you know you can't go back and aren't even sure you want to.

I listened again to the sounds surrounding the trailer. Nothing. "Jen?" I said. I got no reaction, so I said it louder. "*Jen . . .*"

She murmured and mumbled, then opened one eye. A half second later the other eye opened and I could see her focusing. She croaked out, "You *came*."

"Damned right," I said, wrapping the duvet around her shoulders. Then I hooked my arms beneath hers and leaned her toward the door. She stumbled at first and I pulled her into me, gripping one of her elbows.

I led her out of the trailer, down the steps, and across the compound to the back trash gate. I locked it behind me, and then, half tugging and half lifting Jen beside me, I limped up the hill, sucking air like a sun-stroked impala. When I finally reached Zeke, who helped lift Jen out of my arms, it hit me how god-awful tired I was.

I collapsed on the ground next to my sister.

CHAPTER TWENTY-NINE

"**S**tand the hell up, Barr. We got to get."

At different times in my life, I'd been trampled, tossed, torn, cut, shot, and beaten. And I'd usually bounced back pretty fast. Sitting there on the ground, though, looking at Zeke, it occurred to me that sometime recently I must have crossed an invisible threshold into middle age, because just the tension of entering the compound, taking out those guards, and lugging Jen back up the hill had left me completely exhausted. *C'mon, Clyde, suck it up*, I berated myself.

"Okay, okay," I said. "I'm up. Help me move my sister." Together, Zeke and I took an arm and carried Jen up to the horses. A burst of adrenaline helped me along.

"What the hell's *wrong* with her?" Zeke asked as we maneuvered Jen around rocks and trees.

"Pills," I said, hoping that was all. Ducking under a low branch, I saw Zeke leer at my sister.

"Still a looker, though," he said. "Glad you got her, but what else did you find down there? You got any rewards for your buddy?"

It was time for me to show my acting chops. "I pretty

much tore the main trailer apart looking for Lance's stash," I said. "Couldn't find any green or drugs."

"Then you still owe me, and I do need to get paid," Zeke threatened.

"I'll make you whole, don't worry. Martyrs like me don't welsh on our debts," I said, smiling.

"A dead man's marker ain't worth nothing," Zeke complained.

"Then I'll have to stay alive, won't I?"

At that Zeke simply spat on the ground.

Allie watched as we carried Jen up and sat her on the ground by the horses. "Christ," she mumbled, walking over and kneeling next to her. She whispered into her ear, then went and retrieved my bag. "Give me a hand, Barr," she said as she dug out a shirt, pants, and coat. I helped her wriggle Jen's near limp body into warmer clothes; then we set her down in a soft leafy recess next to a tree.

A few seconds later I was back on the edge of our rocky perch, staring at the compound through binoculars. I scanned slowly. No more patrols. No trucks returning. No chatter on the radio that I'd forgotten I still had. I tossed both the earpiece and the receiver in a chokecherry bush.

Zeke came up behind me. "They figure out that Miss Sleepy Pie is missing yet?"

I shook my head. "Not that I can tell."

"Then let's get the hell out of here. Your sister's still out of it, but the horses are itchin'. I can hold Jen on my horse if you want."

"No. I'll put her in the saddle with me. You don't get to touch her." Zeke smiled at me and turned to walk back to the girls and the horses.

A minute later he called out, "Mount up," and climbed aboard his stallion.

Allie helped me lift Jen to the front of my saddle; then she went back to her horse and awkwardly mounted. She rubbed her eyes, then nodded at me to let me know she was ready. We kicked the horses into a trot and headed back.

The horses moved fast, despite the rough terrain, as any horse will do when it knows it's headed home. Jen's eyes were still half-closed. It was clear she was heavily drugged. Whether or not someone else had done it or her condition was self-inflicted didn't really matter at this point. I had to use all the energy left in me to hold her upright as the horses wandered down the steep trails and wove through the trees. Her head wobbled, her dark hair swished across my saddle horn, and it was all I could do to keep us both on the horse.

It felt different, having my tired arms around her waist, embracing her as I hadn't since we were kids—proof that neither of us were those children any longer, hadn't been for years. Yet it brought back memories of why I owed her, why I'd come when she called.

FOR a year after MOM died, Jen and I kept track of Paxton. The bastard rarely left his parents' house, and when he did it was only to walk to a small corner store for 3.2 beer and cigarettes. Every time I saw him, while I hid behind a corner or fence or the dash of Jen's car, I seethed with rage. I was glad the cops hadn't found him, because I wanted to be the one who watched the life fade from his eyes.

That anger drove me to get bigger, stronger, and smarter. That summer I worked every menial job I could find. The harder the better. Bucking hay bales, throwing grain sacks, construction labor, anything to bulk up. I ran two miles a day. And I read everything I could in the library about conflict.

The following fall, when finally I felt a match for the man, Jen picked me up and we went to Paxton's. He left his house at nine, and we knew the route he'd take walking back. He never varied. Jen parked the car a block away, and I made her promise to stay in it, no matter what happened.

I met the son of a bitch in an abandoned lot full of dead elms, tall grass, and shredded plastic sacks. I thought of the rebar, and the sights and smells of my mother dead on a bloody floor. The anger and the adrenaline and the fear mixed into a potent potion that nearly blinded me and made me shake worse in the wind than the dead leaves in the trees. When he saw me he laughed.

He put down the twelve-pack and paper bag, still laughing. He stopped laughing when I rushed him with the knife. I blocked his predictable haymaker and plunged the knife six times into his stomach. Then he knocked the knife from my hand. I remember that number, six, because he only hit me three times before I fell. I'd inflicted twice as much damage, hadn't I? Except I couldn't get up. The last of the three blows had broken something, and I couldn't stand.

Paxton spit on me, clutched his stomach, and bent to pick up the knife.

His hands were about to close on it when the gunshot boomed, and the side of his head blew out.

I turned my aching head to see Jen, standing on the sidewalk at the edge of the lot, holding a pistol. And smirking.

CHAPTER THIRTY

J en stayed in a semiconscious state for most of the return trip from the compound, due to the magical powers of modern pharmaceuticals. Only once did she become coherent enough to acknowledge my presence, issuing a soft, questioning, "Clyde?"

I stroked her hair and told her, "I'm here, Sis. I made it. Everything's going to be okay." Even as I said it, I had a foreboding that everything *wouldn't* be okay. I'd pissed too many people off, thwarted too many best laid plans. It was only a matter of time before someone would show up to deliver payback.

By the time we'd gotten to within a mile of Zeke's place, he'd regaled us with story after story of dumb tourists, dumb cops, and the occasional women dumb enough to stay with him, though eventually they ran away screaming. He was in the middle of one of the latter stories when a strong wind lifted off his hat and he dismounted to get it.

I took the opportunity to focus on Jen. She'd started mumbling, and her eyes twitched back and forth under the eyelids. I called to her again and she mumbled my name, so I dismounted and helped her onto the back of the saddle, then clambered back on. I positioned her arms around me and called over to Allie.

"What now?" she asked.

"Do me a favor and reach into my saddlebag and dig out a long blue strap I have there. I want to get Jen more secured."

Allie found the strap, which had a clamp on the end, and asked, "What do I do with this?"

"Loop it around us at the waist. It'll be backup in case she loses her grip."

"Why the heck do you have that thing anyway?" Allie asked as we got the strap fastened.

"Well, if you want to know the truth, I wasn't sure if we'd be hauling back a body. I'm sure glad we're not."

Allie exhaled and nodded. Then she walked over to her horse and climbed back on.

I whispered to Jen. "Do you remember when you stole the Harley from Mom's boyfriend Reed?" She didn't open her eyes but mumbled something close to yes.

"I want you to hold on like I did then. When you started elbowing me and screaming that I was going to break your ribs."

I could have sworn I saw a smile, and I felt her arms tighten just enough to stay on. I kicked the horse back toward Zeke, felt Popcorn's massive hindquarters bunch and push, and was relieved when Jen didn't fall off.

Behind me Allie seemed subdued. Perhaps she felt the same foreboding I felt? Was rescuing someone from the devil *this* easy? We'd find out soon enough.

Our horses cantered along for another mile until finally we reached the outer gate of Zeke's spread. I continued to ignore Zeke's yarns as we passed through the gate and rode into his ranch, thinking distractedly of where Jen should set up once we got back. I certainly wanted her steering clear of Spike and his ilk. She'd have to find a new place and . . .

I was so trail worn that I didn't register until it was too late the Land Rover parked neatly next to the ranch house and the three men standing next to it, cradling assault rifles in their arms.

A wiry man dressed in slacks and a polo shirt walked around the Rover and stood next to his men, a smug look peeling back his lips. He walked with an air of competence and arrogance, gliding to a spot in between us and the car. He strode like someone who truly believes he rules his world.

It was the same attitude I'd seen in puffed-up African warlords, a smugness based on assumed power and control, backed by mindless thugs. By themselves the thugs were weak, but a mob of weaklings could be more than a little dangerous.

When my mind clicked over to the reality of what was happening I went for my pistol.

"Don't," Zeke said, dismounting. He waved his .44 at my chest. "Let me handle this." The gunmen watched closely, their rifles held loose but ready.

The wiry man walked over to stand in front of Zeke. His men followed, rifles aimed at the ground, spreading out in a semicircle behind him and Zeke. The men looked mean and hard, well trained, and deadly.

Zeke spoke first, his .44 pointed at the ground. "I thought we was gonna meet in town."

The wiry man laughed, a smug and contemptuous guffaw. When he did, I felt Jen's arms tighten and tremble.

"Trust isn't my strong suit," the wiry man said. "You said you'd have Mr. Barr, so I came to collect him here. Your place happened to be on my way." He shook his head solemnly. "I'm disappointed that you had other plans."

Alvis. The man *had* to be Alvis. This was bad. I stole a glance back at Allie, who looked panicked.

Zeke shifted, visibly nervous for the first time since I'd known him. "My plan was always to deliver Barr to you. You're not doin' what we agreed," he said, his thumb moving slowly up the side of his revolver.

"This is *my* mountain now," Alvis said. "I've grown tired of placating you with shipments of willing women. And I'm afraid I won't be able to compensate you for Mr. Barr now that I know you've helped him create havoc at my facility. In fact, you've so thoroughly disappointed me that I've decided you're going to have to die."

Zeke took a step away from his horse and pointed the revolver at Alvis. "I've never been afraid of dying, but I promise you, Alvis, if I go, you go, too. Here's my offer: I let you live and you clear out of here."

Rifles bristled behind Alvis, all pointed at Zeke. Alvis continued to smile and said, "Point that gun in another direction. I *will* take back Jennifer and Mr. Barr, and you will be shot."

There wasn't much time. My stomach clenched as I frantically tried to calculate a way out of this.

There was a long moment of silence with fingers tightening on triggers. Then Zeke grinned. "Fine," he said, and let his revolver fall to his feet. I recognized Zeke's mental wheels turning. He wasn't done yet.

Alvis gestured to his men. "Escort both the lovely bartender over there and Mr. Z to the soft dirt in front of the barn. Then shoot them both." He pulled a Glock, walked to my horse, and aimed it at my head.

The men motioned to Zeke, keeping their distance. Zeke

walked over to Allie's horse and ripped the reins from her hands. As he started to tug the horse toward the barn, he said, "We could have had fun, you and me." He patted the horse's neck, then Allie's thigh. She tried to kick him, but Zeke just dodged and laughed. Some of the gunmen chuckled as they walked behind the two toward the barn.

I tried to control my breathing, tried to will my heart to slow down as the gunmen ushered away the condemned. I'd expected some underhandedness from Zeke, but definitely not this. He'd obviously had betrayal on his mind from the get-go and miscalculated by getting doubly greedy. He'd wanted a payday from both me *and* Alvis.

Now it was Allie, Jen, and me who'd be paying. And yes, Zeke as well.

Alvis had one hand on my horse's bridle, the pistol in the other. "Last smoke?" I asked. He nodded. I reached slowly into my coat and brought out the smokes and my lighter. "Thanks," I said, then shook out a cigarette and lit it.

"It's a shame," Alvis said. He glanced briefly toward the barn. "That dumb miner provided a valuable service. Despite his depravities, he kept the hikers and hunters from stumbling on my facilities. Long-range recon patrols, if you will. I've been told you did something like that, somewhere far away."

I took a drag and shrugged. Jen's grip tightened every time the man spoke.

"Oh, come on, Mr. Barr. You and I did similar work. I'm just better at it."

We have nothing *in common*, I told myself. I kept silent and smoked. Watched Allie and her horse move closer to the barn, led by a lunatic.

"I enjoyed it, you know," Alvis said. "The war. I suppose

in some way you must have, too. When I came back I was beyond bored, until I started building on what my misguided little brother had begun. Now I get to enjoy the same things I did over there."

"I'm guessing a functional vehicle isn't on that list," I said.

"What are you talking about?"

I gestured with the cigarette. "That flat tire on your Rover." It was a simple ploy, one that any chimp like me would know.

But it worked. Alvis's eyes darted away from me for just a second, which was all I needed. I flicked the cigarette at his face, catching him in the eye with the glowing red ember. At the same time I pulled my pistol from my coat, jabbed my horse in the ribs with my heels, and ran over Alvis. He didn't fire or move after the horse's chest and hooves hit him. I kept charging toward the men with the rifles.

Jen nuzzled her head into my back, whimpered, but held on tight.

In the distance I saw Allie moving. She'd kicked again, this time connecting with a distracted Zeke, who was busy pulling a backup pistol from under his vest. Allie gathered up the reins, wheeled her horse, and whipped it toward the gate.

I took five wild shots at the guards, saw one go down, and popped another round in Zeke's direction. He shot once at me, missed, and shot four more times at the guards. Another one fell. The third scuttled away on all fours toward the Rover.

Alvis was still down but moving.

Zeke looked for his horse, which had started loping for the pasture when the gunshots started, and then at me. I put another round in his direction, and he took off low and quick toward his house.

Remembering the rifles in the house, I angled my galloping horse to cut off Zeke's loose stallion, grabbed the dangling reins, and whirled back toward the gate at a full run.

I slowed as I got twenty yards from the gate, just enough to see Allie charging up to it on her horse and throwing it open. She'd just passed through when a rifle boomed in the distance and a tree limb cracked to my right.

So the last gunman had finally decided to return fire. Good for him. I turned my horse with a knee and whipped up the .375. I pulled the safety back and aimed a shot toward the ranch. The recoil was bad, but the sound was worse and my horse shied away, spinning hard and shaking its head. Jen hung on tight.

I got Popcorn under control but almost lost Zeke's horse, since I'd dropped the reins to grab my rifle. I cornered him against an H-brace and snatched up the reins. "Okay," I told the women. "Let's go."

Jen barely seemed to be holding on as we set out in a trot down the road that led to Leadville. Thank God I'd strapped us together. Allie followed third in line. She stayed quiet for a while but it didn't take long before she started asking questions again. We hadn't made it into the trees, had barely made it into the first grassy meadow, when she asked, "How long until Lance or one of his men kills Zeke?"

"They won't, if Zeke makes it to the house," I said. "He's got long guns and is a hell of a shot. They don't stand a chance. And Alvis might already be dead."

"I saw Lance moving when we took off, so he might make it. If he's okay, he and that last goon of his will follow us."

"I don't think so," I said. "That guy will be busy trying to get Alvis out of there." I felt Jen squeeze me harder at the mention of Lance's name. "If he gets Alvis in the Rover, and they try to follow, we'll be off the road, thanks to the horses."

"Zeke will come, though."

"Probably. He doesn't like loose ends. And he knows I'll kill him if I see him."

"Plus there's something else," Allie said quietly.

"What?"

"Jen and me. Zeke still wants his 'payment for services rendered.'"

"He's a sick bastard," I said. "Allie, I'm so sorry I—"

"Yeah, I know, Barr. You thought he was a respected citizen. His shortcomings caught you unawares."

"Well, I thought he had a code. Strength respects strength and all that."

"His code is 'Take and don't stop taking.'"

"Yeah, I guess you're right. Right now, though, we need to find a place to hole up and rest. The horses are tired, I'm goddamned tired, and Jen's mind is somewhere else. She won't be much help until we can clear her head."

"If we stop, Zeke will catch up with us, right?"

"I'm planning on it," I said. I listened to the sound of distant gunfire and pulled my horse off the road and into the trees.

CHAPTER THIRTY-ONE

Half an hour later, as the white sun sank low in the sky, I found what I'd been looking for. We crested a little knoll ringed by craggy limestone slabs. The slabs formed a circular natural wall, like that of a crumbling castle, and I could see only one way in and out. At the knoll's peak, inside the wall, there were patches of crusty snow interspersed with grass and young daisies.

I reined in my horse outside of the rock ring and said, "We'll wait here. And hope he shows before dark. If not we'll camp and wait for him to make an appearance in the morning."

"Okay," Allie said wearily. "I'll take the horses." Even tired and scared, she was ready to help instead of talk. I realized how much I depended on her.

"Thanks," I said. I got Jen unstrapped and lifted her down off the horse. With me holding her under one arm, we clambered through a narrow slit in the gray-and-white rocks.

I hauled her to one of the drier spots in the circle, sat her down, and asked her if she was all right. She didn't reply, just mumbled with her eyes still closed. I sat down next to her and took her hand in mine. It was cold, but she didn't try to rip it away.

Allie came into the circle, saddlebags thrown over both shoulders and dragging packs. She threw them down at our feet, then sat down hard next to Jen, whose pretty face and dull black hair were streaked with sweat. "We need a fire," Allie said.

I stood up and went to gather wood. As I was walking away I said, "Keep her company, will you?" Allie rolled her eyes and said, "What else am I gonna do?"

I limped down the hill, slipping sometimes in shadowy places where snowmelt kept the soil slick, and started picking up dead pieces of pine for the fire. It was a task that came easily and helped settle my mind. I remembered a book I'd read in Nairobi about Zen Buddhism. It said that one of the best ways to keep a calm mind is to do important, simple, physical work. Like raking rocks or carrying water or chopping wood. The book said that these things helped because they felt good and had an immediate result.

I had quite a big pile of dry sticks in my arms, but something kept telling me I needed more. Or maybe it was just that the sticks I was carrying weren't big or dry enough. I wandered around in the dense undergrowth of the pines, talking to myself and picking up and throwing down wood, until I realized I was stalling.

I didn't want to go back up there. There were people up there, and pretty quickly they'd want to talk. At least *one* would. It might take a while before Jen would be gabbing. Down here it was simple. Finally, grudgingly, I headed up the hill. *Time to take your medicine, Barr.*

When I drew to within twenty yards of the campsite and heard a conversation going on, I dropped the firewood in surprise. *What the*— Quickly I regathered the wood and headed into our rocky alcove.

"I don't understand why you're here," Jen was saying. "Is Lance here, too?"

Allie was telling her no, that it was a long story.

"Where is Clyde?"

"Right here, Sis," I said as I walked into camp.

I set the wood down and started building a fire: putting the smallest sticks into a tepee shape, then laying the larger logs around them to look like a log cabin. Jen shook her head slowly. "Clyde, how did you . . . I mean. Sorry"—she ran her hands through her hair—"my brain's all fogged. Tell me who this Zeke guy is."

I shot Allie a look. She glared at me. "I'll explain later, when you're safe. I'm just glad that whatever they gave you is wearing off. Why were you at that compound, Jen? What did Alvis want with you? Why was he keeping you all drugged up?"

"It was a nightmare," Jen said. "I remember Lance and drinks. He seemed interested in my job. Then I was waking up in a hotel room with guards. Lance made me take pills. I spit some of them out and sneaked away and called you. Then a guard caught me and forced the pills down my throat."

"Did it have something to do with a break-in?" Allie asked.

As I waited for Jen to answer, I held my Bic lighter to the kindling and watched the flames hungrily eat their way to the larger pieces of wood. The fire slowly took on a life of its own and I sat down wearily on the ground, resting on my elbow in the black loam.

Jen shook her head slowly, her black hair swaying over her face. "A break-in? Yeah, maybe. He needed something from this place I work at—needed me to get him inside the main storage area. He was waiting for my shift to start back up in . . . a couple days? . . . What day is it? . . . And then—"

"Where do you work?" I asked, watching the flames.

"I work for the government. At the Department of Energy depot outside Junction. I clean."

That made sense. Government building, probably really secure. And as a custodian she'd have access to the whole building.

"What would Lance want from *there*?" Allie asked, puzzled.

Jen mumbled to herself, then pressed both hands against her temples. "I'm still fogged in. It had something to do with . . . with . . . a chemical. In barrels. Big black barrels. They use it to clean up uranium mines." She mumbled again, and her eyelids started to droop.

The sibling in me said, *Enough*. She was too tired, and too drugged, for us to keep pressing. We'd get more out of her after she had some sleep.

While I was away searching for wood Allie had sorted the gear. I grabbed my sleeping bag, unzipped it, and rolled it out next to Jen. I fluffed it, and when Jen's eyes were fully closed, I slowly rolled her into the puffy fabric. An image flashed in my mind of Jen as a kid lying on her bed in the mornings, gripping the big stuffed tiger she'd won at the fair. *So long ago.*

Allie noticed the look on my face. "You okay?"

I nodded. "It's just been a long day."

"She's still out of it," Allie said, "but she's alive. And she's going to be all right. You kept your promise, Barr."

I put my head in my hands, then stared past the fire into the gathering dusk. "This isn't a win until we get away from Zeke and Lance. We've kicked up a hornet's nest and the hornets are flying our way."

"So what do we do?"

I thought for a few seconds. "In a way, it may be easiest to stop Lance. Somewhere in that ruckus back there, I lost my phone. I just need to use your phone to call those Feds who followed us and tell them where the compound is."

"Sounds good, Barr," Allie said. "Just one little problem."

"That being?"

"My phone's with our gear in the Jeep."

"Why didn't you put it in your saddlebag?"

"Because you said just take the essentials. Plus Zeke said the service around here sucks."

"Oh," I said. "Right."

My saddlebags were near a clump of snakeweed next to Allie, so I limped over and grabbed them, rummaging around until I found the shells and my hunting knife. The knife went on my belt. It took me only a minute to reload the pistol and the rifle.

I handed the pistol to Allie. "Time's up. Zeke should be here soon. I'm going to climb up on one of those boulders and watch. I want you to stay in these rocks with Jen, keep her safe. If Zeke somehow gets inside, shoot him, okay?" She nodded.

I looked at my sister, watched her sleep with the same fitful murmurs and leg twitches she'd exhibited growing up.

Then I turned, hefted my rifle, and went to find a rock.

CHAPTER THIRTY-TWO

The hard granite was cold as I bellied down on it and jacked a shell into the .375. The sun was gone, well on its way to the other side of the globe, and the planets were starting to twinkle in the gray sky. In another half hour it would be full dark, and if Zeke wasn't here already, then he'd have to use a flashlight to find our tracks. It would make for an easy target. But if he was *already* here . . . well, then it would be a little more complicated. I should have given Allie the pistol earlier, so she could have shot him when we were at the ranch. If she had, we'd all be on our way back into town now, instead of sitting on a hill, waiting for a madman to come to us.

There were no unusual sounds in the hills below us, only the regular shift change of the forest denizens. There were owl hoots, the conversational croaking of ravens, and the far-off lonely calls of coyotes. When I was little I imagined the chipmunks and squirrels punching tiny time cards in tiny clocks, putting their tiny hard hats on little hooks and wearily climbing the trees back into their little houses and snuggling down next to their loving little wives. Their shift was over now, and everything seemed normal down below.

As I stretched out on the rock, cradling my well-worn rifle,

I couldn't help but chuckle at how unlikely this situation was. I'd finally come home to the Land of Plenty, and here I was getting involved in the same old shit.

It was fun in the beginning, all those years ago, when I was young and the world was simply a wide-open adventure. A stint in the Merchant Marine, then I jumped ship and traipsed across Africa, naive but lucky, camping and hiking my way south. But the money from my year at sea had run out, and so I'd been forced to take a number of dreary jobs. I grabbed the only ones my skills allowed, meaning I spent months watching cows and building fences and digging wells. In a developing country you'd have to work for *years* doing things like that to get out of the country.

So I turned to jobs that paid a little more. Like hunting poachers in animal reserves. Or guiding hunting safaris. Good work, outside, but it still didn't pay much. Then I began helping the underdogs in coups and revolutions, picking the side I approved of. That kind of work proved to be a golden ticket—at least, relative to the other options available.

Eventually I got out. I took a job crewing aboard a ship sailing out of Cape Town and headed for Chile.

In South America I began with a little more money so I wandered around the jungles and deserts, heading north, until the money got thin. And at that point I fell back into old routines, like helping the natives fight against the oil companies. But there wasn't any money in those types of wars, so I started copying the natives, taking a little here and there from the rich companies that came to pillage.

Months became years and one day I woke up in Mexico. Like before, I tried to help the little guys, but it was hard to know *who* I was helping. Eventually my luck ran out and I was thrown into a Mexican prison. Where I met Zeke.

Zeke had been a part of this thing from the beginning, I now realized. Been around the world, have you, Barr? Think you're pretty smart? So why doesn't it smell to high heaven that your old prison buddy just happens to know where this man you're looking for can be found? Zeke had been told in advance that I might be headed his way, and like a spider he lured me into his web.

I must have drifted off to sleep. I jerked my head off the rock when one of the horses nickered and stomped far below me. I looked out and found that it had gotten too dark to see them; there was nothing but a sea of blackness under blinking stars. Needles rustled on the ground near the horses. Could be a deer, an elk, or any of the numerous animals that chose this time of night to come out and graze. But I didn't think so. I put the rifle up to my shoulder, looked hopefully through the scope, and wasn't surprised when I saw nothing but black.

Behind me I heard the faint sound of Allie saying something comforting to Jen, and in front of me more needles swished in response.

I slung the rifle onto my shoulder, slowly slid off the rock, and climbed down silently, heading toward the horses.

No moon had yet appeared, but the stars shining in the cloudless sky provided just enough light to see the ground beneath me and a couple of feet in front, enabling me to creep slowly toward the horses and pick a spot where I could crouch and watch them. It took me ten minutes to make it that far, and it turned out to be a little too long.

Something blurred through the trees, and I heard the slapping of horse flesh. Three horses thundered off down the hill, back toward the ranch. Our horses. As I groggily wondered how they came to be untied, a branch snapped somewhere close. I couldn't determine the source of the sound because of the louder pounding of hooves, and I stood still, waiting for my senses to wake up.

My senses failed, because the source of the sound found me.

"Howdy, you son of a bitch," Zeke whispered as his cable-like arm snaked around my neck and cool steel bit into my throat.

CHAPTER THIRTY-THREE

I tensed, feeling the old feelings surge through my body. My heart raced, my muscles bunched, time slowed, and bile rose from my stomach and turned to acid.

It wasn't the first time I'd had a knife at my throat. If it were, I would have been panicked instead of pissed off. My hands shot up instinctively to the knife, and I pinned the hand holding it against my chest. After that I shot my right arm to the sky, lifting the shoulder and forcing the blade away from my neck. Then I twisted out and away from the crazy bastard, shoving him as I escaped.

He still had the knife. And I hate knives. The primal emergency-alert system in my skull was screaming for me to run away, but I couldn't. I had nowhere to run to, and I wasn't about to abandon the women. My hands searched for the rifle sling, but the weapon had fallen off my shoulder in the scuffle.

"You shouldn'ta shot at me, hombre," Zeke said, holding the knife low and advancing.

Allie must have heard the scuffle. "Barr?" she shouted from behind the walls of our camp.

I shuffled and put myself between the madman and the

camp. Shouted over my shoulder, "Stay put, goddammit. Watch Jen."

I went for my own knife but didn't reach it before Zeke smiled and leaped, jabbing his blade up as he flew at me. I plowed into him, grabbed the knife arm, and tried to drive an elbow into his head. I couldn't connect but managed to use the force of the charge to drive him into the ground.

This wasn't a calculated, testing, playful fight like before. This was now an animal rite, a savage, writhing, biting, clawing, rolling battle. Zeke kept trying to stick me, and I kept a hold on his arm. No one gained any ground; we just clung and rolled and jerked until he somehow managed to get his arm free and stick the knife hard into the outside of my shoulder. Luckily my muscles were hard with exertion, and it only peeled a small chunk off the outside.

I grabbed an ear and twisted and ripped, feeling the flesh pull away like warm taffy. Zeke screamed and I dropped the ear and rolled away, jumping to my feet.

He came up fast, screaming obscenities, one hand pressed to the side of his head as he tried to stanch the flow of blood streaming down his face. The other hand held his knife, and it shone in the starlight as he waved it in circles. He yelled something about my mother being a member of the oldest profession and that I'd die and burn in hell. I didn't really listen, couldn't because of the sound of my heartbeat pulsing in my ears.

"Barr!" Allie screamed from the camp. She sounded closer. "I can't see to shoot."

"Don't," I yelled. "Get back with Jen." I heard her say something, her tone telling me I'd have more to apologize for later.

I pulled out my own knife, took a deep breath, and prepared for the worst kind of fight.

This is something the movies always get wrong. They show two guys waving steel, dancing around and lunging at each other with a string of near misses. Hell, even in Olympic fencing it doesn't work that way. Points are scored quickly, sometimes faster than the eye can see. That's why they rig the fencers with electronic sensors.

And that's how most knife fights are. Quick and dirty and bloody. Most stabs are faster than the eye or brain can register. And the worst part is that your body won't even realize that it has been stuck until much later. It will feel like a pinch, then feel as if you're sweating. You'll look down and realize that the pinch is a deep knife gash and the sweat is blood. Then later, if you're still alive, it'll hurt like hell.

It was too dark to make out Zeke's facial expressions, but I'm sure that if I could've, there would've been a lot of smiling. Even after getting his ear ripped off. He held his knife low, against his leg, and said, "Okay, Barr. One last go-around. You? Or me?"

I was pretty sure I'd been in more of these stab contests than he had. But he was good, and I didn't want a straight-up fight that would end with one of us dead and the other almost that way. So I decided to cheat. "You," I said, and turned as if to run back toward the women.

He moved to follow and I pretended to stumble, put both hands on the ground. He rushed after me, raised his knife, and I kicked hard at his ankle, twisting him off his feet. He landed hard on his face, then rolled to his back, moaning. I jumped up and slammed down on top of him, pinning his knife arm with my knee, the way you would pin a calf's neck during a branding.

And here's another place where Hollywood has it wrong. I didn't hold him down and let him struggle. I didn't try to have one last conversation with him, telling him I was sorry it had to end this way, that I wished we could be friends again. I didn't because those things don't happen in real life when someone is trying to kill you. With a knife. Especially if this someone's next act after killing you will be to rape your sister and friend.

No, there was none of that heart-wrenching sappiness, just me bearing down on him, one hand fighting off his flailing arm, and the other jamming the knife down into his neck, his chest, his stomach, then back up. Again and again until he stopped moving and I was left breathless, retching, covered in blood, on top of someone I used to call a friend. Someone I'd fought with before, side by side, but had always known deep down could *never* be a friend. Because he'd lost his soul.

I pulled myself off the body, then sat back on the hard earth. I wiped the blood off my knife onto my pants, waiting for my heart and lungs to slow. After my body had calmed down, after my knife was shiny again, after I'd dry heaved for the last time, and after I'd wiped blood off myself using sand and leaves, I went back to Zeke's body. I took his gun and five hundred in cash out of his wallet. Then I kicked sand over his face.

I somehow managed to drag my tired, broken, and exhausted body back to the campfire and the women. Jen was still asleep, nestled deep in my sleeping bag against a rock by the dying fire. Allie clambered down off one of the rocks and sprinted over to me. She put her arm under mine and helped me limp to the fire.

"Are you hurt?" Allie asked, wide-eyed.

"I've been better," I said. I swayed by the dying fire.

"Zeke?"

"Dead."

I heard her sigh. Then, "What do we do now?"

"We get some sleep."

"Shouldn't we alternate, in case someone else followed us up here?"

I couldn't imagine how anyone else could. Zeke knew this place, and he knew me, so it was easy enough for him to find us. I doubted anyone else could. "I'll take first watch," I said. "Come and get me when you wake up."

"You should crash first, Barr. I've slept twice as much as you in the last couple of days."

She had a point, but I had the experience and the rifle. "Sleep next to Jen. Make sure she doesn't wander off if she needs to use the bushes. I'll be on a rock."

She was about to argue again but gave up with a yawn. "Fine. But just a few hours; then we'll switch."

I nodded and found a spot in between rocks where I could see in the direction of the faraway road. I went prone and cradled my rifle. Every time I blinked I saw blood, and the blinks came more and more frequently. I heard Allie's and Jen's soft snoring and murmuring, heard the grass swish in the breeze, and stared at the stars.

Just a few hours, and I'd finally get some goddamned sleep.

CHAPTER THIRTY-FOUR

I thought it was a dream at first. In the dream I'm throwing on my pack and walking into the wilderness, and Allie is standing at the trailhead, crying and telling me not to go. I kiss her on the cheek and tell her it will be okay. But she doesn't stop crying.

That's when I realized I was lying facedown in the dirt and it wasn't crying but cursing that was coming from behind me. Allie was pacing the far side of the camp and swearing.

I'd fallen asleep at my post. Yup, that was it. I hadn't been attacked. I hadn't been conked on the head by a sap. I'd simply *fallen asleep*. Still, my noggin felt like a smashed pumpkin and my shoulder burned as if sand had worked its way under the skin. All my joints protested with the smallest movements, and even breathing was excruciating. Other than that I felt fine.

Allie paced her way over to stand beside me. "Barr," she said. "You fell asleep."

"Yeah, I gathered." I looked at her with one eye open. "But apparently so did you."

"I did. And now we have another problem."

"Such as . . ."

"It's a big one."

"Out with it, woman," I said, opening my other eye. It was bright. The sun was almost directly above me. I guessed I must have really needed the sleep.

"You can be such a bastard, you know that?"

"I've been told. What is it now?"

"Jen's gone."

I sat up quickly, too quickly, and nearly blacked out. I waited for my vision to return to normal and said, "What do you mean, she's gone?"

"She's gone."

"You mean she just up and walked away? Where the hell did she go?"

"I don't know. I woke up and looked over and she was just . . . gone."

"Well, she sure didn't take a horse."

"How do you know that?"

"The horses have scattered. Zeke chased them off before he and I met up."

"Damn it . . ." Allie looked both angry and exasperated.

"It's my fault," I said. "You were right about keeping watch." I pushed myself to my feet and stumbled over to where Jen had slept. The tracks there, though trampled in places by Allie's pacing, told me everything I needed to know.

What I saw were drag marks and the deep prints of a man carrying something heavy. What an idiot I was. If I were more flexible, I would have kicked my own ass.

"We need to go," I said. *"Now.* Alvis's man didn't drive off with him; he followed us. And he took Jen while we were getting our beauty rest."

Allie didn't argue. She helped me fill our small packs with what little we needed and hide the rest of the gear.

"How do you know it was the man from Zeke's?"

"That guy was big, and those tracks over there"—I pointed at where Jen had lain—"are size thirteen. I can't be a hundred percent sure, but I'm pretty certain. Alvis must still be alive and calling the shots. He sent his man after us."

Allie helped me make sure the fire was completely out, and then we buried the ashes to erase the fact that we'd been there. "I don't understand how he could get in here," said Allie. "I mean, how could he take Jen and leave without us knowing? And if we were sleeping *that* hard, why didn't he just kill us?"

"Couldn't take the chance," I said, guessing. "He was out-numbered and didn't know how deep we were sleeping. Plus I was off to the side. Maybe he didn't spot me. If I were in his situation I'd use a gag or a chemical-soaked rag and get the hell out without making a sound. Make myself a hero to Alvis. Get a promotion."

"I guess so," Allie said. "Still, he'd have to be good."

"He was. I think I might have underestimated Alvis and his men."

"You think?"

We both stared at each other, immensely frustrated. Yesterday—recovering Jen, almost dying at Zeke's ranch, surviving Zeke's attempt to deliver payback—had seemed like climbing the tallest mountain imaginable. It had pushed us both to the edge, demanded everything we had. And now all our gains had disappeared. It was as if we were at the base of the mountain again, staring up at its towering summit.

Allie rallied first. "The good news is that they need her for something. And they'll keep her alive until then. We just have to get her back, again, before they don't need her."

"Yeah, that's all we have to do," I said.

"You thinking of giving up?"

"What?" Her question startled me. "*Hell* no." Not for the first time I marveled at this woman who'd come into my life, at her fierce resolve. "Let's get to it."

As we slung the packs onto our backs, I told Allie to stay directly behind me—to try and walk in my footsteps.

"Like a good woman should?" she asked.

"No," I said, "so you don't accidentally ruin sign."

It was maybe one o'clock, well past the prime morning tracking time, where the slanting rays of the sun would cast shadows on one side of the tracks and make them easier to see. I'd have to wait for twilight to have the same light, and that was too long. I circled the inside of our little rock castle, cutting sign, and found the big boots. I started on his trail, following it through a gap in the rocks.

"Are you just guessing where he went, or do you actually see something on the ground?" Allie asked as she clomped behind me.

I crouched down, the pounding in my head increasing, and pointed the track out to her: large, size-thirteen tactical boots with extra weight on the outside of the right foot—due to carrying my sister. "See?" I said, tracing the print softly with my fingers, memorizing the feel in case I had to track by touch alone.

"No. Wait, yeah. Barely. Can't we just go to the compound, or Zeke's? That's got to be where he's going."

"We *could*. But what if they had a rendezvous point somewhere else? What if he's taking her to town? What if Jen fights, and they're stopped until he can settle her down? What if the guy breaks an ankle and is laid up between here and the road?"

"Okay, I get it. Track on."

I went prone, tilted my head, and looked across the ground for the next track. With the different light from that angle, I was able to see the depressed pine needles six inches in front of the first track. That position, though, also made me want to take a nap.

The tracks showed that we might have a chance to catch up with them before they got to the road, depending on what time the man came into camp. I noticed a single wave in the middle of the tracks, which meant a very slow gait. Also, there were occasional wobble marks on the sides, which indicated resting and heavy breathing. It's not easy to carry a body for miles, no matter how good you are.

Some of the prints had clean peaks at the top, showing that they'd been made only a couple hours ago. In the daylight. God, we must have crashed hard. One of the human body's greatest flaws is that when the brain demands sleep, it gets it. No amount of caffeine or drugs or adrenaline can keep someone awake forever.

"We can catch them," I said. I pulled my aching body up, and almost fell before Allie grabbed me.

"You sure you're all right? We should go to town, get you to the hospital."

"I'm fine," I said. I wasn't, but I'd been worse and knew I could push through. I *had* to. Jen needed me.

So that's what I did. I brushed Allie away and went into the trance you need while tracking. I took off fast, keeping the tracks on my right, watching for prints, kicked gravel, compressed pine needles, flattened grass. When a track was faint, I used the average gap between steps to find the next one.

A quick hour later, we'd tracked Mr. Size Thirteen to the main road leading to Zeke's, maybe four miles from his place.

There'd been multiple stumble marks as the man grew fatigued, even a few spots where he'd fallen, and by the end his stride had shrunk to two inches. At that speed, we should have caught up with them.

But they weren't there.

Instead I found the twin-oval marks where the man had rumped down. Allie called me over and pointed at the tire tracks in the road. The pickup and Jeep marks were gone. Run over at least twice by the wider, knobbier tires of the Rover. Meaning that Alvis had driven out, and back.

The only tracks out of place were the tire prints next to where the man had sat down. And the footprints of a lighter male. He'd exited the vehicle from the driver side and walked to the side of the road. Jen's tracks scraped along beside the tracks of the two men on the way to the vehicle.

On the other side of the road a mess of torn and flattened new grass showed where the Rover had turned around. The trees on our side were starting to sway, and leaves blew across the road. The wind that whipped across smelled like cold rain.

"What's it mean?" Allie said, staring at the ground in confusion.

"Means they're gone. Either to the compound or somewhere farther away." It also meant that everything we'd done had been in vain. I sat down hard, in nearly the same spot that the man had.

Allie sat down beside me, put a hand on my leg. "So . . . what now?"

I threw up my hands, exasperated. "I don't know. Walk back to the ranch, grab the Jeep, and start all over. I need to think about if and when to call the Feds now that Jen is at risk again. I have no clue what the Feds' priorities will be if she's back at the compound and they decide to storm it."

Allie squeezed my leg. "Well, that's just great," she mumbled, before jumping up and pulling me to my feet.

Now that Alvis knew I was out here somewhere and aware of his compound's location, I was pretty sure he'd be more on guard than ever—and likely not even at the compound. Which meant that my next plan would have to involve finding his location and building in an element of surprise. I'd just started running through options when the storm hit.

CHAPTER THIRTY-FIVE

Maybe two hundred yards down the road, the wind doubled in intensity. It slapped at our faces and dragged small rocks across our path. The trees whipped in crazy circles, the smaller ones leaning over so far that their needles touched the ground. Allie stopped, her hands over her face, her back turned to the wind. I jogged over to her and shouted, "We aren't going to make it. Not today."

"Why?" she said. I could barely hear her because the wind pulled her words away as soon as they left her mouth. She sounded miles away.

"Look," I yelled, and pointed at the horizon.

A wall of inky-black clouds rumbled down off the peaks toward us. The occasional lightning strike lit up whole sections of the wall as it advanced. Allie looked, saw the clouds, and put up her hands. I couldn't hear her, but I could read her lips: "Now what?" It was easy to read; she'd said it so many times it could have been her personal slogan.

I pointed up the slope at a ridge with a jumble of rocks that looked like our best chance of shelter. Allie nodded and we took off at a run, letting the wind push and occasionally throw us toward our refuge. We soon found a suitable spot: a medium-size cliff carved at the bottom into an overhang. We ran inside and threw down our packs. It wasn't large, maybe twenty by thirty feet, but it would do.

Outside our cave the wind continued to howl, only slightly slowed by the tall, thick pines that ringed the opening. Inside it was much quieter. The floor of the cave was soft, dry soil without any miniature gullies or washes. Meaning we'd be dry in the coming storm.

I sat down on my pack and Allie did likewise. She hugged her knees and rocked back and forth. "Why don't we just keep going, make it to the cabin? Where it would be warm?"

"Thunderstorms bring more than rain. There'll be lightning and flash floods and mud. Better to wait it out. If it lasts until dark we'll camp here."

Allie didn't reply. She just sat there and kept rocking. This woman continued to surprise me. She had to be exhausted. She'd been through as much as I had in the last few days. But she kept going.

In her own way, over the past week Jen had shown resiliency, too. She'd been kidnapped, dragged into the mountains and dosed . . . then kidnapped *again*. Her toughness never ceased to amaze me. Like when we were kids: she'd taken beatings worse than the ones I'd gotten and still had the nerve to talk back. *Hold on, Jen*, I said to myself. *Just hold on a little bit longer.*

"Here it comes," Allie said, pointing. The clouds had caught up with us, and the first fat raindrops started falling, spattering the rocks and pooling to form small lakes and rivers in the low spots. Thunder boomed and rattled the sides of the rock, followed almost immediately by a bright white flash. We both scooted farther into the cave and stood close to each other, following some primitive human instinct.

"Barr?" Allie said, looking over.

"Yeah?"

"You're bleeding."

I looked down, saw the dark stain on my shoulder. The sand hadn't stuffed it well enough, I guessed, and the piece of flesh that Zeke had cut was dripping again. It didn't hurt though, not compared to how exhausted I felt.

"There's a medical kit in one of our packs," I said, looking beyond the cave's roof. The rain outside fell harder and the large drops were so frequent that the air looked solid.

Allie found the medical kit and tossed it to me. I pulled off my shirt and set it on my bag.

"Nice," Allie said, looking at my shoulder.

"If you like half-chewed meat."

I couldn't see the wound very well. It was on the back of my deltoid, near the triceps. I poked at it, then found an alcohol wipe in the kit and tore it open.

She pointed at her pack. "Sit down."

"I got it."

"Just sit down and shut up," she said, grabbing my shoulders and pushing down. "You might pass out. Let me do this."

"Do you know what you're doing?"

"I can fix a little boo-boo, Barr," she said. "Although, if the hole was any bigger, I'd have to put you down."

I sat down. I felt, more than saw, her wipe the wound and slather antibiotic ointment on it. Then she opened a four-inch square bandage and taped it on. She did a great job, but it felt so strange having someone else take care of me. It hadn't happened much when I was little, and very rarely since. Having a woman like Allie do it meant more to me than I wanted to admit.

After the wound was cleaned, dressed, and taped well

enough to last a couple of days, Allie stood and put away what was left of the medical kit. I started to stand and grab my shirt.

"No," she said, coming back over. She pushed my shoulders down again and left her hands there. "I need to check the rest of you."

"I'm fine now. Thanks."

She shook her head. "You don't look fine. You look like you fell off a goddamned mountain. I'm going to check the rest of you, whether you like it or not. Take off the pants."

"Yes, ma'am," I said, sliding out of the pants and putting them with the shirt. She squatted beside me and looked me over.

"You're different, you know that, Barr?"

"I've been told."

"I mean, you *look* different," she said. "Like these scars, for example. There's so damned many." She ran a warm finger lightly over some of the bullet and shrapnel scars on my shoulders. Whether or not she'd intended it, the touch excited me. She continued, tracing her finger along the calligraphy of past pain, first on my shoulders, working her way around and down my back, then past my boxers and onto my legs. She lingered on the bad leg.

"This where the hyena tried to make a snack of you?"

"One of the strongest sets of jaws in Africa," I said, somehow ashamed that she was seeing me like this.

She rubbed the hyena scars, then hunched up next to me. "You lived through that, I guess you'll make it through this."

Both of us didn't say anything for a moment. Outside, the rain continued to pound. "Hey," I said finally. "You're a pretty good nurse, you know."

She smiled. "That's me, Nurse Martin. Always on call."

"It's only fair I check *you* over, though, too," I said. "Make sure you aren't in need."

"Uh-huh. What did you have in mind?" We both knew where this was going but were having fun pretending we didn't.

"I'll need that shirt off."

"And the pants, too, I suppose?"

I nodded.

She scrunched her face, wriggled out of her shirt, and pulled the pants down. Kicked them both into the pile and shivered. "Okay?"

"Let's take a look." I took hold of her shoulders and slowly twirled her around, looking at the green bruises, the crusty cuts, and the road rashes. "You seem okay," I said—if you ignored the injuries. She looked like she'd fallen off a smaller mountain, but the way her pearly pale skin contrasted with her black underwear looked better than okay. So did the way the little scars and old tattoos stood as markers of a complicated life. They made her look real.

I stepped back, said, "Wait a second." I took the kit and started to fix her up. I took my time cleaning the cuts, rubbing ointment on the bruises, and washing out the abrasions. I wasn't very good at taking care of someone else's injuries, but I pretended to know what I was doing. It gave me an excuse to run my hands up and down her soft, goose-bumpy flesh, to get close enough to smell her intense womanly smell.

"I think you need a shower," I said.

"Really? I had one this week. Isn't that enough?"

"Usually. But you're getting pretty ripe. I think you could use one now."

Before she could say anything, I picked her up and carried her, confused and kicking, out into the pouring rain. Then we both screamed. The spring day may have been warm but the water wasn't. It was as if a glacier had suddenly turned liquid and fallen on us. My heart missed a couple of beats and it took me a while to catch my breath after that first scream. Allie caught her breath before me.

"Sweet-Holy-Christ-Mother-ColdAss-PissRain-God-dammit-Barr!" she yelled.

I agreed, threw her over my shoulder, and ran back into the cave. We ripped through our gear, flung the sleeping bags onto the ground, and fell onto them in a heap.

"Damn you, Barr. That was cold!" She rolled over on top of me.

"Yup. And we won't be able to start a fire, either. All the wood's wet." I grabbed her around her waist.

"Well, then, warm me up."

So I did.

CHAPTER THIRTY-SIX

I woke to the sounds of birds. Gritty yellow sand covered my face and had worked its way into one of my nostrils. A warm rump pressed hard into the small of my back and I reached around to stroke its owner. A little beyond and above Sleeping Beauty were two eyes—small, yellow, and intense—hovering on the cave wall. They bored into mine, prying for a moment, and then they were gone. The light slowly filtered into the cave, and I saw two large rats standing on our packs against the far wall. They caught me staring and took off—one with the last piece of jerky in its fanged mouth.

My mind drifted and soon traveled down one of those twisty tunnels, shifting from the rats to the men my mom had dated, to Paxton, to Jen, to the night of Paxton's death.

THE SOUND OF THE GUNSHOT had given me enough of an adrenaline boost to drag my busted body back to the car in a hurry. Jen and I took off into the night with rubber screaming and drove aimlessly for hours, trying to wrap our heads around what we'd done.

Eventually, after we calmed ourselves and rationalized

Paxton's death, we drove to the river and tossed the gun—Mom's pistol that she should have used earlier—into the middle of the roaring brown waters. We spent the next three days in the desert, sleeping in the car, eating rabbits, and listening to the radio for news. There hadn't been any witnesses, and the police were asking anyone with information to please come forward. We went home, and when the cops eventually showed up to ask questions, we alibied each other out. It cemented our promise to always look out for each other.

ALLIE STIRRED AND PULLED ME back down into our nest. "Morning," she said, then kissed me hard.

"That it is," I said. "We need to get going."

She pushed me away, stared me down. "We could just stay here," she said. "You could go and shoot something for breakfast; then we could make a fire, maybe finish what we started last night." Her eyes brimmed with hope, and I hated like hell to say what I said next.

"We need to move. We need to find Jen. Things undone stay undone and wear on you like a bad-fitting saddle."

"Just how are we going to do that?" she asked, reluctantly standing and sliding into her pants. "We don't know where she is."

I threw on my clothes, checked my rifle. "I'm ninety percent sure she's with Alvis, and I'm almost as sure he's left a trail. We'll sneak into the ranch first, and if no one's there, we'll take the Jeep and figure out our next move."

Allie sighed, started picking up her things.

I watched her for a long moment, and then said softly, "Hey, Allie . . ."

She turned around. "Yeah?"

I couldn't look her in the eye. "I'll understand if you want to call an end to this, take the Jeep to town. I can take one of Zeke's horses. I'll be okay . . . really. Maybe it's better, you know?"

"You trying to get rid of me again?" she said. "You don't want me around?" She walked over to me, lifted my chin. "Look at me, Barr."

Our eyes met and I pulled her toward me, kissing her forehead. "I just don't want you to get hurt . . . I couldn't live—"

"You can live through *anything*, Barr," she said. "That's what makes you who you are." A single tear appeared at the corner of her eye and she wiped at it and sniffed. "How about *this* . . . how about we figure out where Lance is, but we do it quietly? We don't rush in this time without an army to back us. Maybe we get the Feds involved."

I didn't say anything for a moment, then finally nodded. She was making sense, of course, but I didn't picture things playing out that way.

We readied our packs quickly and were walking in the early morning light as the sun clambered its way over the eastern horizon.

THE MOUNTAINS WERE FULL OF enthusiasm after the rain. Sunlight glistened off the dew on the grass and through the silver strands of spiderwebs dangling in the trees. Ghostly white steam rose from the rocks where ravens stood croaking.

It didn't take us long to reach the ranch, as we really hadn't gone that far the night before, it just felt like it in our hasty exit. I left the road, Allie following closely behind, and we worked our way through the trees to the hill behind the ranch. From there we watched the buildings closely for any kind of activity. Seeing none, we walked down slowly, my rifle at the ready, until we reached the main house.

"I'll start the Jeep," she said. "You do your thing."

I nodded and she ran off.

I heard the Jeep start as I kicked the house door open, rifle pulled tight against my shoulder. Nothing happened. The place seemed abandoned but hadn't been completely cleaned out. On the table were two empty bottles of vodka and torn white paper packaging from medical gauze. I swept through the house quickly with the rifle, then slowly after I was sure it was empty. I searched Zeke's room, and when I opened his footlocker I realized just how dark a human being he'd actually been.

Inside were pictures of terrified women, chained to beams in the barn. And stacks of DVDs with women's names Sharpied on them. Next to the DVDs were two sets of handcuffs. A minute later I searched Zeke's closet shelf and came across a small revolver stuffed into a sock.

I checked the barn quickly, finding nothing; just the horses we'd ridden staring dumbly back at me. I made a quick sweep through the corrals and outbuildings, then ran back over to the main house.

I ransacked the liquor cabinet, stuffed a pint of whiskey in my coat, and broke the rest of the bottles against the walls and the floor. I hesitated on my way out when I saw a map on a chair by the books. It had the Alvis compound circled. I grabbed it and stuffed it into my coat.

Then I pulled out my lighter, lit a torn piece of gauze wrapping, and dropped it onto the floor as I stepped outside. I felt the sudden rush of hot air on my neck and heard a muffled roar as I walked to the Jeep. As I opened the driver's side door, I looked back briefly and saw flames dancing behind the windows. "Time to go," I told Allie. "Let me take the wheel."

I hadn't driven much past the main gate before I brought the Jeep to a halt.

"What's wrong?" Allie asked.

"I need to watch the place burn."

We got out and stood as the ranch house quickly became unrecognizable. The flames crept out of the windows, licking at the roof. Even from there we could hear the snapping and popping of the hungry fire. Black smoke rose into the crystal blue sky, drifting lazily toward the high-flying ravens. They croaked and circled, watching us and the fiery remnants of a madman's domain.

Back in the Jeep, heading down the rutted two-track, I thought of how crazy this all was. I'd seen evil on three continents, some of it unspeakable, but it seemed worse in this place I called home. On a different continent, *everything*— good and bad—can seem strange, alien. But you don't expect to come back to places that seem so familiar and discover the greatest evil of all.

I made the mistake of slowing the Jeep to a crawl a couple miles away from the ranch, to check the map and consider whether it might be worth trying to get within viewing distance of the compound. It turned out to be one of the worst mistakes of my life.

CHAPTER THIRTY-SEVEN

I'd just reached into my jacket for the map, my hand pushing past the pistol, when the first bullets crashed through the windshield.

As glass shattered around me and Allie screamed, I jammed the brake to the floor. The sound of the automatic fire rattled the air as glass tinkled down into the Jeep. Through the ragged hole in the windshield, I watched two tan SUVs appear and stop nose to nose in front of us. Black-barreled weapons jutted out the windows.

"Down!" I said, throwing the Jeep in reverse. Allie flung herself below the dash as I rocketed the Jeep backward over brush and into the trees, attempting to turn around on the narrow road. Before I could get moving forward again, though, two men on four-wheelers slid to a stop behind us. They were already firing as they jumped off.

Bullets whanged off the side panel, and some tore through the roof. I got my pistol out, held it on the dash with both hands, and cracked off a shot. One of the four-wheeler shooters spun away and fell like a doll onto the road. The other ducked behind his machine.

The men in the SUVs opened fired again. "Move!" I yelled

at Allie. She yelled back, "Give me a gun." I squeezed off two more shots at the remaining four-wheeler shooter and, without taking the time to see if I hit him, shoved Zeke's pistol into Allie's hand. In what seemed like a single motion, but was actually a series of frantic movements, I grabbed the rifle and pack from the backseat, tossed on the pack, laid the rifle on the hood, flung off the safety, and shot the first man who came into my scope, aiming by instinct alone. I caught him in the chest and he fell where he stood, a chunk of flesh flying off behind him into the trees. Bullets made furrows in the hood as I ducked back down, one coming close enough to graze my cheek.

Lead smacked hard into the engine block as I yelled into Allie's ear, "I'm going to take another shot. When I do, you run past the four-wheelers and head into the trees. See anyone, shoot them." She nodded, her eyes wild with fear. This was much worse than anything we'd done together so far.

"Ready?" She took the revolver and pulled the hammer back, then nodded. I threw the rifle up and she took off.

I spotted one man next to the two vehicles and fired; the large .375 bullet smacked hard into his thigh, causing it to disintegrate in a red mist. At nearly the same time I caught a glimpse of men moving in the trees and heard shots behind me. I'd jacked my last round into the rifle and started to turn when the Jeep and I were ripped off the ground in a brilliant flash of white. As I was thrown into the air, I tried to recall the last time I'd had a grenade thrown at me.

Then there was only blackness.

A blackness followed by . . . ringing in my ears and something that sounded like Allie screaming. Her terror dragged me back to consciousness. I moved an arm, patted my body—everything seemed to be where it was supposed to be. But my whole torso pulsed with pain and there were wet spots in strange places.

Got to move.

I sat up, saw my rifle out of reach, and heard movement. From somewhere deep and primal, I summoned enough energy to roll and grab the gun, holding it on my chest as a man walked into view from behind a scrub oak. He raised his assault rifle and I shot him. I was aiming for his chest but couldn't use my scope in that position, and the bullet went high. It collapsed his head, leaving a tattered, spouting wreck on his neck. His body fell forward, almost crashing into me.

I wiped the man's blood off my face and tried to stand up. I was almost entirely drained and didn't know if I could. But the sound of Allie screaming fired my adrenal glands once again and I jerked to my feet. I'd been knocked well away from the now burning Jeep, and the sound of the cry had come from somewhere back up the road. I tried to run toward it, but my legs wouldn't cooperate and I fell hard onto the headless gunman.

I looked down and saw a jagged piece of plastic protruding from my leg. It had lodged square in the middle of my thigh, right above the knee the hyena had gnawed on. Of course it couldn't be the *other* leg. I wiggled my toes to make sure the problem wasn't nerve damage, and was happy to feel them responding. I decided not to remove the piece of plastic in case it had lodged next to a major vein or artery. That's when I spotted the headless gunman's rifle. I slung my .375 on my back, picked up the new weapon, checked the magazine and the slide, then pulled myself up and started limping toward the sounds of gunfire.

I crouched low and used the brush and the trees for cover. All was quiet for a moment; just my heavy breathing and the scraping sound of my wounded leg dragging in the dry leaves. Then a burst of automatic fire erupted from my left. The tree between me and the gunman started shredding, little chunks of white aspen bark flying like confetti in the air, and I flung myself to the ground.

I held the rifle over my head and fired a short burst at where I thought the firing had come from, then rolled to my right behind the exposed roots of a pine tree. Bullets tore into the ground where I'd been lying a moment before, some burrowing into the loamy earth and others ricocheting off into the distance after hitting buried rocks.

I still couldn't see who was firing at me. And I couldn't hear much at all over my own labored breathing. I waited, my ears and eyes searching for anything out of place, ready for the gunman to make the next move. I was trying to wipe the sweat-soaked dirt off my face when I heard Allie scream in pain. It sounded much closer this time.

I was about to slither toward Allie's voice when the gunman moved and started for it instead. He ran past my position and I raised myself just enough over the roots to pop off three rounds. All three hit him: the first slowing his step, the second spinning him lazily around, and the third tearing through his face as he fell.

I jumped up, checked around me for any other threats, then, when I was pretty sure my position hadn't been spotted, ran and grabbed the extra magazines off the dead man. The adrenaline was still pouring; even so, I could do little more than shuffle my broken body toward the sound of Allie's last scream.

More gunfire came from that direction. A pistol shot, followed by automatic fire. Then a louder, sharper crack from farther away. I willed myself closer, dragging an almost destroyed leg behind me, my arms lagging and barely able to carry the rifle. Days like this were the reason I kept finding more gray in my beard.

By the grace of some deity, I made it to a wide valley. At the bottom was a small, rocky, treeless rise. Staccato rattling from automatic rifles surrounded the hill. The rocks on the crest were pockmarked with bullet holes. A pistol cracked on the top of the hill, followed by a volley of return fire.

I settled myself down behind a fallen pine and threw duff over myself. Then I worked my way out of my backpack, threw my newly found rifle on the ground, and unslung the .375. In the backpack was my last box of ammo for it, from which I quickly loaded the magazine, easing back into a familiar routine. I put the .375 to my shoulder and started sweeping the base of the hill with the scope, centering my search on the sounds of the automatic fire.

I quickly settled the crosshairs on a man dressed like all the others in black tactical clothing. His chest heaved, his face a tight grimace. He mouthed a few unsociable words and put his rifle back to his shoulder. Four hundred yards away. Light wind out of the north. I adjusted my scope a few clicks as light snow started to drift down through the trees. I steadied my breathing, watching the white vapor in the quickly cooling air. Then I squeezed the trigger slowly.

The valley filled with a reverberating crack and I watched the man, after a slight delay, flop down dead with an unnaturally large hole in his chest. The carbine fire stopped immediately.

Allie's pistol fired again, and I almost yelled for her but didn't want to give away my position. I was about to start searching for the next man when a large section of the log I was hiding behind disappeared, followed shortly by an echoing boom. Someone on the other side of the valley had a high-powered rifle and had either seen me or made a pretty good guess where my shot had come from. I was pinned down until someone else made a move. *Touché, assholes.*

Allie bailed me out, taking a potshot with her pistol in the general area of the sniper. He responded immediately, the roar of his rifle followed by another scream from Allie. I moved, tucking both rifles and my pack under my arms and rolling over the log and down the hill. Metal and rocks and bushes jabbed me in all of my soft spots as I tumbled over and over, the world nothing but a dark blur.

I slammed to a stop at the bottom, my already injured shoulder hitting an unmovable aspen tree. Of course it couldn't have been the *other* shoulder. Lucky me. I forced down a cry of pain, gathered up my gear, and made a run for it up the hill. I tried to zig and zag, tried to keep low under the brush, tried to keep quiet, but I didn't really have enough energy to do any of that. Instead I simply wished for luck and barreled in a fairly straight line up the hill.

Lead flew around me like deer flies in the summer, but this time luck didn't abandon me, and I made it to the little jumble of rocks that Allie lay in, both of us swearing heartily by the time I threw myself and the gear in the little nest where she lay. I didn't look over at her, didn't say anything, just manhandled the carbine up and put down some covering fire in every direction, holding the trigger until the slide clicked open, and then I ducked back down.

The gunmen's return fire threw chunks of rock high into the air and filled the entire valley with thunder. I pulled the extra magazines out of my pockets, slammed one into the carbine, and looked over at Allie. She lay moaning and swearing against a rock, curled in the fetal position. Her black hair was still in a ponytail, but the tail floated in a spreading pool of blood. She clutched her stomach.

"Oh, Allie. I'm sorry," I said.

"For what? You aren't the one that shot me through my goddamned pancreas." She tried to laugh through the tears, ended up choking.

"You sure that's where you're hit?"

"No. I'm not sure. I don't even know where my god-damned pancreas is. I caught one in the guts." She coughed hard, and I saw a slow trickle of blood run out of the corner of her mouth. It mixed with her tears and turned pink, then dripped onto the ground. Her face turned white and started to slacken, life quickly draining. I bit my lip until it bled, then reloaded the .375. I set the loaded carbine next to Allie and asked, "Can you shoot the pistol?"

She smiled faintly. "Ran out. So, no."

"Okay. I'm going to give you this auto. Aim it in the air and pull the trigger. I need to take out the sniper."

She nodded slowly, scooted back against the rock, gingerly took the rifle in a limp hand, raised it, and pulled the trigger. The rifle swayed back and forth like a loose fire hose. She dropped it, smoking, into the rocks.

When she fired I was already in place, scanning the pre-sumed area of the sniper. I saw the flash, felt a hearty smack on the rock that Allie leaned on, then heard the shot rumble through the valley. I bared my teeth, gripped the rifle tight enough to pop knuckles, then fired. Red spray shot above the bush where I held my sights. No large-caliber return fire. Just the smattering pops from the remaining men with carbines.

I grunted and sat down next to Allie. With the sniper out, there wasn't much the other guys could do from where they were. They'd work their way up and try to clear the hill, I knew, but so be it. Let them come. It didn't matter anymore. I turned and got to a knee, then started to lift up Allie's shirt.

"Let me get a look at you," I said.

"Clyde," she said, her voice soft and girlish. It was the first time she'd used my first name, and that scared me.

"Just a second." I peeled up the blood-soaked shirt and examined the entry wound.

"Clyde?"

"You're going to be okay. It doesn't look all that bad," I said. But it did. There were multiple ragged, oozing holes. Two circular ones, as big around as my little finger, inches away from her belly button. A section of her midriff was missing. Blood rushed hot and warm over my hands as I ran them across her belly, searching for other leaks. I wiped my hands on my pants and looked in my bag for the medical kit. Not much left in there, and nothing for something of this magnitude.

"Clyde?" she asked again, this time in little more than a whisper.

"Yeah?" I took off my coat, then my shirt, which I bunched up and pressed against her wet stomach.

"I . . . " she started, then said, "I'm cold."

"It's the snow," I said. "I'll get you out of this, kid."

She looked up at me, smiled. "Sure," she said. "But I'm not a kid, Clyde." Then she closed her eyes, her head fell forward, and she was gone.

CHAPTER THIRTY-EIGHT

Gone.

No. I didn't believe it. Couldn't believe it. I checked her pulse twice. Nothing.

I shook her, screamed her name, my legs giving out. I slumped down beside her. The tears came then, in hot, salty waves, trickling through my beard. She couldn't be gone. Not now, when we were so close to finishing what we'd started.

I wrapped my arms around her small body, even smaller now somehow, and pressed my face into her neck. Kissed her cheek, her forehead, her now breathless mouth, and brushed the brittle snowflakes from her hair. I smelled the now receding scent of smoke on her skin and remembered the night of the pumpkin soup, how she'd looked so beautiful in the orange light.

We should have stayed in the cave.

I started to think that I should have left her in Junction, but then we wouldn't have had those dances in Steamboat, or that night at Zeke's in our life raft of a tent, or the cold shower and warm nest in the cave. Her death was something I'd never forgive myself for. Something I'd never forget. It was a gaping chest wound that would never heal.

I wished to every god in heaven that I'd shown more emotion, more affection, told her how I really felt. Because now it was too late. I kissed her forehead one last time, slowly, softly, lingering until shots from below brought me back to the world. Then I grabbed my rifle.

I jammed shells into the magazine, dropping a couple because of something slick on my shaking hands, then rammed the bolt so hard I thought I'd crush the casing or cause a misfire. I stood, snow stinging my naked, red-streaked torso, and put the rifle to my shoulder. I caught one of the men in the open, walking quickly up the hill with his rifle held at port arms. I pulled the trigger and spun his worthless corpse to the ground. I jacked another shell into the gun and yelled something. It sounded right in my head but came out wrong. The bellowing echoed down the valley, sounding not unlike the roar of a wounded lion.

Shots popped from two different directions, my two o'clock and my nine. They didn't worry me. They were coming from a bad angle, and I had the high ground. Both literally and metaphorically. One or both of these men had put holes into a beautiful woman who possessed ten times their guts, and they would both die for it. Or I would. Either outcome seemed acceptable. So I spun and searched with the scope for the two o'clock man. Saw a glimpse of arm to the side of a newly budding scrub oak. Aimed up and to the right, fired, and the man was knocked off his feet, dead before he hit the ground.

A long burst of autofire came from my eleven. The man had moved, must have been running, because the shots were close. The bullets that didn't fly dangerously close to my head smacked into the rocks, sending small pieces of granite shrapnel into the air and, in a couple cases, into my chest. *Sonofabitch.*

I turned and looked for him in the scope. Couldn't find him, so I yelled, "You want me, come get me." I kept the rifle up, searching the area he'd fired from. Then one of the little spindly trees moved in the direction opposite the prevailing wind. *Gotcha*.

I wanted to run down the hill, strangle the man with my bare hands, squeeze his head until it popped off his scrawny neck. But I had the rifle, and the cold stock felt good in my hands—natural, like an extension of my body.

I fired into the tree. Twice. The man rolled out from behind it and let loose with a short burst of inaccurate return fire, then scrambled on all fours back and away behind a larger tree. It was the first time I'd missed in years and it pissed me off.

I climbed up onto the rock, pulled shells out of my pants pocket, and thumbed them in, mumbling to myself. The tree the man was hiding behind swayed in the wind, and I dragged my crosshairs up and down the trunk. I saw the flaking bark and the gnarled, sappy knots where former large branches had once protruded. I saw the scars of bear and porcupine scratches. And at the base I saw new grass and a couple of ferny, young yarrow plants—and a foot, sticking out slightly from behind the tree, next to a large root. So I shot again, aiming for the laces on his combat boot, and missed.

A vision of Allie pulling me along by the hand fueled the rage burning inside me. It wouldn't do to keep shooting, because, with the way my hands were shaking, I wouldn't be able to hit anything smaller than the proverbial side of a barn. So I jumped up, onto, and over the rocks I was standing behind and started running down the hill toward the man behind the tree. As I ran I ejected the spent casing, rammed the bolt home, and roared hard enough to surprise myself.

I ignored the twinges in my leg and shoulder, ignored the biting flakes of snow, ignored the bitter wind, and focused instead on revenge. The man moved from behind the tree when he heard me coming, raised his rifle, fired a wild round, and ran out of ammo. He was enough of a veteran to know that he couldn't reload in the open.

So he ran for better cover. As he moved, he dropped the magazine, pulled another from his webbing, and shoved it home. He was diving behind a moss-covered rock when I caught up with him. I shoved a knee in his back, and drove the butt of my rifle into his skull.

With no one to stop me, and with my madness coming to a head, I continued driving the rifle stock into the man's skull until it was a caved-in melon. I would have continued hammering him had exhaustion not overtaken me. Entirely spent, I rolled onto my back and stared at the falling snow.

In the time it took me to walk and crawl back to Allie's body, I started shivering uncontrollably. The temperature was falling dangerously close to freezing and an inch of snow had accumulated on the ground. I put on my coat, sat across from Allie, and stared, watching the snowflakes float and flutter to the ground.

There was a part of me that thought I'd climb back up and she'd be fine, that maybe she was just sleeping, or passed out, and would wake when I returned. But I'd seen too much death to truly believe that, and I quickly put it out of my mind, focusing instead on the present.

Her body was cold enough that the snow stuck to her skin, making her look like a winter maiden from one of Grimm's fairy tales. I contemplated packing her off the mountain but realized I had nowhere to take her. So I stroked her lovely face one last time, then dropped to my knees, grabbed a jagged piece of rock, and started digging a shallow grave.

For me it was an act of contrition. Had someone else been there to observe, they probably would have viewed it as the act of a madman. I punished myself for most of the night, finally settling Allie into a hole only a couple of feet deep. With blistered and bloody hands I covered her face with her coat, and then pulled over her a layer of soil and rocks. As I pulled the last handful of dirt onto the barrow, I fell to the ground.

Night closed in, and as my eyelids pressed shut, I asked the cold to carry me away, to freeze me so thoroughly that I'd never again feel any emotion.

CHAPTER THIRTY-NINE

But my request wasn't granted.

A day later I pulled next to the curb in front of my sister Deb's new house, once again back in the valley where I'd grown up. The sun shined bright that spring morning in Grand Junction. The sky was a hazy blue without any trace of the spring storm that had rolled across the mountains I'd just escaped from. All of the houses in the neighborhood looked almost identical; each was a two-story stucco affair with an immaculate bright green lawn and white vinyl fencing. The street and the front yards were empty.

Despite all that bluffing I'd done about surveillance by the Feds, I half expected to see one of Alvis's vehicles parked somewhere—but the only vehicle of his was the one I was sitting in. I reached for my rifle as I got out, but instead left it on the passenger seat of the Excursion, covered by my dirty coat. I grabbed my backpack and limped up to the front door and knocked.

Deb answered the door dressed in a robe, with her short black hair still dripping wet from the shower. She scowled, then saw the state of my clothing. "What the—Clyde, get in here. What happened?" She led me through the clean house, too worried about me—or Jen?—to ask me to take my boots off. I felt bad tracking God knows what onto her plush white carpet.

We sat in her brightly lit kitchen at a wooden breakfast nook. She handed me a cup of coffee and asked, "So? Did you find her?" Her small frame seemed even smaller in such a large house, but her lifted chin displayed self-confidence.

I stared at the pictures on the wall: Deb and her husband at their wedding, shots of her two boys as they passed through toddlerhood and into elementary school, family reunions, everyone smiling. I'd missed all those occasions. The stainless-steel fridge was covered with crayon works of art. "I need a shower," I said. "Where's Nick?"

"He's at work, why? What's going on, Clyde?"

"I'll need to borrow some clothes," I said, wandering off into the living room to admire the house.

What struck me about the place wasn't the fancy furnishings or the impossibly big rooms but what *wasn't* there. Children lived here, but, aside from the pictures on the fridge, I couldn't see any evidence of it. Where were the toys? Where were the discarded clothes, the scuffs on the walls, the scattered shoes? And the smell was missing: that strong aroma of dirt and day-old granola bars. Instead the house smelled like pine oil. If both parents worked, and I supposed they did to keep a place like this, how the hell did they keep it so clean? *Too* clean, if someone were to ask me. It needed some children-related chaos to feel like a family home.

I stared at the expensive leather furniture and the shiny brass and stainless fixtures. It was obvious that Deb had escaped our family's past through upward mobility. I'd chosen the opposite. "Where's the maid?"

Deb huffed, said, "She only comes on Wednesdays and

Sundays, and she's going to be pretty upset next time." She grabbed my arm and led me through the living room.

"Why?" I asked.

"You're bleeding on my carpet. Come on."

I followed her through four more cavernous rooms, up a flight of stairs, down a hall decorated with framed pictures of the ghost children, and then into a small bathroom. "Take a shower, clean yourself up, and when you're done you're going to tell me what the heck is going on." She slammed the door and padded off down the hall. I stood for a moment, the door opened again, and Deb handed me a pile of clothes.

"They'll be big on you," she said. I knew that from the pictures. Though I'd never met Nick, it looked like he was pushing three hundred pounds—not much of it muscle. He must be living the good life.

"I found Jen," I called out just before I shut the door. "I'll tell you about it when I get out."

I stepped into the shower, picked up the suction-cupped green plastic frogs, set them in the organizer next to the children's shampoo, and turned the water on as hot as it would go. As mud and blood swirled down the drain, I tried to piece together the events of the last couple of days.

It was all a blur, just a series of distorted images. It was as though I'd been drunk on anger and depression. Today was the beginning of the hangover.

I'd made it through the night after Allie died, had managed not to freeze even though I'd willed myself to. And at dawn I'd raised myself up and sat next to Allie's grave. With a project in mind, I gave myself permission to build a fire—and then, newly warmed and somewhat rejuvenated, I spent the rest of the sunlit hours building a six-foot cairn that would keep digging predators away. Each rock I placed brought me closer to acceptance; each rock placed me further and further away from Allie and made her death a permanent, fixed thing. By the time the sun was down I'd come to terms with her going. And I knew what I had to do.

Getting off the mountain must have been the easy part because it's the part I remembered least. I must have walked to the road, past the burned-out shell of the Jeep, and commandeered one of the soldier's vehicles. I had no memory of the drive back—nothing until I parked at Deb's new house.

At some point I must have found a better first-aid kit. The hole in my leg was nicely sewn and the shoulder was patched again. It hurt like hell when I removed the bandages, but, with the right medication, it looked like I'd heal.

After I showered I made a quick inspection of the medicine cabinet. Kids' stuff: cartoon-labeled toothpaste and mouthwash, laxatives, some adhesive bandages, and Neosporin, but no antibiotics. I'd need to find some soon or risk losing my leg. I dressed quickly in circus-tent-size pants and a polo shirt. Before heading to the kitchen I took another inventory of my small backpack.

Inside was a new medical kit, minus the bandages from yesterday and today. The pint of whiskey I'd found at Zeke's. Also the old staples: a few stacks of cash, some books, my knife, a meager but essential survival kit, and a new Glock 9mm that I must have found in one of the gunmen's vehicles. A new cell phone, also from one of the gunmen, sat next to a heavy box of shells on the bottom of the pack, and I moved them, checked the false bottom, and found the small cloth bag holding the majority of my wealth. I breathed a sigh of relief knowing I still had the essentials.

Deb had bacon curling and popping on the glass-topped stove when I made my way back into the kitchen. I sat down, put the bag under my feet, and wrapped a leg in the strap. It was a residual habit from harder times and places. I stared at the wedding picture again as Deb slowly flipped the pieces of pork in her cast-iron pan.

In the picture Deb had long black hair. Nick was maybe fifty pounds lighter with a sandy goatee. In the tux he looked like he was buried up to his neck in black sand. But Deb looked good, and there was something about her youth and vitality and perhaps her happiness that . . . well, it reminded me of Allie.

I brushed the thought aside and said, "You know how long it's been since I've had bacon?"

"No," she said. "You still like it, don't you?"

"Of course. It's a miracle food. First time I've had it in years. It was Angie who always hated it."

Deb smiled. "Angie *is* a picky eater."

"How's she doing?" I asked, thinking that the last time I'd called her she'd told me to go to hell.

"Great. She and Steve have their own business—they're both CPAs. She's supposed to visit me tomorrow, go for a dip in the hot tub—just hang out."

A hot tub? I hadn't noticed that. I guessed hot tubs were standard for houses like this.

"Uh-huh."

Both of us were silent for a second.

"Jen's okay?" Deb asked, taking the crisper slices off and putting them on a separate plate covered with paper towels.

"She's alive."

"Where?"

"Don't know."

"What do you mean you don't know? I thought that's why you went—"

"Listen," I said. "I'm sorry I dropped in like this. Thanks for the shower, the coffee, and the food. But some shit went down in the mountains and I need you to—"

"Watch your language," she said, handing me a plate. There were eggs on it, too. "The boys will be home soon. I'd rather they not see you. But if they do, you *will* be civil."

"Got it. Sorry. But some things happened. Sit down for a second, will you?"

Deb caught my tone, put the fork down, pulled her robe tight, and sat down next to me. Her chair squeaked on the hardwood floor.

I told her most of what had happened. An abbreviated citizen version. I told her that I'd found Jen and tried to get her home. But she was in bad shape and had been snatched up again by the people who'd taken her in the first place. I left out most of the unsavory details. Then I told her that the man who had Jen was rather angry with me and that, well, I'd tried bluffing him into standing down, but he might try to come after the rest of my family. Her and Angie.

She stood up, her small five two looking like a full six, and said, "What the *hell*, Clyde? You come into my house and tell me that someone hates you, that they might be coming after me? And my kids? After I told you we were done? This is the same crap all over again. The same insane crap from high school. But this time, instead of cops coming to the house, it's someone who's trying to kill us. That's just great."

What was there to say? I'd made a complete mess of this, and my expression told her that I would accept any punishment she cared to mete out.

"Look," she said, trying to calm herself. "It's not like we don't care about Jen. We do, we always have, and you can bring her here and we'll get her the help she needs. But I cannot allow you to expose my family to danger. That is *totally* unacceptable." She looked flustered. Some part of her realized that the problem wouldn't just go away by giving me a tongue-lashing.

"I don't think it'd be a good idea to call the police," I said, anticipating her next move. "The police can't handle people like this. I'll call someone who can."

Deb was fuming now. "You need to *leave*, Clyde. I wish it wasn't the case, but I think you have a target on your back. You need to stay away from here."

I stood, stuffed two pieces of bacon in my mouth, and shouldered my pack. "I'll keep you and Angie safe. I promise," I said. Then I turned and let myself out.

Out on the street, I realized the irony of what had just happened. I'd gone and made another promise—one I might have a hard time keeping. Something told me that to keep my promise to Deb I'd first have to keep my promise to Jen.

CHAPTER FORTY

I needed to be around people, otherwise I might find myself thinking of Allie and fall into a dark place that I'd never escape from. I considered finding a bar but feared that one drink could easily lead to ten. Chugging boilermakers was a lazy way to dull the pain. So I drove to the nearest indoor shopping mall.

Inside I wandered past useless shops until I found a nice quiet bench. It was next to a too-green plastic tree where I could make some phone calls and still be able to watch the shoppers as they passed. I decided to make the hardest call first. Teenage couples walked past hand in hand, some stopping to kiss and grope each other under the neon-green exit sign.

The inspiration for the call was that fanciful idea I'd tried out on Alvis the first time we spoke—that the Feds had my sisters under constant surveillance, believing I, Clyde Barr, was the key to finding Lance Alvis. Maybe it wasn't such a far-fetched idea after all.

With the phone I'd taken from one of the dead gunmen, I called information and was connected with the local DEA office. I asked the bored secretary if I could leave a message for the officer in charge. "Tell him," I said, "that the man you tried to follow in Rifle wants to talk." I told her he could call me back at this number. I hung up the phone, realizing that I'd spent more time on this little nuisance machine in the last week than I had in over fifteen years.

While I waited I watched the flow of shoppers as they walked numbly in and out of stores. It struck me how different they were from the villagers I'd seen crowding markets in the third world. There was no vitality in this place, just slack-jawed men and women trading for things they didn't need. People walked by with plastic sacks (themselves a waste) full of useless trinkets and gewgaws that required electricity to function. No one talked to each other; most simply stared at their phones as they shuffled across the dirty tile.

The phone in my pocket buzzed.

"Yeah," I answered.

"This is Special Agent Peters. With the DEA. Are you the one who left the message?"

"I am. I want to make a trade. Information for a favor."

"Who is this?"

"Doesn't matter. Can we trade?"

"If you have information, call our hotline." He paused but didn't hang up. I could hear him chewing loudly. It sounded like he should take smaller bites.

"You know I have more than that. That's why you followed me. You were looking for Alvis, right? Before your boys got in a little pickle up on the mountain?"

"About that—you need to come in and we'll have a little talk."

"Won't happen. But I can give you some of Alvis's crew right now."

"You can, huh?" More chewing and mouth smacking. "How's that?"

I recited my sisters' addresses. "Put your guys outside those houses, and they'll come to you. If you keep the people in those houses safe, I'll give you more. Call me after you do that." I hung up.

The phone buzzed again immediately. I pushed decline. He tried to call back three more times. I declined them all.

I put the phone in the bottom of my bag and walked to a wireless store, where I bought one of their prepaid models from a pretty little blonde with metal in her eyebrow who smiled at first, then rolled her eyes when she saw my oversize clothes.

So I walked to a clothing store and bought a brand-new pair of blue jeans that had already been washed and distressed—"distressed" meaning that someone other than me had put holes in the knees, and someone else's keys had worn out the thighs. I guess it was worth the high price if the look could save me a couple of years of actually wearing the jeans. It took a while to find a pair that fit me, since most of the jeans in the store were made for people whose legs had atrophied.

The only shirts they sold were too-tight designer crap, so I gave an exorbitant amount of cash to an acned teen and walked out with just the worn-out jeans. Then I walked past the central café to a shop called the Ranch Store. The place had nothing to do with ranching; instead the clothes there resembled what I'd seen people wearing years ago in the movie *Urban Cowboy*. I bought a gray long-sleeve snap-button shirt, then went and changed in the mall's overly used bathroom.

Back at my bench I called Juan with my new prepaid phone. Maria answered and said Juan would call me back. He did, from an unavailable number.

"Barr, you on a disposable?"

"I am."

"Good. How you holding up?"

"Fine," I said, lying. "I just need to know if the enemies of our friend are still in the picture."

"I can give you that. That whole social circle in Rifle, they're gone."

I smiled. "Well, that's one item checked off the list. One last favor, brother? Then I won't bother you again."

"You're pushing it, Barr. I told you I didn't want to get sucked back into the life."

"I hear you. Really, I do. Just one more, Juan . . . please."

Juan sighed. "Okay, shoot."

"You know that little beach by Corn Lake, where they put rafts in? If Alejandro is still around, have him meet me there tonight. Say, six thirty?"

Juan hesitated. "Why would he want to meet? You two don't know each other from Adam."

"I want to volunteer my services—as a fill-in for our friend. Even if that particular social circle is no longer with us, the big honcho still has to be dealt with, yes?"

Juan chuckled. "I thought you were going to handle that yourself, Barr. Remember how you called me to make sure Alejandro didn't interfere with you and that army of yours?"

Good point. For perhaps the hundredth time in my life, I kicked myself for displaying such inexcusable arrogance. This time my inflated ego had caused Allie to pay with her life.

"It looks like I'm now an army of one," I said quietly, but then my voice gained strength. "But I'm seriously *dedicated* to taking this guy off the board. Alejandro should be interested in that."

"Okay, Barr, I'll give him the message."

I nodded to the phone and hung up. Then I pulled the

card from inside the phone, crushed it, and threw both it and the phone in the trash can by the bench. A young boy passed, staring at me in astonishment, as if he'd just witnessed someone burning a Bible.

Outside the mall, my eyes took a second to adjust to the blinding sunlight. Then I got in the Excursion, shoved the selector into drive, and drove to the nearest park.

In the asphalt lot I got out, checked the area, then locked the vehicle and walked to the center of the park and sat down in the plush grass under a large ash tree. I was on the opposite side of the children's playground, close enough to hear their happy screams and laughs, but far enough away to avoid being mistaken for a creep. I pulled out the phone and scrolled through the numbers on it until I found the one I was looking for, then punched the green icon.

Alvis answered after three rings. "Tate?" he said. "Is it done?"

I waited, simply breathing into the phone.

"Tate?" Alvis asked again.

"Afraid not," I answered.

Silence. Then, "So I've made another bad investment. Where are my men, Barr?"

"All dead."

"That's very unfortunate. Can I assume you still want your sister back?"

"You can."

This time the silence lasted for a while. "Well," Alvis said finally. "It seems that you have the better of me in this negotiation. I will have one of my men drop off your sister at a place of your choosing. Just tell me where."

I rifled through the bag and found a pack of cheap cigarettes. I lit one and said, "You ever been to Africa, Lance?"

"No. And I don't plan to. What's that got to do with—"

"South America maybe?"

"No. What are you getting at?"

"I have, and a lot of other places people rarely get to—places where the rules are pretty loose."

"Your point being?"

"That I've been around. You don't come back from those places if you haven't developed an ability to smell obvious bullshit. Keep Jen with you."

"Are you sure?"

"Absolutely. I'll come pick her up."

CHAPTER FORTY-ONE

I walked back to the Excursion and drove downtown again, parking at the first pawnshop I found. As I was getting out the phone rang.

"This is Barr."

"Special Agent Peters."

"So?"

"No sign of Alvis's crew yet. My guys aren't babysitters, Barr. And I'm an impatient man."

"Give it another day," I said, buying for time. "Even if you have to put on two shifts. It's not a question of if but when . . ." Okay, so I was just writing myself an insurance policy—but I wanted Deb and Angie protected while I made my last play.

"What is your connection with all this?"

"Just a concerned citizen with information."

"Yeah, and I'm Little Bo Peep. We pulled some surveillance tapes in Rifle. You were involved in a shooting at a rest stop. Now this."

"I believe at the rest stop everyone involved was drug or gang affiliated. I was just in the wrong place at the wrong time."

"Whatever. We picked up four of his guys."

"Like I said."

"You said there'd be more info."

"You going to keep watching those houses for me?" I asked. What he said next was important. He could shine me on just like I'd done to him, but I sensed he was a straight shooter.

"That depends. Government protection costs a lot. How are you going to earn it?"

"Okay, fine." I gave him directions to the compound in Leadville. I told him that Alvis might not be there—in fact, I was convinced he *wouldn't* be there; Lance was too smart for that, now that I'd discovered his location and was at liberty to drop a dime on him—but there'd be enough evidence at the place to convict him when he was finally run down. Peters didn't thank me, just hung up.

I got lucky in the pawnshop. The old man with the twitchy eye behind the jewelry display wore an NRA cap. His camouflage T-shirt was stretched to breaking around a midsection built by years of beer drinking, and one of his forearms sported a faded green Semper Fi tattoo. He glared at me as I walked in, pointing two fingers at his eyes to show he'd be on the lookout for any five-fingered discounts.

I lingered far longer than most patrons, because I felt comfortable in there—much more than I'd felt at the mall. The shop was full of well-used, passed-down artifacts. Nothing new, nothing wrapped in thick plastic packaging. In here were the kinds of things you'd see in the third-world: rows of VHS and cassette tapes, black-and-white tube television sets, saddles, and kids' toys.

I grabbed a well-used Carhartt coat from a rack and went up to the counter. The man still eyeballed me. I asked him about ammunition for my rifle and pistol. He told me he didn't carry any ammo. I mentioned that I'd just returned from fighting overseas, which wasn't a complete lie. He went in back and brought out a box each of .375 and 9mm shells and set them on the glass case. I paid in cash, no questions, and as I grabbed the boxes I noticed that the case was full of pawned wedding rings. Men's gold and women's diamonds. It said a lot about the state of marriage in this country.

I drove down to the river, parked under an old cotton-wood in the hard-packed dirt parking lot of a rafting put-in. I watched a fit man in sandals and a floppy hat unload a raft frame with the help of a cute blond woman in cutoff jeans and a bikini top. They used hand pumps to inflate the raft, taking turns whenever one of them got tired. I reloaded both weapons and wished I was going with them.

It was a waiting game now—except I didn't want to wait. I wanted to move, go forward, hurt someone. Like a grassland fire, I'd swept across the dry stubble, the flames growing larger and hotter at the mercy of the wind, only to stall at the edge of the water. I was afraid I'd burn out if I stopped moving.

I had a couple of hours to kill until six thirty, so after the raft disappeared, I climbed out of the vehicle, locked it, and walked upstream. I found a spot underneath the highway bridge where the river eddied, stripped down to my boxers, and jumped in.

The cold, brown water sucked the air out of my lungs. Once I had it back, I swam out into the middle of the strong current, let the river take me a few yards down, then fought back. Using powerful kicks, good form, and strong quick strokes, I was able to keep from going downstream. I kept swimming, hard against the current, relishing—despite my still-beat-up state—the feel of muscles burning and lungs heaving. It felt good to be fighting, but I knew I couldn't keep it up for long, so I breaststroked over to the eddy and let the slower water carry me in circles.

I rolled to my back, stared at the thick clematis vines covering the bank and bridge, and tried not to think about my mom . . . or Allie . . . or Jen.

It didn't work. It *couldn't* work, because somewhere in the mud below me lay the rusted gun that Jen had used to blow out Paxton's brains. As my body drifted slowly upstream, my mind drifted back to the last years I'd lived here.

THE COPS HAD PUSHED HARD. There wasn't any evidence: no gun, no witnesses, nothing to tie us to the body. But we had motive. Damned good motive. So the cops came around daily, sometimes taking one of us into the station. They reopened our child welfare case and forced us to move in with Deb, hoping she could get us to talk. But we didn't tell her what happened, and neither of us broke. The cops had nothing.

Jen and I, though—we were never the same. We both tried to pretend it never happened, and that worked for a while, about as long as the cops kept looking. When they stopped, we were forced to start thinking about what we'd done.

Kids shouldn't have to deal with that kind of blood and guilt, and it broke us. Jen dropped out of school her senior year. Started hanging out with folks who dressed like they were extras in a Dracula movie. Began using every drug that went through the valley.

Me, I would have dropped out, too, but in my junior year I met Maria, and she kept me sane. Or as sane as an adolescent boy can be when he's hopped up on hormones. Jen ran away to live with the black-lipsticked people. I spent most of my time at Juan's.

As graduation approached, though, Maria wasn't enough to keep the demons from coming to me in the night. I needed to *move*, see new mountains, deserts, the jungle, and the sea. So I said my good-byes, by this same river, and took off for the coast.

I CONTINUED PADDLING AROUND THE river aimlessly, enjoying the feeling of the deeper currents tickling my feet, and kept trying to work through all those tough questions I'd never found good answers to. I must have been pretty rapt in my aquatic navel-gazing, because I didn't hear tires crunch on river rock. Didn't hear four doors slam on an SUV or see the four men dressed in oversize white tees and Dickies work pants who were standing on the bank by my clothes. I noticed them only when I rolled to my stomach and started paddling toward the bank.

By then they had their pistols aimed at my head.

CHAPTER FORTY-TWO

"**Y**ou Barr?" one of the men said, waving his gun.

"Who's asking?" I said, preparing to dive. Water usually makes a decent shield against a bullet.

"Shoot him," the man said.

I took in a deep breath and was just about to shove my hands up and my body down when the same man said, "Just kidding, homie. Put the guns away." The others laughed and put their guns back in their pants, and the man talking extended a hand. I took it and he pulled me up and out of the water. "My brother called."

I stood there shivering, dripping brown water into the sand, as the man who must be Alejandro continued talking.

"Shame about Chopo," he said. "Damned good gun, that one."

I nodded. I wanted to say I was sorry he died, but guys like these didn't get all sentimental.

"We won't need him now. *Or* you," Alejandro said. "I just dropped by to thank you for stirring things up. We got Alvis on the run now. We still don't know where he is, but he's pulling back his troops. We're taking back the business in the valley."

"Good to hear," I said.

"We already moved on the Cellar. As of yesterday, Alvis's little brother is selling for *us*. He was willing to betray his big brother without blinking. Ask me how much I trust him?"

I smiled. "Not too much, I'll bet."

"It won't be long before Spike is history. I just need to figure out some of the angles he's been playing with the customers."

The mention of Spike had my wheels turning. "Mind if I get dressed?" I said, still shivering.

"We'll leave you to it," Alejandro said, waving his hand in a *be my guest* gesture. He motioned to his men and they all turned and began walking away. They'd moved off about thirty yards when Alejandro turned and called out. "Hey, Barr . . ."

I was buckling my belt. "What?"

"Next time you arrange a meet-up with a guy like me, keep your pants on."

I nodded. "Good advice."

I SHOULD HAVE FOUND a place to bed down and get some sleep. But I was too restless. I didn't know where Alvis was, but I knew where to start looking.

So as soon as I dried off, I drove straight from the river, ripping up 32 Road, and roared to a secluded spot a block from the Cellar. I parked, checked my pistol, shoved it in my coat, and started walking. Cars rumbled down F Road, their drivers oblivious to what had happened in the mountains and what was about to happen here. I envied them.

Once again there weren't any people outside the bar. I kicked the door open and strode inside.

The place still smelled the same: piss, stale beer, and despair. But there were now the faint traces of fear. And blood. The narrow room was empty, except for the three men at the bar: two gray-bearded bikers in dusty leather and denim, and Spike wearing a Hawaiian shirt, khakis, and a walking cast. All three turned and stared at the sound of the door slamming against the wall.

Spike said, "Oh, shit," and reached under the bar.

"Don't," I said, whipping my pistol out and pointing it at the idiotic face under the expensive haircut. He put his hands up and grimaced.

"You two," I said, pointing the pistol at the bikers. "Out." They creaked and cracked off the stools, then shuffled outside. I waited until I heard the sounds of their Harleys drive off, then said, "Where's your brother?"

Sweat dampened Spike's immaculate hair. His left eye twitched, and his hands shook. "Look, man. I ain't got nothing to do with him no more. Even when he was running things, I never knew where he was holed up."

"I think you're a lying sack of *shit*," I said, moving closer to the bar. "I think you knew what your brother's plans were for my sister the first time you saw my face. I think that Allie is dead because you sent your posse after her and drove her in my direction."

His eyes grew wider. "Allie, dead? How—" Sweat started to drip onto the collar of his bright shirt. His lip twitched in unison with his left eye.

I pressed the barrel of my pistol directly into his chest. "I want you to tell me *now* what you know about my sister."

"Please, please, you gotta believe me. All I know is, I mentioned to my brother that your sister worked at this government place, and he was all ears. A couple minutes later, he was chatting her up, talking about all those chemicals she worked around. They walked out that night together and that was it. End of story."

I pressed the gun barrel harder into his chest. "I don't think so. There's more to it, isn't there?"

In that moment Spike looked like he was desperately trying to figure whether to open his mouth or keep it shut. Panic finally made him open it. "All right, yeah . . . I might have overheard my brother talking on the phone a little bit after you first showed up. A day or two later. Something about a break-in that's supposed to go down tomorrow night. He mentioned 'the Barr girl.'"

Tomorrow. The first time Jen had called me for help, she'd said that whoever had her—Alvis, as it turned out—would kill her after whatever was supposed to happen happened. "Tomorrow" meant there was very little time left. There had to be some way to figure out where Lance stayed when he wasn't at the compound.

Then it came to me. I remembered something Allie had said to me about Lance the first time she and I had met: *No one knows exactly what Lance does or where he goes, except maybe whatever woman he's screwing.*

Why didn't that comment stand out to me the night she'd said it? How many more people might be alive—Allie included—if I'd just been concentrating?

I lifted the gun and stuck it just below Spike's twitchy left eye. "I need a name," I said. "The name of whatever female your brother was keeping company with before this week."

Spike didn't get it. "Why do you want—"

I pushed the pistol harder into the soft flesh below Spike's eye socket and saw the outlines of a bruise start to form. "Just . . . give . . . me . . . the . . . *name*," I said.

"Beth Corrigan," Spike blurted out. "She cuts hair over at Mesa Mall on US 6. She only came in here a few times, but she was his latest."

The look in Spike's eyes was one I'd seen before. It was the look of a man who fully expects to be killed in the next few seconds. That's why I reckoned that he was telling me the truth. So I drew back my pistol a couple inches. "That'll work. Give me your cell phone."

He reached slowly into his pants, pulled the black plastic square out of his pocket, and tossed it on the bar. I pulled it out of a liquor puddle and shoved it in my coat.

"Now forget that I came in. If you even *think* about calling your brother—if you even *think* about calling anyone close to him, I swear, I'll come back, cut your nuts off, and shove them all the way down your throat, you got that?"

Spike nodded furiously.

I walked out the door and into the night air. The streetlights buzzed. *Where to now?* The Mesa Mall wouldn't be open at this hour. I began driving aimlessly through the little city where I was raised. I noticed how much it had changed since I'd left. Progress. Homes torn down to put up shopping centers, more people moving into what used to be farms on the outskirts, all of them driving cars that clogged the streets and subdivisions. I didn't want to be there anymore.

I decided to head north into the desert. About thirty minutes out, I stopped on a secluded barren ridge, reclined my seat, pulled my hat over my eyes, and tried to see something other than blood and fire.

CHAPTER FORTY-THREE

At nine the next morning I walked into the salon.

The place reeked of industrial chemicals and nail polish. Expensive bottles of skin and hair potions lined shelves near the four chairs designated for walk-ins. Two ladies were working on other ladies sitting in swivel chairs. Around one customer, piles of hair littered the floor. The other customer had her feet up as a stylist buffed her toenails.

"Beth in?" I asked no one in particular. My voice boomed in the small room.

"Sure am, hon," the stylist who was cutting hair said. "Someone send you in for a cut?"

"We need to talk."

She stopped cutting, put her hands on her hips, and squinched her eyebrows together. She was tall—unusually tall—and had the body of a college girl: hard muscles and soft curves. Her face, though, seemed harder. It was the face of a woman who was on her third lap around the track and trying too hard to make it look like the first.

"What you need is a haircut," she said.

I took off my hat and ran a hand through the ragged mess. She was right. But today could very well be Jen's last, so I didn't have time. I glanced at the price board behind the chairs and found the rate for a man's haircut. "I'll pay for twenty of them, if you'll talk to me."

Before, her face had looked like a battered puppy's—open but ill-treated. Now it looked like a coyote's: hungry and greedy. "Give me five minutes to finish up here. Then meet me at the coffee shop next door."

I nodded, put my hat back on, tipped it to the ladies, and walked next door.

Six minutes later Beth Corrigan came in and sat down across from me at the small table.

"My sister's missing. A man you know has her," I said. "You know where he'd be if he was in town?"

"You a cop?"

"Not even close. My sister's in trouble."

She thought about it for a moment, then shook her head. "Haircut money first."

I slid two of the five hundreds I'd taken from Zeke across the table.

"This man you're looking for, his initials L.A.?"

I nodded.

She looked around, suddenly wary. "I don't think I can talk to you about him. He's bad news."

"But you're seeing him, aren't you?"

"*Was* seeing him . . . past tense. That ended last week, when he did this to me." She held up her left hand, which was missing a pinkie. A bandage covered the stump. "I guess I should count myself lucky that he didn't do it to the other hand. I cut hair with my right."

"What did you do to deserve that?"

"I laughed."

"What?"

"I laughed at the way he was cutting his steak. He doesn't like people laughing at him."

I shook my head. Every story about this guy seemed worse than the next. "So you know where he stays when he's here?"

"I told you. I'm *not* talking to you. It's too dangerous."

"I'll buy some more haircuts then." I laid two hundred more dollars on the table.

She stared at the bills for a moment, considering. The waitress came over and I ordered two medium coffees, black. After the waitress had returned with the steaming cups, and after she wandered to another table, Beth said, "You gonna kill him?"

I nodded.

"Good," she said. "You look like you might stand a chance. You don't, though, and we're both dead, okay? I give you his address, you have to promise me that that man won't wake up tomorrow. Can you do that?"

I nodded again.

She gave me the address. As we sipped our coffee, she also gave me more intimate Alvis details than I cared to know.

I thanked her and stood. "You did the right thing," I said reassuringly, then turned to go. I was headed to the door when I saw the cop.

Through the front windows I saw the Mesa County Sheriff's car parked crosswise in front of my stolen SUV. A stout bald deputy stood next to the driver's side door, talking into the mike on his shoulder.

I groaned. *You should have known better, Barr.* A guy can't drive around in a vehicle associated with a wanted drug lord and not attract the attention of the law. If I wasn't in a hurry, I might have been able to sort things out at the police station with a call to the Feds. But now that I had Alvis's possible location, I couldn't think of anything else but getting there.

This presented a major problem, though. I couldn't get my gear without being noticed. I couldn't get the SUV out because of the cop car. And I couldn't just elbow the officer and take his car. This wasn't Africa, where the police and military are just a part of a regime that changes monthly, where the cops of last month were the militia of this.

I went back to Beth's table, where she sat sipping. She was obviously still mulling our conversation.

"Back so soon?" she asked.

"I'm going to need to borrow your wheels."

"On account of our being such good friends and all?"

She had a point. She didn't know me from Cain. I hadn't bothered to tell her my name. All I'd said was that I was planning to kill her ex-boyfriend. I wasn't exactly the first choice of someone to hand your vehicle to. "Look, I know we just met. I know you have no reason to trust me. But believe me, I'm just a guy who's trying to save his sister. And I'll get your ride back to you."

"What's with *your* vehicle? Or don't you have one?"

I nodded my chin in the direction of the sheriff, who was now walking slowly around the SUV, writing something down in a notebook. "That Excursion belongs to the man who likes to cut off fingers," I said.

"You stole it?"

I nodded.

She grinned approvingly. "How am I gonna get home, then?"

I took out my last hundred and handed it to her, flashed my most charming look, then opened my palms at an angle as if to say, "We have a deal?" She crossed her arms and took another couple seconds to deliberate. "What's your name anyway?"

"Clyde Barr."

"Clyde, if I give you my key, will you promise me I won't regret it?"

"I promise."

"Okay, I'm probably crazy for doing this, but . . . there's a red Honda Interceptor parked in the back of the salon. You do know how to ride, right?"

A motorcycle? I hadn't ridden one in years. "Been riding all my life. I'll have it back to you tonight or tomorrow morning."

"You better."

As soon as I stepped out the back door, the rain started. Misty rain at first, swirling in like fog, then quickly turning to a cold, steady drizzle. *Great motorcycling weather.*

I spotted the red bike next to the brick wall and swung on. After some fumbling for a kick-starter, I realized it didn't have one and I managed to find the electric starter button.

I pushed my hat down, zipped up my new coat, and walked the bike away from the building, then whiskey-throttled and popped the clutch. I ripped through the lot, swerving and weaving, almost hitting a tree and a trash can. Then I let off the throttle, got it under control, and lurched down the pavement like a toddler on a tricycle.

I tried to remember how to ride. Counter-steering and leaning and foot gears. It had been so long since I'd been on a bike, and the little dirt bikes and scooters of the third world were light-years behind this one in terms of technology. This one had a computer display that told me things I didn't understand. Buttons on the handlebars did God knows what. I finally figured it out well enough to keep up with traffic and headed west.

On the highway, I felt the small raindrops burrow into my skin and tried to recall the route to the address I'd been given.

If my mental map was still correct, it would be simple: I-70B to Fruita, then south on 19 to the river. On a bike that could go as fast as this one, I'd make it in a matter of minutes, if I cared to push it.

Which I did. Normally I didn't care for speed, but Alvis was on the move. He'd either be at his place or on the way to where Jen worked to begin the job of stealing whatever chemical it was they were stealing. I needed to be there yesterday.

So I laid my body flat, my stomach resting on the gas tank, and flew through the gears. I took the bike up to fifth in residential areas—sixth on the wider main highways. Over one hundred miles per hour. I prayed that I'd stay on the bike, that the cops wouldn't get involved, that Alvis was at his house, and that Jen was still unharmed.

My luck held, and I made it into Fruita. I pulled over at a golf course and hoped my luck would continue.

I was going to need it.

CHAPTER FORTY-FOUR

A s I stood shivering next to the road, water and oil and grease dripping off my sodden clothes, I formed a semblance of a plan. I pulled a phone from my coat and called Alvis.

The call connected, but he didn't answer right away. Just panted into the phone. I hoped the hard, ragged breathing was from packing.

"I've changed my mind," I said.

"So nice to hear your voice, Barr," Alvis said, his voice communicating the opposite. "What have you changed your mind about?"

"About that idea you had of dropping my sister off. I'm too tired to come get her. How about Stocker Stadium? The park just south of there? I'll be there at noon. Drop her off on North Avenue, have her walk to the park. I'll pick her up and you can keep running your business in peace."

There was a pause while he tried to figure out how dumb I was. "That sounds feasible. Noon it is." He hung up.

I got back on the bike, having no intention of being at Stocker. But if Alvis played it safe, I'd have less to worry about when I got to his place.

The road that led to Alvis's house ran straight south along

the edge of the golf course, then curved past ponds ringed with Russian olives and tamarisk. These ponds were once gravel pits used to build the interstate, but this close to the river the developers simply let them fill with water and then built fancy houses around them.

One of which would be Alvis's. The address I had put his place at the end of 19 Road, just north of the Colorado River. Made sense. It would be secluded, with road and river access. Twenty bucks said that Alvis would have a boat tied somewhere on the water. He'd also have guards and maybe a few layers of security surrounding the house.

I stopped the bike at a pond and parked it under a low-hanging olive, getting ripped by three-inch thorns in the process. As cold as I was, I didn't feel any pain. Then I pulled the pistol, left the road, and hiked into the jungle of olives, fallen limbs, and tangles of vines that ran between the river and the road.

I ended up crawling most of the way. Following the animal trails, which were more like tunnels, I had to duck and wallow underneath the large lower branches. Mosquitoes congregated and drilled my exposed skin. The black greasy mud covered me from head to toe. I smelled of rotten vegetation and motor oil.

Five minutes of slopping later, I arrived in a small opening close enough to watch the house at the end of the road. The opening was dense enough to hide me from anyone looking out of the building, but I was far enough back that I couldn't hear any sounds from the house.

The crawling had warmed me up, and I'd stopped shivering. The rain had gotten worse, however, filling the air with a roiling wetness that made it hard to make out what was going on in front of the colossal three-story adobe. Two black

SUVs were parked next to the Land Rover, and through the misty air I watched five men walk from the house and climb into the SUVs. They drove off in a hurry.

As I was about to stand and try to circle the house, my phone buzzed.

I pulled it out and pushed OK.

"Stocker Stadium will not work for me," Alvis said, calmer this time, his voice steady. "We'll have to change the location. And time. Two o'clock at the Botanical Gardens."

I delayed answering to make him think I was calculating how to make my play at the Botanical Gardens. "Okay," I said grudgingly. "I just want my sister back."

"And you shall. She'll be waiting for you in the lot."

He had no intention of bringing Jen there. Just like I had no intention of going to Stocker. He was a smart guy, and he figured I wasn't. Alvis's thinking went like this: *Barr wants a meet at noon. He picks the place and gets there early to ambush. So I'll call back, change the time and location, and have my guys already on the way when I call. That way, no matter how early Barr is, I'll take him down.*

Nice try. He had no way of knowing where I was. And it meant that most of his goons would be at the Gardens, waiting a long, long time for a man who'd never show.

"Wait," I said.

"Yes?"

"Let me talk to Jen. I need to make sure she's still alive if I'm going to meet your men."

A pause, and then some shouting in the background. Finally Alvis's voice came back on the line. "Here," he barked. There was another pause, and then I heard Jen's trembling voice. "Clyde?"

"Are you okay?"

"Better. Still fuzzy, but better. Where are you?"

"Coming. I need you to be strong, Jen. Starting right *now*. I need you to do what we did every time someone hurt us in our old house. Right now, okay?"

She breathed into the phone, confused at first, then said, "Yes. Please hurry. We're leaving and after—"

There was the sound of a slap, and Alvis got back on the phone. "Two o'clock, Mr. Barr." For a moment I heard the sounds of scraping and struggling. Then Alvis hung up.

I wasn't sure if Jen had caught my meaning or even had the ability to do what I asked. I wasn't sure under what conditions she was being held. But I thought back to all those terrifying nights when she would use her dresser to block the door, and decided it was worth the try.

How many of Alvis's men were still in the house? I figured at least one, prayed there were no more. Resigned to just trying my best and hoping luck was on my side, I checked the pistol, made sure a round was in the chamber, then stood and worked my way closer to the house.

CHAPTER FORTY-FIVE

As the heavens unloaded more cold rain, I crawled and crouched my way through the jungle, circling around the house. Although it was hard to be completely certain due to the rain, I was reasonably sure there was only one guard patrolling the grounds. And when his route took him to the back of the house, I made my move to the front. I ran across the clearing, boots squishing in the grass, and ducked behind the engine of the Land Rover. No shots fired.

I eased to the driver's door, found it unlocked, and opened it. Then I popped the hood. I went back around, staying low, and pulled up the hood another foot. Though I don't know much about fixing cars, I've disabled a few, and it didn't take more than a minute to pop off the spark plug wires and rip the fuses and relays from the fuse box.

After I closed the hood, I went back to the door and crawled inside. I checked for a rifle, weapons, anything I could use once I went inside to find Alvis. The vehicle was clean. No weapons.

I got out, eased the door closed, and listened. No shots. Nothing but the steady splattering of rain. When my lungs had stopped heaving, I pushed away from the Rover and took off for the house. Water streamed off my hat and beard as I ran to the side of the building. There, I slowed to a walk and cautiously went toward the back, where the guard was currently patrolling.

Before I got around the last corner, the raindrops turned twice as fat, and lightning flashed in the east. The first giant thunderclap boomed as I eased around the corner and scanned for the guard. He had his back to me, fifty feet away, searching the nooks and crannies between the trees. Likely he was noticing last night's deer beds, and maybe, if he was good, the tracks I'd made as I circled the house.

A bright blue bolt of light arced from the clouds and hit the top of a ridge just about a mile away.

Which was the break I was looking for.

I raised the pistol, braced my arms against the corner of the house, and counted to five. When I hit five, I squeezed the trigger. The thunder cracked at the same time my pistol bucked, masking the sound, and the guard fell to the ground.

I wanted to run over and take the man's rifle, ammo, and vest, but just then I heard what sounded like a scream from inside the house. Jen might have just decided to do what I'd asked her to. On an impulse, I moved toward the back door. Finding it unlocked, I slipped inside.

The house was bigger than Deb's but similar. The ground level looked to be all great room, offices, kitchen, and dining room. Sparse but expensive decorations broadcasted the owner's wealth. A large statue of Mars stood guard by the door, across from a larger statue of Apollo by the stairs.

The stairs would lead to the bedrooms, where Jen would be if she'd done what I'd asked.

After a second of listening for another soldier roaming

the building, and hearing nothing, I mounted the stairs two at a time, my pistol held low and ready. Halfway up the wide stairs, I heard the pounding, then Alvis yelling, "Open the goddamned door, bitch!"

I topped the stairs and swung around the corner, into a long, wide hallway. Alvis was halfway down the hall, trying to kick in one of the doors. He must have seen me out of his peripheral, because he spun immediately to face me.

I didn't get a chance to pull the trigger, because two things happened at the same time. A pistol appeared in Alvis's hand as if by magic. He was good, and he was fast. Also, plaster flew off the wall next to me. Someone had fired shots from below.

I fired once at Alvis and missed, and he went prone and fired a quick double tap my way that also went wide.

Then I was moving. Down the steps, firing twice at the soldier by the Mars statue. He took cover behind the god, and I vaulted over the rail, falling for a second before crashing into the hardwood near the center of the great room. My injured leg gave out. I crumpled and rolled, reacquiring the soldier with my front sight.

The jump had hurt, but it had put the stairs in between me and the soldier. When I rolled, I became visible to him again, and he shot, but too high. I fired twice, hitting him in the upper leg, and he went down screaming. Blood from his femoral spurted onto the floor, and a few seconds later he passed out.

I crawled across the floor, aiming to take the man's rifle, and was almost there when Alvis started shooting from the railing. Wood chips flew, and I rolled away from his line of sight toward the kitchen.

The shooting stopped and the pounding started again, followed quickly by a scream and Jen yelling my name. Before I could get to my feet, Alvis had managed to drag Jen down the stairs and position her in front of me. His pistol was pressed hard against her temple.

"Drop the gun, Barr," he said. "Drop it or I kill her."

I saw Jen's frightened eyes. But I'd already entered that place I went to at moments like this. Instinct took over and I laughed.

At first Alvis didn't know what to make of me. Jen also looked confused. Alvis glared at my pathetic body sprawled on the floor and seemed to take satisfaction in seeing me clutch my injured leg as I limply held a pistol in the other hand. "Why the hell are you laughing, Barr?"

I smiled. "Because you're *not* going to kill her. You need her for that big score you're counting on. Today is D-day, right?"

While Alvis's mind worked to process how much I knew, Jen used that moment to stomp on his insole. "Fucking bitch," he said, pulling his arm back to pistol whip her. That's when I decided to take a chance. Though my arm was shaking with pain and exhaustion I sighted along the end of my pistol's barrel and pulled the trigger.

I missed.

Or rather, I missed the head I was aiming at, and hit the arm holding the gun. At the elbow. My first love, Lady Luck, hadn't forsaken me.

Alvis grunted, dropped the pistol, and tried to pull Jen to the door with one arm. It didn't work. I was on my feet limp-running toward Alvis when Jen jabbed a hand in his face. She curled her fingers, got one in an eye, and scratched her nails down to his chin.

Alvis grunted again, pushed her away, saw me coming, and took off for the front door. He threw it open and ran to the

Rover. I lurched toward the door, tripped over a sofa, then got up and followed him out.

Alvis was sitting in the Rover, pounding on the steering wheel. In his side mirror he saw the reflection of me coming and jumped out. He ran south, toward the river, cradling his bleeding right arm.

CHAPTER FORTY-SIX

I followed, heading down the trail toward the river as the thunder boomed nearby. Thankfully, the rain had stopped. For now. I limped as fast as I could and paid close attention to the ground.

Alvis's arm was destroyed, and my leg was close to the same, so he covered ground almost twice as fast. But he left tracks. Blood spots and footprints. I followed them across the clearing, onto a path through the trees that would lead to the river.

The blood spots were bright red, meaning highly oxygenated blood from an artery. And they appeared more and more frequently as we got closer to the water. That told me he was slowly bleeding out and wouldn't make it to the boat that was surely tethered somewhere on the bank.

The truth was, I had no idea what I'd do if Alvis took off down the river or if he had a cache of weapons on the boat. I tried devising some alternative plans, limping as fast as I could down the trail. Soon it occurred to me that he was doing what every seriously wounded animal does. They head downhill, or toward water. They also become erratic, and when I thought of that it brought me back to the trail I was following.

There was blood on *both* sides of the trail. Before, the

red stains had only been on the right side, because they'd fallen from Alvis's injured right arm. I stopped abruptly and listened. Not hearing anything over the splattering of rain and the occasional thunderclap, I pulled the magazine from the pistol and checked the remaining rounds. The magazine was empty.

So I had one round left. And sometime, while I was deep in thought, Alvis had doubled back. He was somewhere to the side of the trail, either circling wide to the river or lying in wait. It depended on whether he considered himself prey or predator.

I turned, intent on following the backtrack, when I saw a bare-chested apparition with a rock in his hand lunge out of the brush.

I shot, low from the hip, and missed.

Alvis swung for my head with his good arm, intent on crushing my skull, and I ducked under. I hit him hard in the solar plexus, causing him to bend over slightly, then I slapped my useless pistol to the side of his head and jumped back.

In what seemed like a long drawn-out moment but was only a slice of a second, I took in the man before me. He'd pulled off his shirt and tied it around his ruined elbow, then cinched his belt above the elbow as a tourniquet.

He should have been dazed. I'd hit him hard twice, and he'd suffered significant blood loss. But he seemed weirdly calm and collected.

"I was wrong about you, Barr. You're *worse* than an irritant. You're a nasty, hairy, nosey cockroach, and I'm going to stomp you."

"Bring it," I said, eyeing the rock he still held in his hand. I began raising my pistol, counting on him not to know I was out of ammo.

But he was twice as fast as me and had closed the gap before I got the gun to chest level. Instead of swinging the rock, he slammed it on my foot and tagged me with an uppercut that lifted me to my tiptoes.

I didn't fall. Not until he put a foot behind mine and shoved my chest. Then I went over his leg, hit the soggy earth, and he was on top of me. My lungs accordioned inward, but I got my legs up and hooked my ankles over his back. He punched me once in the jaw, and then his good hand wrenched the pistol back, nearly breaking my trigger finger and wrist.

As he ripped the pistol away I grabbed his bad elbow with one hand and dug my fingers underneath his makeshift bandage and squeezed. He screamed and tried to head butt me, but I lowered my chin into his chest, ducking under him. I might have heard footsteps coming down the path then, but I was too busy pulling Alvis's head toward me so I could get my teeth on his neck. When I did, and bit down hard, Alvis screamed even louder.

In one last spasm Alvis's hand brought my pistol up and fired it at my head—with no effect, of course. That's when I lit into him. I rolled him under me and pummeled him with everything I had. Punches. Head butts. Palm strikes. Eye gouges. With each hit, I thought of my mom . . . and Allie . . . and all the women and children I'd laid to rest on three continents over the years—innocents in a world of evil.

I wore myself out trying to replace the back of Alvis's head with his face. I pictured the human being under me as a fleshy effigy, and I would have kept hitting until Alvis was pulp if it weren't for the sound of my sister's voice pleading.

"Stop it, Clyde, *please*, STOP," she was begging. At that moment I probably didn't seem human to her; I probably seemed like a monster. Vaguely, I felt her arms pulling at my shoulders.

"It won't *help*, Clyde. It won't bring them back." She was sobbing hard now.

I slowed my punches then, knelt back, and dazedly accepted Jen's embrace. She put her arms around me then and we both cried.

CHAPTER FORTY-SEVEN

Cars were parked in the driveway of Deb's towering house when I pulled up on Beth Corrigan's Interceptor, Jen seated directly in back of me like she had a few days before when I'd worried she might fall off my horse. This time, riding with her arms locked around me and a small duffel bag between us, she did just fine, and we'd only caught a little rain. I'd phoned Deb's house about forty minutes before but just got her machine, so I simply left a quick message saying the "bad guy" had been caught and all was back to normal. Now, sitting in front of my oldest sister's house, I wasn't sure we'd find anyone home. So I did something I'd done only once before. I sent a text. I asked Deb if she was home, told her I had Jen, and asked if we could come in.

She didn't reply. Instead she opened the door. And standing next to her was my sister Angie, whom I hadn't seen in sixteen years.

Jen ran and hugged them both, and all three girls spun in a circle, laughing. Grabbing the bag that Jen and I had brought with us, I followed behind, suddenly feeling awkward in the midst of this family reunion. As I stepped across the threshold and dropped the bag just inside the door, Angie broke free from Jen to give me a *you're crazy but I still love you* look. She seemed blonder and more beautiful than I remembered. "We're all so glad this thing is over, Clyde."

"You look great," I said, and meant it.

She smiled back and made a show of appraising my sodden, blood-smeared self. "And you look—"

"You don't have to say it—*like hell*. It's been a tough few days."

As we sat down at the kitchen table, Jen swung her gaze around to take in the expensive decor. "This house is *amazing*," Jen said. "Even better than the old one."

"I forgot you hadn't been here since we moved in," Deb said, handing her a blanket. She handed me one, too. "You know how it is—buy a new house, get a chance to make new memories." She looked over at me. "Can I fix you two something to eat?"

I opened my mouth to answer but Jen beat me to it. "I'm fucking starving," she said.

I waited for Deb to chew her ass, like she'd done to me on my last visit—and like she'd done to both of us when we lived with her as kids. But she didn't. She just went into the kitchen and pulled a pan out of a cabinet. "Beef and broccoli, okay?" she asked. She smiled when she heard enthusiastic grunts.

"I'll give you a hand, Deb," Angie said, joining her at the counter.

"Kids aren't home?" I asked.

"Nick took them to the park," Deb said as she went into the fridge. "Everyone breathed a sigh of relief after we got your phone message. And the kids were going stir crazy. So when the rain let up—"

I nodded. I was about to apologize and launch into the

speech I'd prepared on the way over, but Jen spoke up first. "Thanks for cooking, you two. And these blankets are heaven."

"Anytime," Deb said.

While our two older sisters busied themselves in the kitchen, Jen and I flashed a look. It was one of those *I can't believe this is over* looks. The truth was, we were probably both still in shock. We'd barely said anything to each other since leaving Alvis's house.

I'D DONE EXACTLY FOUR THINGS before retrieving the Honda, coaxing Jen onto it, and roaring out of Alvis's front gate. The first was to phone Deb and leave that message. And the second was to give the Rover another quick check. That turned out to be a good decision. Underneath a panel in the rear of the vehicle, where a spare tire would normally be, was a small brown duffel. Inside were hundreds of bundles of large-denomination bills.

My third move was to call Agent Peters and tell him about a rumor I heard concerning Mr. Lance Alvis. I gave Peters the address and suggested he might want to send an ambulance.

My final act before throttling out of Alvis's driveway was to ask Jen what that break-in had been about anyway.

"All I know is that those chemicals were very valuable to him," she told me. "Some of his men talked among themselves about a special formula they were making at the three cookhouses he'd set up—yes, there were two others. The formula all depended on this hard-to-get ingredient. I could get them into the facility. I had the clearance, the pass-through. But at the DOE depot we work in one-week-on/one-week-off shifts. For security reasons. So Lance needed me bottled up until my next shift started. And then he was going to discard me—like a used needle." She wiped away a tear. "If you hadn't come . . ."

"But I *did*. I *did*—because that's what little brothers are for, right?"

She smiled weakly and nodded.

"Okay, so hold on tight," I said, and then we zoomed out the front gate, leaving behind for good Lance Alvis and his demented visions of empire.

BACK IN THE PRESENT, WITH a full meal in their bellies, Deb, Angie, and Jen were poring over some of Deb's photo albums, and I noticed at the corner of one of the pages an old photo of Mom—one of those schoolgirl shots. The girl in that photo was young and beautiful and no doubt looking forward to a bright future. At some point in our childhood, we *all* look at life that way. What happens to us?

My sisters called me over, asked me to look at a runty photo of me when I was in the third grade. They all began laughing at my big ears. I laughed, too, and realized I was enjoying myself. Hell, I'd gone at least an hour without sweeping the horizon for a threat. It felt good.

"I love you guys," I suddenly blurted out. Everyone stopped talking and looked at me.

"What?" they said, almost in unison.

I'd never said it to *any* of them. I'd insinuated it, when we were little, and I'd tried to show it, but I don't remember using the words. I'd missed my chance with Allie, and that was a lesson I'd have to live with—live with and, I hoped, benefit from.

"You heard me," I said. I looked at Jen specifically. "From now on, you need anything, I'm a phone call away. No matter how far away I am. Swear. You just have to promise me one thing."

"What?" she asked.

"No more drugs."

"Promise," she said. She smiled at me like she had when Dad was still around, and our lives hadn't been flushed down separate sewers.

Deb and Angie flashed broad smiles, too, which was when I heard the front door swing open and the wild, animated voices of two young boys, followed by a booming "Take off your shoes, varmints—you're going to muddy your mother's carpet." That could only be Nick.

Our brother-in-law meeting wasn't as awkward as you'd think. Nick caught the mood in the room and rolled with it. We even found that we both had something in common— our hatred of modern technology. Or learning how to *use* it, at least.

As for my nephews, they were a hoot. They seemed fascinated to have another uncle. And they were even more fascinated by my scars. They wanted to know how I got them and I told them "working construction."

After I'd visited for another hour, I knew it was time to go. Too much had happened that day. There'd been too many intense emotions. I needed to be alone—organize my thoughts.

"Welcome home," I told Jen as I stood up awkwardly from the couch. I left her in the capable hands of Deb and Angie, shook Nick's hand, gave the kids affectionate punches in the shoulder, and headed for the front foyer. On the way out, I grabbed the duffel I'd set down by the door.

I rode to the nearest hotel, used some of the cash in the duffel to check in, and took the hottest shower the place allowed. Then I pulled the sheets and comforter off the second bed, piled them on the one closest to the door, and burrowed into a blanket nest. Finally warm, dry, and more at peace than I'd been in a very long time, I fell into the depths of much-needed sleep.

CHAPTER FORTY-EIGHT

With no goddamned cell phone to wake me up, I slept until almost noon. I had to pay for a second day, according to the angry little woman who could barely see above the registration desk. I didn't care, since it wasn't my money.

Remembering my windfall, I went back up to the room and counted the contents of the duffel. A little less than 500K. I shoved one of the bundles into my pocket, unscrewed a ceiling vent, crammed the duffel into it, then replaced the grill. As I left the room, I hung a "Do Not Disturb" sign on the door. Downstairs, I told the clerk I'd be back and made her promise not to have the room cleaned. Then I went outside to the parking lot and climbed on the Honda.

Beth Corrigan was greatly relieved when I returned her bike. I tried to give her an extra two hundred for getting the Honda back to her so late, but when I told her there'd be no more finger cutting going on in Junction for a while, she stuffed the bills back into my hand.

"You done good, Clyde Barr," she said.

I tipped my hat and walked out.

I continued walking to a cheap used-car lot three blocks away. One of those places that trade cash straight across for the title. No paperwork, no questions. For now I figured I'd get myself a temporary rig. I knew a guy five hundred miles north who'd help me out with a deal on something more permanent. After ten minutes of wandering a lot full of dented and rumpled cars, I traded the flighty woman in the bulletproof kiosk a grand for the keys to an AMC Eagle. The four-wheel-drive car was an obsolete, rugged precursor to the more complicated, less tough, modern crossovers. Not as cool as a pickup, but it would do.

Then I headed to the nearest sporting goods store. I bought three backpacks and the basic supplies that would allow me to hit the trail on foot if I chose to. Water purifier. Cooking kit. Cordage, poncho, sleeping bag, and some extra lighters. I'd pick up a rifle somewhere on the road.

Back at the hotel I retrieved the duffel from the vent and divided the money into the three packs. I put 245K into two of them, and the last ten thousand in mine. I left the duffel itself in the room and checked out.

At the central library I sweet-talked a young woman with a nose ring and orange hair into helping me find two addresses. Using a series of arcane computer tricks, she tracked down the last two people in Junction that I needed to find. If I'd known locating someone was this easy, I might not have been as tired and sore as I was. Maybe technology isn't so bad after all.

The sun burned off the last of the clouds as I drove the Eagle to a place called Mountain Top. After filling out reams of paperwork—and lying on most of it—I left one of the backpacks with the nice round man in the office, who assured me that the money would be put into the account of Mrs. Martin. I figured that amount of money would take care of Allie's mom for at least twenty years. Someday soon I'd write the woman and tell her how brave her daughter was, but I didn't have it in me just yet. I left the assisted-living place in a hurry, vowing to myself that I'd wander into the woods and die of hypothermia long before someone wrangled me into a place like that.

My next stop was Mack, a small farm town just a few miles from the Utah border. I guessed it to be about four in the afternoon when I opened the white vinyl gate and walked to the house that matched the address the orange-haired librarian had given me. It was a little brown modular, well kept, with a tidy little lawn surrounding it like a moat. Outside the yard, close to two hundred squat, short meat goats roamed in groups. They nibbled the weeds and sparse grass inside the heavy fences, wandered to and from the little sheds, and frolicked in the sunshine.

I knocked. No one answered. I heard pounding from the side yard and headed that way, figuring it was someone working on a fence or a machine. It wasn't. It was a little girl, maybe four or five years old, and she was very busy pounding the side of a coffee can full of dirt, trying to liberate the muddy contents.

She looked up at me, and I saw the bright green eyes and the faint beginnings of freckles. Her dark black hair was cut in a bob, and my eyes watered. I coughed. She wasn't scared or startled to see me, simply annoyed that I'd interrupted her work.

"Your parents around?" I asked.

She looked back at the can, continued pounding, and pointed over to where I'd seen the goats.

I found one of the parents in a milking shed. As I entered, I heard the distinct tinkling of milk hitting a pail, and next to it mellow bleating. I called out, "Hello? Is this the Otterman place?"

A tall, thin woman in muddy jeans and a checkered shirt rose to greet me. She wiped her hands on her pants and stuck out her palm. "It is. I'm Liv."

I shook the proffered hand, felt a grip strong enough to break bones. "I'm Clyde, from down the road."

Liv looked me up and down warily, taking in the hat and the bag I was holding. "Can I help you?" she said, glancing over to the house and seeing the Eagle parked out front.

I handed her the bag of cash, which she took reluctantly. "Your girl?" I said. "This is for her. Her mom wanted her to have it."

Before she could say anything, and before my eyes started to water again, I turned and walked away. I climbed into the Eagle and didn't look back.

IN THE DESERT FIFTY MILES west of Mack, along a stretch of highway that was barren of cars, as the sun disappeared and smeared the sky with crimson, I saw them.

A band of eight wild horses, their heads and tails held high, ran through the sparse brush atop a ridge to the northwest. Their dark bodies poked holes in the streaming light of the dying sun, and as they ran along the skyline, it seemed as if they were being chased by billowing purple dust.

They weren't being chased, however. They were running because they felt like it. Because they were free. They were enjoying the blissful moment in between storms, kicking up their heels, snorting, and tossing their heads.

Up until I saw them, I'd been staring out my windshield, feeling sorry for myself and wondering where I was going. *Going* in the deeper sense. Jen was safe, back in the folds of family. And Allie was gone. There was no denying that, not after the finality of seeing her daughter. There was nothing for me here, nothing left to do.

The horses ran off the far edge of the ridge, out of sight, chasing the sun. It was then that I remembered what Allie had told me, and it hit me hard, seeing the horses following her sage advice. They weren't running away from a past. Or toward greener pastures. They were living in the moment.

I decided then that maybe I didn't need to go all the way to the north to find contentment. Maybe the Yukon was just a way of running from memories and looking for something that didn't exist. I could drive, or gallop, or walk in whatever direction I damned well felt like, doing whatever needed to be done.

There was *always* something that needed to be done. I was sure of it. The trick was to stay in the moment and accept each situation as it came—the way Allie would have.

ACKNOWLEDGMENTS

Writers are just a small part of the publishing process, and it's here that I get to thank the other people who made this book possible. My sincere gratitude to them all.

To my agent, Darley Anderson, who believed in me and Clyde: thank you so much for finding this book a home, for the constant kind words of support, and for the wise and tenacious way you've built my career. Thanks also to the wonderful staff at the Darley Anderson Literary, TV and Film Agency who have been nothing but helpful, supportive, and friendly.

To Rick Horgan, my brilliant editor at Scribner and the worthy heir of Max Perkins: thank you for taking a chance, and for making this book, and me, better than I thought possible. We do make a good team! Also, thanks to David Lamb and everyone else at Scribner who have put so much time and effort into this project.

To my parents, who raised me right: thank you for teaching me to love reading and to work hard, and for giving me the chance to spend so much time outside. Thanks also to my brother and sisters who supported me on this journey.

To Mr. Cummings and Mr. Kruger: I promised you'd be

mentioned in here, if this ever happened, and I didn't forget. Thank you for teaching the classics, encouraging reading, and for being the first to suggest that I write. Your early encouragement meant a lot.

Thanks again to my wife and daughters for putting up with me during all of this. I know it wasn't easy, since I was mostly a horrid beast, but your love and support means everything. You are the reason I live, and write, and love.

To readers everywhere: you are a dwindling and unique breed, and I thank you for trading money and time to enjoy books when there are so many other things competing for your attention. A special, huge thanks for choosing this one.

To everyone I've ever met: you've helped me in some way, even if not consciously, and I thank you all.

Erik Storey is a former ranch hand, wilderness guide, dogsled musher and hunter. He spent his childhood summers on his great-grandfather's homestead or in a remote cabin in Colorado's Flat Top wilderness. He has earned a number of sharpshooter and marksman qualifications. *Nothing Short of Dying* is his first novel. He and his family live in Grand Junction, Colorado.

Find out more at www.erikstoreybooks.com

Turn the page for an exclusive extract from Erik Storey's
next novel, featuring the tortured hero, Clyde Barr:

A PROMISE TO KILL

CHAPTER ONE

The second time I saw the old Ute, he was dying.

It was late summer, hot and drier even than usual. I was riding a new mare and leading a reluctant mule named Bob across the lowlands of northeast Utah that lay between the hump of the Book Cliffs and the higher Uinta Mountains to the north. When I saw the old man's truck idling in the bar ditch, I let go of Bob's lead rope and kicked the mare into a half gallop. I jumped off and let the reins hang as I checked on the old man.

He sat slumped against the steering wheel of his twenty-year-old rusty pickup and was complaining that his arm hurt and that he had some serious indigestion. I told him to hang on, rummaged in my pack, and pulled out a bottle of expired aspirin.

"I'm fine," the old man said. "Just ate a bad lunch. You don't need to worry about me."

"No, you're not. Here, take these."

I shoved a couple of pills in his mouth and made him chew. He grimaced, which made his aged face look even older.

"Tasty, huh?" I said. "I'm no doctor, but I think your ticker's giving out. Try not to die for a second, I'll be right back." I tied my mare and the mule to some nearby piñons and went back to the truck.

The old man looked like he was concentrating, trying to control his breathing. He rubbed his arm and clutched his shirt. "Ain't my ticker. I have the heart of a warrior. Strong." He thumped his chest feebly, and the grimace returned.

I dug back into my pack and found my cell phone, which was dead. Of course. There aren't many places to plug a charger into a horse.

"We need to get you to a hospital."

He nodded, grunted, and tried to unbuckle his seat belt. I slipped my knife from its sheath and cut the strap before he could struggle it off, then ran to the other side of the vehicle and helped him into the passenger seat.

Once I got him halfway comfortable, I hopped in the driver's seat and tried to remember how to drive an old ranch pickup. The gears were sloppy, the clutch slipped, and the engine loped like a panicked Appaloosa I once owned. The knack of relying on *mechanical* horsepower, not the animal kind, came back to me a few miles down the road. As the old codger and I rattled down the dusty, narrow highway, I thought back to the first time we'd met, twenty minutes before.

I'd been sitting atop my horse, trotting across the gray asphalt, when the old man had stopped and waved me over.

"Nice pony," he'd said. The clipped way he said it, combined with the dark, wrinkled skin, told me he was a Native. That was the politically correct term these days. I remembered playing Cowboys and Indians as a kid. These days, I guessed kids played Cowboys and Natives—the ones without cell phones and Xboxes, anyway.

According to the map in my pack, I was getting close to

the Uintah and Ouray Ute Indian Reservation. This old man proved I was closer than I'd thought.

"She's a little tall to be a pony," I said as an understatement. The mare stood at least sixteen hands tall.

The old man laughed, his skin a map of deep canyons and craters. "I raise ponies just like that," he said. "On my ranch. Quarter horses. Not as full of fight as the ponies my great-grandfather rode into war, but pretty good." He laughed again, then asked where I was going.

I shrugged. "North, I guess." It didn't much matter where, as long as I was moving. Although it would be nice to get up into the range that I'd been riding toward the last couple of days. The cold granite, crystal water, and tall, fragrant pines would help fix what was eating away at me.

"You should come by," he said. "Cook me dinner and I'll tell you some stories."

I told him I would, and I'd planned on it, but I'd barely ridden two miles before I came to his idling pickup.

Now, as the sun sank low in the sky, and the surrounding stubby juniper and piñon trees cast grotesque shadows across the road, I divided my time between trying to keep the old beater of a truck on the pavement and glimpsing over at this man I barely knew, whose condition seemed to be worsening.

"You still with me?" I asked.

He grunted and motioned vaguely with his hand. "Go to Wakara. Straight ahead five miles. My daughter works at the clinic there. She's a doctor—a good one. She'll take care of me."

I did as he said, driving through a long narrow cut that had rock walls rising up on either side, but I had to stop a couple times to remove some debris that had probably fallen off a flatbed and would have shredded the truck's tires. When we finally got into what barely passed for a town the sun had disappeared behind the rocky horizon and the clinic was closed.

"Where's the nearest phone?"

He shrugged and pointed to the only building out of the ten or so in town that had a light burning. I drove there, told the man to sit tight, and walked toward the door.

As I neared the slumping building, I heard the rumble of laughter and jeering. The place looked like it wouldn't make it through the winter. The outside walls were a mix of peeling plaster, missing windows, and artful graffiti. The inside was worse.

CHAPTER TWO

Once I opened the front door, my nose caught the pungent scent of dried leather and manure, and my eyes took in the sight of rows and rows of haphazardly placed goods for sale. On one wall were tightly packed clothes, and on another was an assortment of hunting and fishing supplies. Occupying the room's center were stacked cases of canned goods and packaged food. Where the back wall should have been was a recessed area that featured a bar. And in front of that bar were at least twenty loud, burly bikers in leather jackets and chaps. Surprisingly, all were white. No Natives in sight, despite the fact that I was officially now standing inside an Indian reservation.

There was no one manning the small check-out counter by the door, so I waded into the boisterous room.

"Hey," I yelled, barely able to make my voice heard above the drunken racket. "Is there a phone here?"

The room went quiet. Which gave me time to notice details. Like the patches on the bikers' jackets. Their club was apparently called the Reapers, and they were one-percenters. I'd met bikers before and seen outlaw patches similar to these. Normally, they wouldn't have bothered me. What *did* bother me was the way the men held themselves. Most were leaner and more muscled than the bikers you see on TV or in the movies. But more important were their eyes. They were full of menace. For some reason, this crew reminded me of the Janjaweed—a deadly horseback militia in Sudan that I'd once made the mistake of upsetting.

The biggest of the men, a giant who must have topped six feet six, shoved his way to the front and moved to stand in front of me. His patches said he was the club's president and that his name was Jury. "No phone. Store's closed for a private party. *Leave*."

His men smiled. I said, "I've got an old man outside—he's in bad shape. I need to borrow someone's phone."

Jury grabbed a beer out of the nearest biker's hand and slammed it to the floor. Glass shattered and tinkled against my boots. "Let him die."

For an instant I tried to assess how much of this stone-cold-killer response was an act. Maybe he was just testing me, waiting to see if I'd offer the secret "bad guy handshake" or something. *Should I say something clever?* At that moment, I couldn't think of a single comeback other than "I can't."

At that, Jury's friends' eyebrows all rose like coordinated curtains, and twenty heads shifted slightly to see what the president's next move would be.

"I think you will."

"Won't." I didn't move. Instead, I matched his stare.

"Listen, bumpkin," he said. "When our club rolls into a little town like yours, we own it. We make the rules, and we make the demands." He stared hard at his men, paying special attention to a couple of the sloppier Reapers wearing Nomad patches—the only ones who weren't yet coiled for action. "We also say who lives and who dies. And if you don't leave in the next three seconds, you and your friend outside will both be dead." Time slowed as I fought to control my adrenaline. Twenty bikers continued to stare at me, like hungry hyenas at night, waiting to see if they could feed. My hands shook. I wanted, more than I'd wanted anything in a long time, to pop Jury in the throat and wade into his friends with chin jabs. But there was an old man dying outside. So I put my hands up and backed away.

"That's right, walk away, bumpkin. Go play with the Indians. And if you *ever* interrupt us again, I'll stomp you into six kinds of flat."

CHAPTER THREE

It was full dark when I hurried back outside and climbed into the truck. In the glow of its overhead light, the old man seemed paler. Beads of sweat broke off his forehead and ran into his eyes. He didn't wipe them away. "Still hanging in there?" I asked.

It took him a moment to answer. "Don't worry about me. Even at eighty, I'm stronger than you."

"Probably," I said. "Where's the nearest hospital?"

"No hospitals. They're full of Mormons who poke you with needles and try to convert you at the same time. Take me to my house."

"I could, but then you might be dead in an hour. We're going to the hospital. Point the way."

This time, I noticed, he didn't put up any fight. For all his stubbornness, he probably knew he was in a bad way. He pointed north. "Thirty miles that way, in Vernal," he said, then curled up tighter and clutched his chest.

I shifted into drive and was about to pull out when a teenage Ute boy ran around the corner of the building and grabbed at the truck's door handle. He tried to talk, but his run had left him breathless. He wore a dishwashing apron and a flat-brimmed ball cap over his long hair.

"What's wrong, kid?" I asked, wanting to get out of there.

Panting, the kid pointed at the old man and said, "My grandpa. I heard you say an old man was hurt, and I hoped it wasn't him, but I came out to see, and . . . and it is."

The old man mumbled, "Taylor?"

"I'm here, Grandpa."

"This guy wants me to get poked by Mormons."

The boy looked at me for an explanation and I said, "Your grandpa's heart is giving out. You want to come with me to the hospital or not?" He hesitated only a second and jumped in the back. The rear door was just slamming shut when I peeled out and pushed the rattling pile of metal up to its max speed of sixty. Above us, the stars shone brightly in the thin desert air.

The old man groaned again and looked over at me. "Why are you helping me?"

My eyes never left the road. "You offered a fellow horse lover dinner, right? If you die, I'll never get to eat it."

I thought about what would happen when we got to the hospital. Some insurance lady would probably have us fill out ten forms while the old man was taking his last breath. It seemed smart to phone ahead. I called into the back seat, "Hey, kid, you got a cell phone on you?"

In the rear-view mirror, the kid's face looked genuinely anguished. "It was almost dead when I got to work. I need to charge it. Damn, my mom should know what is happening."

I sighed. Why is it that all the machines that are supposed to make life easier go on the fritz when you really need them? I pushed my foot down harder on the gas pedal and hoped this machine I was counting on to eat up the miles wouldn't give out, too.

CHAPTER FOUR

We made it. *Barely*. The insurance lady must have been on break. The blond nurses who took the old man away on a gurney told us if we had been five minutes slower, he'd be dead. They said he was going into intensive care and to take a seat in the waiting room for god-knows-how-long. So we did. The facility was much bigger than I'd expected. Acres of shiny floors and clean walls and beeping machinery. It smelled of cleaning products. I hadn't been in a hospital this modern in my life. Most of the times I'd been patched up, it was in some godforsaken place, with foreign languages being spoken and people screaming in pain from lack of anesthetics.

Taylor and I found open chairs with plush cushions and took a seat. Magazines of every variety were splayed in a circle on a table in the middle of the room, but most of the people waiting were glued to the television hanging from the wall by the entrance.

Taylor looked away for a moment and wiped at his eyes, hoping I wouldn't see. He knew his grandpa wasn't out of the woods, and he was obviously rattled. As I stared at the ceiling tiles and consciously tried to drain away some of the adrenaline that had been surging for the last hour, Taylor plugged his phone into the wall, then put on his toughest mask and asked, "Is he going to be okay?"

I wasn't going to tell him there was nothing to worry about. "Intensive care is never a good thing. But your grandpa seems pretty stubborn. I wouldn't bet against him."

He nodded, seemingly lost in thought. Then he pointed at the giant screen. "Have you seen the news?"

The display showed a newsperson I'd never seen before talking in an excited rush about something big. Words ticked across the bottom of the screen as he spoke. The guy continued for a few minutes, describing an escalating event somewhere two hundred miles south of us. He mentioned a terror alert, and the moving words at the screen's bottom reported that all major concerts and sporting events would be canceled until whatever was occurring to the south was resolved. I shrugged, looked away, and picked up a fishing magazine.

Taylor, however, continued staring at the TV. "That's just south of here, man. Down by Green River, on the interstate. I canoed all the way there once. Sounds like the government is looking for something there, and that terrorists might be involved. Can you believe it? In Utah?"

I shrugged again and returned to the article I was reading about catching lake bass. My ho-hum response must have reminded Taylor where he was, because, a few seconds later, he took his partially charged phone into an alcove, presumably to call his mom. If her car was faster than the rattletrap truck I'd driven, she could be here in twenty-five minutes.

As I surveyed the waiting area, I noticed that most eyes were still fixed on the TV. This terror news was exactly what I was trying to get away from by going into the mountains. Death, fear, and worry—what was the point of brooding on all that stuff, anyway? The situation would blow over eventually. Even if you were caught in the middle, you'd deal with it then. Why spend your life stressing over *might bes* and *could bes*?

I finished the lake bass article and was just beginning a story that rated the best rods and reels when I noticed that Taylor had wandered back and was once again staring worriedly at the TV. "Hey kid," I said, "you need a diversion. Why not grab some fine reading material?" I reached into the pile of magazines, pulled out an issue of *Cosmo*, and handed it to him.

"*Cosmo*, man? Really?"

"It's got lovemaking tips. Plenty of pictures of good-looking women, too. Read up."

The kid smiled for the first time and riffled through the pages. "Ugh," he said, pointing to a model who seemed to be pitching moisturizer. "Too skinny." He flipped through more pages for a couple minutes, then tossed down the magazine. "I hope my mom gets here soon. She was trying to sound calm when I told her, said how they really know what they're doing here and everything would be okay. But I could tell she was barely holding it together."

"Is she really close to your grandpa?"

"They have this running thing. Each pretends that the other is exasperating. Grandpa is always pushing the old ways, and my mom reminds him that the old ways didn't work out very well. But you can tell that they both love each other, you know?"

"Family is important," I said evenly. For me, family was simultaneously lots of great memories and lots of horrible memories. Sometimes I preferred not to go there.

"Hey," Taylor said, brightening. "My mom asked what your name is and I didn't know."

"Clyde Barr," I said, and stood to stretch my bad leg.

"My mom says to tell you thanks, but you don't have to stay. She says you can borrow my grandpa's truck to get back to town, if you want."

"I'll stay," I said, taking my coat off and stuffing it under my chair.

"Why? You don't know us."

I shrugged. Why *was* I staying? I guess that, after seeing so many people who crossed my path end up dead, it felt important to see someone survive. There was something else, too.

"Your grandpa reminds me of a man I used to sit up late with, watching the campfire die. He told stories about his people, and I listened."

"Who were his people? Ute?"

"He was Mayoruna. Met him in Peru, near the Brazilian border. Good guy."

"You've been to Peru?"

"I've been around." We were killing time, so I took him on a ten-minute tour of the countries I'd visited, especially places in Africa and South America. I emphasized the cheery sights I'd seen—the marketplaces, the temples, the festivals. I left out the bodies I'd seen lying bloated in the streets, and the fetid smells that hover over battlefields long after the last life has been snuffed out.

"Sounds cool," he said.

I smiled. I'd been like that once, always believing that what lay over the horizon was way more satisfying than my current surroundings. Maybe I was *still* like that.